The Nuns Of Nara

An Akitada Novel

I. J. Parker

I•J•
2019

Published 2019 by I.J.Parker and I·J·P Books
3229 Morningside Drive, Chesapeake VA 23321
http://www.ijparker.com
Cover design by I. J. Parker.
Cover image by Kawase Hasui
Back cover image : unknown artist.
Publisher's Note: This is a work of fiction. Names, characters, places, and incidents are a product of the author's imagination.

The Nuns of Nara, 1st edition, 2019
ISBN 9781096283799

Praise for I. J. Parker and the Akitada Series

"Elegant and entertaining . . . Parker has created a wonderful protagonist in Akitada. . . . She puts us at ease in a Japan of one thousand years ago." *The Boston Globe*

"You couldn't ask for a more gracious introduction to the exotic world of Imperial Japan than the stately historical novels of I. J. Parker." *The New York Times*

"Akitada is as rich a character as Robert Van Gulik's intriguing detective, Judge Dee." *The Dallas Morning News*

"Readers will be enchanted by Akitada." *Publishers Weekly* Starred Review

"Terrifically imaginative" *The Wall Street Journal*

"A brisk and well-plotted mystery with a cast of regulars who become more fully developed with every episode." *Kirkus*

"More than just a mystery novel, (*THE CONVICT'S SWORD*) is a superb piece of literature set against the backdrop of 11th-cntury Kyoto." *The Japan Times*

"Parker's researlch is extensive and she makes great use of the complex manners and relationships of feudal Japan." *Globe and Mail*

"The fast-moving, surprising plot and colorful writing will enthrall even those unfamiliar with the exotic setting." *Publishers Weekly,* Starred Review

". . .the author possesses both intimate knowledge of the time period and a fertile imagination as well. Combine that with an intriguing mystery and a fast-moving plot, and you've got a historical crime novel that anyone can love." *Chicago Sun-Times*

"Parker's series deserves a wide readership." *Historical Novel Society*

"The historical research is impressive, the prose crisp, and Parker's ability to universalize the human condition makes for a satisfying tale." *Booklist*

"Parker masterfully blends action and detection while making the attitudes and customs of the period accessible." *Publishers Weekly* (starred review)

"Readers looking for historical mystery with a twist will find what they're after in Parker's latest Sugawara Akitada mystery . . . An intriguing glimpse into an ancient culture." *Booklist*

Characters

Japanese family names precede proper names

Main characters:

Sugawara Akitada	nobleman, official
Sadako	his new wife
Akiko	his sister
Tora	his retainer
Fujiwara Kosehira	his friend
Captain Katsuura	Nara police officer
Doctor Hayashi	Nara coroner

Characters involved in the disappearance of the majordomo:

Sanekane	majordomo
Sanekata	his son
Kiyo	widow of a guard
Otoyo	her daughter
Sachiko	Noodleshop owner
Midori	prostitute
Ushimatsu	gambler
Kosuke	crippled boy
Otomo	pharmacist

Characters associated with the case of the missing nun:

Shosho (Lady Hachijo)	imperial concubine
Lord & Lady Yoshido	her grandparents
Yoshido Masatada	her brother
Chozen	a novice
Enchi	an elderly nun
Kanren	another novice
Wakita Tsunetaka	layman, temple *betto*
Minamoto Yoshitomo	nobleman, captain
Fujiwara Noritoki	nobleman, poet
Fujiwara Korechika	governor of Yamato

(Also a prime minister, an abbot, an abbess, assorted nuns, pharmacists, bandits, and several dead people.)

1

Cold as the Moon

Her terror was so great she did not notice how the ice cut her naked feet as she ran. The moonlight on the snow had blinded her at first and now she did not know where she was or where she was going. She kept running because she knew she would be killed if he caught her.

The moon was full and brilliant on the new snow, but the houses of the city were dark. So clear and cold was the moon that its light seemed to turn to ice beneath her feet.

She could not scream for help. That would give her away, and he would find her quickly and finish what he had started in the darkness.

Under her loose robe she was naked. She had torn it scrambling through the small, high window. She was ashamed of her nakedness and ashamed of what had happened to her.

Fear and shame outweighed the cold, which she barely felt while she was running. She fell twice but scrambled back up. She wished she had her socks at least, but her new life's austerities forbade socks unless you walked far in the snow. She had not anticipated the need.

She had not anticipated any of this, though she had known he was angry with her.

Where was she? The night looked unfamiliar. She did not know how much longer she could run. She was gasping for breath and a stitch in her side grew into agony, yet still she ran down streets she did not recognize.

A long way back, she had passed through a gate into the city she did not know. The streets were empty and quiet. She slowed a little and looked back. She saw the dark figure detach itself from behind a tree and start for her. With a small sob, she took off again, clutching her skimpy robe, hoping to see some stranger. Anyone. Because surely there could not be two such monsters in this city.

What he had done to her, brutally, grunting like some animal, had been less frightening than what he said when he locked her in.

"I'll be back," he said, baring his teeth. "I might give you another taste of that. Your last. The dead do not embrace, I fear." He had taken the light with him and left her in the dark. His prisoner.

Now she was running for her life.

She had followed him obediently. It had been farther than she had thought, and when they got there, he had pulled her into his house. His grip on her arm had hurt and she had cried out in protest. He must have hit her, because when she became aware again, she was lying on the floor, naked, and he was on top of her, inside of her, grunting. Her head hurt and she felt sick.

She had lashed out at him feebly, but he had caught her hands, finished, and then struck her again. "Bitch!"

And then he had made his promise to come back and kill her.

Somehow she had escaped and now was lost in this strange city that was asleep.

Alone with the moon and the sound of him behind her.

Ahead was a river, the water black between the snowy banks. She ran along the shore toward a bridge, sobbing now, calling to Amida and all the saints, praying to the gods, and then she fell again.

The last thing she saw was the cold moon in the water.

2
Snow at Night

Winter moonlight cast black tree shadows on the new snow. Akitada shivered. He had stepped on the veranda to see the brightness of the first snow. The world was silver against the blackness of tree trunks and shadows. When the sun came out, those shadows would be blue.

It was an unearthly beauty — and deadly. Somewhere, someone, far from home, might fall into the white softness to die. A gentle death.

In his own experience, dying had been a terrifying business. There had been no beauty in it. Death had been a violent separation of living human beings from all they held dear. He shivered again and pulled the silken quilt more closely around himself.

A soft voice from the darkness behind him asked, "What are you doing, Akitada? The cold air is coming in. Close those shutters and come back to bed before you catch your death."

He smiled and obeyed. "It has snowed."

Sadako held open her cover for him and he slipped in next to her. "Oh!" she breathed. "You are frozen."

She was warm, warm as life itself. He felt her shiver in his arms. "Let's get warm together, my love," he murmured against her soft neck. "Allow me to show you how warm I can become at a moment's notice."

She laughed and reached for him, accommodating herself to his sudden urgency.

Later Akitada held her. She sighed contentedly and drifted off again into her interrupted sleep, while he thought how sleep was much like death.

Suddenly fearful, he held her closer and said, "I went to look at the snow in the moonlight. So beautiful. And I thought of death."

She was startled awake. "Death? No, not death. You are safe, alive, here with me."

He sighed. "You forget that my work all too often deals with death. And now I have once again someone to lose."

She sat up. "Oh, Akitada, don't. It's bad luck. Don't ever think of such things."

He pulled her down into the blankets and murmured, "I'll try, if you are very kind to me."

She laughed softly and curled up against him. He listened until her breathing told him that she was asleep again, and then slipped from their warm cocoon to get up. Throwing on his plain house robe, he padded down the cold galleries to the bath. The water was only lukewarm, but he washed and shaved by the light of the wax candle, then walked back to his study, where he used the candle to light two more and an oil lamp.

His desk was covered with papers he had brought home, cases for which he wanted to consult his law books. His father had left him a fine library that had been passed down through generations of Sugawaras and had been added to as every heir took up his court duties.

Now his own son Yoshi was also enrolled at the university, though his father was not at all sure he would please his professors. They made allowances for the very young boys, and Yoshi had had excellent tutors, but the boy's mind was on horseback riding, kick ball, and stick fighting. Tora was responsible for the last, having been a stick fighter of renown in his day.

Akitada worked for an hour or more, listening to the watchman call the time. When it was near dawn, he got up, stretched, and went in search of a warm bowl of gruel. His study had become unpleasantly frigid and his padded robe failed to keep him warm.

The cook and maid were in the kitchen, hovering near the fire. He startled them and they apologized that they had not looked after him. Reassuring them, he ladled gruel into his bowl. The maid filled a large brazier with live coals and walked with him to his study. The brazier spread its warmth quickly, the gruel warmed his insides, and the maid returned with a steaming pot of tea which she left on the brazier.

A smoothly running household.

Contentment.

Love at long last.

Alas, the dry legal work awaited him. He could have worked at the ministry where the archives held all the legal books he might need, but he had chosen to return to his home, drawn by the happiness it held. This could not go on, of course. Later that day he would have to put on his court robes and report on his work.

But by midmorning he received a visitor and his plans changed abruptly.

3

Kosehira Brings News

Fujiwara Kosehira was Akitada's oldest friend. They had met when both were students at the university. Kosehira, a short boy, had attached himself to the tall Akitada and together they had faced any number of difficulties likely to terrify young students. Kosehira disliked sports and was mocked by others until Akitada appeared on the scene. And Akitada, who lacked an influential family, had Kosehira, the son of one of the powerful Fujiwara families, to intercede for him whenever professors tried to ignore his achievements while giving awards to the sons of men who would be grateful.

Akitada's troubles had followed him to his appointments in government service, and even then Kosehira had done his best to smooth the way for him. But now it was many years later and life had created problems and damaged their friendship.

After the death of his first wife, Akitada had been devastated. Kosehira had invited him to spend some time with his own family, and there Kosehira had done his best to bring his lonely friend together with his oldest daughter Yukiko. Akitada was already past forty; Yukiko was eighteen. He resisted, but she had become infatuated with him through the stories her father had told her of Akitada's past. She had thought him a hero. And Yukiko was lovely and young and full of life. And her father approved. So they had been married.

The real Akitada was a great disappointment to a young woman raised on hero worship. She soon saw he was after all only a dry old stick who spent his days with dull paperwork, while she dreamed of a life at court. Being Kosehira's daughter, she became a lady-in-waiting to the empress, while Akitada left to serve as governor in another province. Their marriage was predictably headed for disaster. When Yukiko expected another man's child, Akitada agreed to accept it as his own to avoid a scandal that would have ruined her reputation and reflected on her father. But Yukiko refused to live in his house and, tormented by her influence on his own daughter, he eventually divorced her.

And now the rift in his friendship with her father could never be mended. Guilt and shame on both sides made their meetings difficult and painful. Kosehira was only too aware that he had wanted the unequal marriage, and Akitada knew that he should have had the sense to refuse.

Kosehira entered shyly, looking embarrassed and apologetic. Akitada put on a smile and said brightly, "What a surprise! How are you, Kosehira?"

It was clearly not what he would have said years ago. He would have gone to embrace his friend and expressed his joy at seeing him.

Kosehira looked for a moment as though he would turn and run. "Erh, I hope I don't interrupt?"

"Not at all. Please sit down. Is everyone well?"

Kosehira was flustered. "Everyone" in this case surely meant Yukiko and her child. He gave Akitada a shamefaced smile. "Yes, yes. All are well. And you? You look happy. I trust your lady is in good health?"

"Excellent health, thank you."

"And Saburo and Genba are quite recovered?"

"Genba is doing well. Saburo was far more seriously wounded and still suffers pain and has some trouble breathing. That knife went in quite deeply and he lost a lot of blood. It was a miracle he lived long enough for us to find him."

"I heard. I'm sorry for him. Brave man."

"Yes."

The conversation faltered.

Akitada offered wine, and Kosehira accepted. He seemed grateful for the excuse to make more small talk. Akitada was beginning to smell a rat. He clapped for a servant and gave his order, then asked, "So, what brings you?"

"Oh, umm, yes. Do you like Nara?"

"Nara? I like it well enough. Why?"

"Hmm, yes. Very pleasant place. I have a house there. All those magnificent temples! Our ancestors were brilliant builders. We have nothing like it here."

Akitada said dryly, "With good reason. Our illustrious emperor who founded Heian-kyo, was very particular about keeping the Buddhist clique at a distance. He had learned how adept they are at troublemaking and meddling in national affairs."

Wine and food arrived, were served, and the maid departed.

Kosehira sipped the wine and nodded. "Good. I was quite parched. Erh, about Nara: there's been some trouble there, it appears. I thought you might be interested."

Akitada said repressively, "I've only been back a few months. There is a great deal of work at the ministry."

Kosehira sighed. "You've changed," he said with some of his old frankness. "You used to like any excuse to get out of the ministerial archives and into a murder case."

Akitada relented. It was true, he had no relish for the paperwork. "Someone got murdered? I think they have a very capable police force in Nara. Have to. All those pilgrimages by members of the court."

"Yes. That's it. Exactly. Nara is very close and everybody around the emperor has become religious. The ladies are forever traipsing off on pilgrimages."

A sense of doom settled over Akitada. His former wife Yukiko was one of those ladies. She was by now quite an important person, said to be the empress's closest confidante. Heaven forbid that Yukiko should drag him into a case that was not only dangerous because it involved imperial women but also because it could jeopardize his new marriage. Yukiko had proved to be vengeful in the past. Akitada said nothing, but he bit his lip.

Kosehira, who watched him anxiously, said, "It has nothing to do with Yukiko."

"I'm glad." Akitada's relief was palpable.

Kosehira chortled. "I don't blame you. That daughter of mine is a handful to turn any man's hair white."

They laughed a little, and some of the tension left the room.

Then Kosehira sobered. "Well, this is something I wouldn't have put past her, but this time, the troublemaker is another young woman. May her family forgive her."

"What happened?"

"She's vanished."

Akitada raised his brows. "You mean into thin air? As in one of those stunts devout monks always pray for?"

Kosehira gave a snort. "Not quite, though there are similarities. You'll keep this to yourself?"

"I don't see how I can find your young woman if I'm not to mention her."

Kosehira, taking this for acquiescence, nodded. "Fair enough, but hear me out." He emptied his cup to give himself strength and said, "This is Lady Hachijo. Hachijo-in."

Akitada blinked. The suffix "in" was reserved for the emperor's women. It marked the fact that they were favorites, usually mothers of male heirs. In this case, the "Hachijo-in" was a retirement palace given to the concubine in recognition of her service to His Majesty. It also became her name.

Kosehira saw his face and nodded. "Yes. Awkward."

"I'll say. How does an imperial concubine disappear? I'm not familiar with her, by the way. Haven't stayed in touch with the palace."

"No. I know." Kosehira smiled. "One of Yukiko's complaints about you."

Akitada said coldly, "Precisely."

Kosehira sighed. "Hachijo-in is a Yoshido. She is now nineteen years old. She is a beauty and His Majesty was enchanted even though her family no longer has any power. The affair was very upsetting to the rest of his ladies."

"I can imagine. I daresay it offended any number of Fujiwara concubines and empresses." Somewhat snidely, he added, "And their families."

Kosehira looked hurt. "You know I've never played that game. Even if my daughter did. Yes. They tried everything to blacken the Yoshido lady's reputation and, I hear, eventually resorted to poisoning her food, though that may be an ugly rumor. By that time, though nobody knew it, she was pregnant with the emperor's child."

Akitada sat up. "She was poisoned?"

Murder in the imperial family? Could such a thing be?

"She survived but she lost the child. His Majesty was beside himself. He almost sent the prime minister into exile."

Akitada shook his head. "Surely you don't expect me to investigate an attempted murder in His Majesty's women's quarters?"

"No, of course not. I told you the lady has disappeared."

"Probably afraid to stay around for another attempt on her life."

His friend made a face. "Don't be flippant. She's in no danger even if someone planned such a thing. She informed His Majesty that the loss of the child and her near death convinced her to renounce life and become a nun. She's no longer one of his ladies."

"Ah! Then why disappear?"

"Exactly. The emperor is distraught, as you may imagine."

"Yes. Understandable. I expect so is her family. From rich expectations to nothing."

Kosehira sighed. "Your work has made you bitter. Or perhaps my visit is too unwelcome." He prepared to get up, and Akitada was ashamed.

"No," he cried. "Go on, tell me. I shall listen without further remarks."

Kosehira looked at him uncertainly.

Akitada said, "Come! We used to be able to joke together. What's happened to us, my friend?"

After a moment, Kosehira nodded and sat. "Lady Hachijo left the capital and went to Nara. There she entered Hokkeji, a convent that is connected with Kofukuji." He paused, as if waiting for a comment.

Akitada said nothing. Kofukuji, the largest temple and monastery in Nara was the Fujiwara clan temple. Anything affecting it would have been of the greatest concern to a member of Kosehira's family.

Kosehira took up his story again. "I mention it because you may have to deal with the Kofukuji monks. That is, if you agree to take the case." He gave Akitada another uncertain glance.

"Go on! So the imperial lady became a nun and a member of Hokkeji?"

"Yes. Well, several of the nuns used to be high-ranking women. I suppose that's what made her choose it. They have a great deal in common. In any case, she suddenly seems to have disappeared. Nobody knows exactly when this happened. At first they thought she'd gone on a retreat or pilgrimage. But when the family asked, nobody knew where. Her family had not seen her since she became a novice and they are very upset. It is also causing great distress to His Majesty. So, please, Akitada. Just go down to Nara and ask a few questions. You can stay at my place."

"You forget that, unlike you, I'm not free to leave my post without permission."

"Oh, that's taken care of. His Excellency, the prime minister, has informed your minister that you'll be looking into the administration of Hokkeji. Can't trust those nuns to run the place properly, you see." Kosehira grinned.

Akitada scowled. "So the decision never was mine, was it?"

His friend's face fell. "Not really. I'm sorry that you hate the idea, Akitada. I thought you'd welcome some diversion."

"Hardly. After this summer's troubles, which left two of my people severely wounded, and my recent marriage, I'd hoped to be left in peace for a while."

"Oh. Yes. You're right. Lady Sadako has cause to resent my request." Kosehira's face brightened. "But why not take her along? Ladies like to go on pilgrimages."

"I'll not put my wife into danger. And my cases always seem to turn out badly."

"Not this one, Akitada. What could happen? You'd be dealing with some nuns and a monk or two. They're not violent. The Buddha forbids it."

That was laughable. "Are you serious?"

"Well, not really, but this is nothing to do with the religious business. This is about an imperial lady. Your wife could be a great help."

4
Akiko

Akitada admired how well his bride looked in the deep green gown she wore. He had selected that silk for her some months ago and enjoyed that shopping trip because he was once again buying clothes for his wife. Their marriage had only been days old, and he had walked among the silk merchants as if on clouds.

"Kosehira came," he said absently, studying the graceful way in which she held her head. He was enchanted by her neck, usually hidden from sight by her long hair. Today she had tied it back because she was airing out the clothes boxes. He went a little closer and saw that she was unpacking the trunk of spring clothing. "Those look pretty dull. I think you need new clothes," he said, smiling in anticipation. "Something in a very pale rose color perhaps?"

She turned with a laugh. "I'm much too old for that, my dear, but thank you for not noticing. What did Kosehira want?"

"Hmm." He bent to put his lips to her enticing neck. "You're young and desirable. Much too desirable. I am to go to Nara and talk to nuns."

She looked startled. "Nara? Oh, you lucky man to be able to visit Nara!"

It struck him that she sounded wistful. "Umm, would you like to come with me?"

Lady Sadako dropped the red robe she held and flung her arms around his neck. "Of course! How can you ask? I've never been there. Oh, how I wish to see it!"

Leaving his wife to make her travel preparations, Akitada sought out Tora.

Tora was on the front veranda, leaning on the railing and watching the stable boy clearing away the snow that had fallen during the night. He turned and grinned at Akitada. "I'm bored. You, sir, have no such cause to complain. When I think back to the days when Hanae and I started life together, I had no time to think of anything but her."

Akitada smiled. "That's a little unkind, Tora. Do you mean you no longer value your wife?"

"Well, yes, I do. But having her wait for me every day is no longer a surprise, a sort of reward for having worked during the day."

"Ah, that explains why I find you lazing about at this hour."

"I usually do some stick-fighting with Yoshi, but he's already gone to the university."

"Yes. Some things are more important than stick-fighting."

"Bite your tongue."

They both laughed. Akitada said, "We're going to Nara tomorrow. Lady Sadako is coming with us."

If anything, Tora's joy was greater than Sadako's. He clapped his hands and shouted, "Another case! Finally another case. It was terrible of you to enjoy all the excitement without me last time."

"Hardly enjoyable," Akitada said dryly, but he smiled. "We'll ride. Lord Kosehira has a house where we can stay. It shouldn't take too long, but tell Genba and Saburo. I'm going to see my sister."

Lady Akiko was engaged in a sewing lesson for her two daughters who were thirteen and nine years old. They were in her pavilion with many-colored fabrics spread across the *tatami* mats. The shutters to the outside were closed, and a brazier spread pleasant warmth while several large candles lit the space and made the colors in the painted screen brilliant.

It was a lovely scene, no less bright than the snowy world outside. Akitada had grown fonder of his sister Akiko as the years had passed, but he had never loved her like his other sister, Yoshiko. Yoshiko was the gentle one, though she had proved stronger and more stubborn than Akiko. Akiko's main fault was that she had inherited a few traits of her mother, Akitada's stepmother. She was ambitious and manipulative and valued status above all else. However, she had also proven her loyalty to him. Perhaps most interesting was the fact that she shared with Akitada the sort of curiosity that solves crimes and ferrets out secrets.

Seeing her at this domestic and maternal activity astonished Akitada, but she quickly reassured him by jumping up, scattering fabrics, with the words, "Thank the gods, you've come. You have no idea how dull life has been with all this snow."

Akitada embraced her, greeted the girls and nodded to the maid. "You're a good mother," he lied. "And you make a lovely picture all together like this."

"Pah! I had planned to go to court. But never mind. You and I shall sit and you shall tell me what is going on in the world."

"Then you'll be disappointed to learn that I've come to you for the same reason."

She laughed. Directing her daughters and the maid to take the sewing elsewhere and send someone with refreshments, she made Akitada comfortable beside the screen and sat down across from him.

"Marriage agrees with you, Brother," she said with a smile. "I hoped you would bring me good news."

He chuckled. "We're happy as we are. No need for any more children."

Her eyes widened. "You're joking. Mind you, you're both no longer in your first youth, but you have only one son. What if something happens to him? You must have more children. And you can well afford them."

"Yoshi is healthy and has reached an age when we can trust fate."

"Akitada, don't put it off too long. But never mind, what brings you, if it wasn't that?"

Heaving an inner sigh of relief, he said, "I am to go to Nara to find one of His Majesty's ladies. I thought you might know a bit more about this story than Kosehira."

Akiko's eyes sparkled. "Oh! Tell me more. A mystery? Who is the lady?"

"A Lady Hachijo."

Her face fell. "Not that woman! There's nothing to investigate. She's gone for good."

"What do you mean, 'gone for good'?"

"She's a nun. Thank the Buddha for this mercy. The nuns at Hokkeji took her in. Now she's their problem."

"What problem? I know she's a nun, but she seems to have disappeared."

Akiko's eyes widened. "Seriously?"

He nodded.

"Don't do it, Akitada. It will cause nothing but trouble."

"Kosehira came to me this morning. It must be serious. He rarely visits."

"There! I knew it. She's making more trouble. Let them deal with it. Nobody cares about her."

Akitada cleared his throat at his sister's callous comment. "It appears His Majesty cares a great deal."

She grimaced. "Men!"

"Seriously, Akiko, what can you tell me about her? Why, for example, do you hate her so?"

She glowered at him. "I serve Her Majesty. And I've seen Her weep because of that woman."

"That seems rather excessive. What did she do?"

Akiko tossed her head. "You wouldn't understand. You know nothing about the imperial women and how they live."

"I recall being married to someone who was determined to become one of them. And who nearly seduced my daughter into following her. I'm fully aware it's not the paradise some seem to think it."

Akiko sighed and relented. "Not everyone behaves well. Your former wife and the Yoshido woman certainly don't."

"Be specific. Did Hachijo engage in affairs with other men?"

"That, too."

It dawned on Akitada that he had not considered the atmosphere of political maneuvering when ruled by the female temperament. Akiko, though not in service to Her Majesty as a lady-in-waiting, was a frequent visitor to Her apartments and a friend. And Akiko was very loyal.

He asked, "Did she make trouble for Her Majesty?"

Akiko nodded. "And how! Her Majesty was frequently in tears."

"Because the emperor chose Hachijo as a new favorite?"

"He didn't choose. She seduced him. We all watched her flagrant behavior. I do not for a moment believe she was expecting His child. Not for a moment. Women who choose to sleep alone in eave chambers do so because they expect night visitors."

"Surely someone would put a stop to this once His Majesty expressed an interest."

Akiko pursed her lips. "They tried. She would have none of it."

"And yet the emperor still seems to be fond of her."

"Men are fools."

It crossed Akitada's mind that Lady Hachijo had made enemies, and that these enemies were likely behind her disappearance. Perhaps the tale that she had chosen to become a nun were mere fabrications to cover the fact that this thorn in the side of Her Majesty and Her powerful relatives, among them the prime minister, had been removed permanently.

"I take it she had few friends at court. What about her background."

"She comes from one of those minor families that never quite made the move from Nara. Their name is Yoshido. No money, but they claim to be direct descendants from the gods. As for friends, she had none but those men who crept into her bed at night."

"I assume she is beautiful and talented?"

Akiko tossed her head again. "Pah! A small girl. Pretty enough. And she plays the *koto* and sings a little."

Akitada translated this to mean that she was quite beautiful and played and sang charmingly. He said, "Those men you claim visited her in secret, who are they?"

"I don't know. It was a matter of someone hearing voices or seeing shadows moving in the dark. There was a lot of talk, but no details."

Akiko was at least honest in this matter. Akitada pursued the issue. "Come, sis, name names!"

"Well, I've heard that Captain Yoshitomo is an admirer. And the governor of Yamato, Korechika, and Fujiwara Noritoki, the poet. It could be any of these, or all, or someone altogether different. Maybe even that handsome monk who comes down from Mount Hiei to instruct the imperial ladies."

Clearly life at court was even more depraved than Akitada had assumed. A monk? He knew of the other three. Yoshitomo was a young Minamoto, a rather dashing figure at court. Korechika was one of the Fujiwara nobles. He was close enough to the capital for frequent visits at court. The poet lived on his family wealth, taught at the university and spent the rest of his time composing verse which he recited at poetry festivals.

Akitada said dryly, "They were hardly friends under the circumstances."

Akiko snapped, "Men don't sleep with women out of friendship."

This made Akitada chuckle. His sister was shockingly outspoken for a well-brought-up woman. He would not be surprised that it was this part of her character that made her so welcome in the women's palace.

He asked, "What if she was murdered?"

That gave her pause. She frowned. "I trust not. The scandal would upset Her Majesty."

"And the emperor."

Akiko grimaced. "I beg you, don't touch this. It could be dangerous. And it might hurt Her Majesty. She's suffered enough."

"If I don't look into the matter, someone else will."

Akiko thought about this, then nodded reluctantly. Akitada decided his sister had shared what there was to share. And she was clearly prejudiced. He must search for the truth about Lady Hachijo in Nara.

5

Nara

The weather stayed clear and cold and the roads were good between the capital and Nara. They made excellent time on horseback, comfortably wrapped into quilted trousers and coats and wearing boots. Sadako also wore a silk head covering against the cold, but the men were bare-headed. All three were red-cheeked and cheerful.

They were not alone, in spite of the season and the new snow. Pilgrims and monks walked or rode, and messengers dashed by from time to time. Once they had crossed the mountain range at the provincial border into Yamato Province, they descended gently through the snowy foothills into another plain.

Sadako exclaimed when they reached a look-out and saw the city spread beneath them. "It's all white. And it looks like the capital! But, oh, there are so many temples. It's a holy city."

Her husband, pausing beside her, snorted. "Hardly. It's a city of monks."

She shot him a glance. "You really don't like them, do you?"

Akitada hesitated. Disliking the Buddhist clergy was not diplomatic in his world. But honesty made him say, "No. I've met too many bad ones."

"They aren't all bad, Akitada. Some are good men. And women. Do you hate nuns also?"

He said stiffly, "I don't hate anyone. As for nuns, women are easily misled."

"Oh, Akitada! Think of the young woman who traded life as the emperor's favorite to serve the Buddha."

He raised his brows. "Perhaps even becoming a nun was preferable to life at court."

She turned away. "You're impossible. I'm looking forward to see those wonderful temples and the treasures they contain."

Tora was becoming restive. "I could do with a warm meal and some hot wine. They have some fine eating places in that city."

Akitada laughed. "All those devout pilgrims demand good food and wine for their exertions."

It took another hour until they passed through the northern gate to the city. Sadako pointed out that this, too, was much like in the capital.

"Both are built the Chinese way," her husband said. "The soothsayers have a hand in the planning. The most auspicious place is protected by mountains in the four directions, and the palace is always in the northernmost part."

"Yes. Our houses are built that way also. And I stay in the northern pavilion."

Akitada laughed. "So you do! A wife is the most precious treasure of the household."

She blushed and they smiled at each other. Akitada's heart beat a little faster. He could not remember ever feeling this happy, though he must have in his youth when he and Tamako had first been married. But then he thought: we were young. The young are careless because they know nothing of death and loss and loneliness. And fear seized him again that he might lose Sadako also.

Whatever we hold most dear makes us most afraid.

He reached for her hand and murmured "I love you."

She squeezed his fingers, but before she could reply, Tora called out, "There's the market. They should have some good eating places there."

Akitada, who was eager to discover the mystery of the missing concubine, protested. "We should go on to Kosehira's house. They're probably expecting us."

Tora's face fell. Sadako said, "Can we be sure they expect us? Surely the place is only used when the family visits the temples. There are probably only a couple of caretakers there."

Akitada submitted and they dismounted in front of a large eatery facing the market square with all its booths and stands. Even in winter, there was a good crowd here, and it was midday. People shopped, ate, and gossiped with friends. He had noted that Nara's streets seemed cleaner than those in the capital. Someone had worked diligently to sweep the snow and keep the roads open.

A waiter came quickly, alerted by their fine travel clothes. Hungry travelers from the capital, he decided.

Food and hot wine appeared quickly. They warmed their frozen fingers on the cups before drinking.

Tora smacked his lips, then eyed a mountain of food so hungrily, that Sadako told him to start. She and Akitada still held hands and smiled.

"You're enjoying this," Akitada stated.

She nodded. "It's wonderful. I shall never forget this trip."

Tora lifted a full bowl to his lips, shoveling fish and vegetables into his mouth and regarded his master and mistress complacently. It had been his doing. You could not leave love to those two. They had had no notion how to proceed. Now look at them. There would be little ones in the house again in no time at all. He swallowed and burped.

Eventually, Akitada and Sadako remembered where they were and ate.

The meal proved to be more expensive than any Akitada could remember, but the food and wine had been good.

They found Kosehira's place after asking some questions. It was a comfortably large residence with stables in the northern part of the city. The gates stood open and they rode in. Little had been done to remove the snow. Akitada dismounted and went to help Sadako down. A stable boy of about fifteen years appeared and took the horses. He stared when Tora told him that Lord Sugawara and his Lady had arrived.

Tora glanced at the main house. "Where are the other servants?"

The boy said, "Just me and Ma."

"Really? No maids?"

"Sanekane went to get them. He never came back."

Akitada asked, "Who is Sanekane?"

"He hires the servants."

"Ah, the majordomo. Thank you. He'll surely return shortly. See to the horses."

But Sanekane did not return.

They were left to fend for themselves. Akitada and Sadako walked through the house and found all rooms empty of servants and slightly dusty. They were pleasant rooms with thick *tatami* mats, painted screens, reed curtains, and the necessary utensils such as oil lamps, candle sticks, and braziers. There was a small bath with a wooden tub, but the water was ice cold. They chose their room, which gave onto a small courtyard with snow-covered bushes and a small pine. Sadako remained here to inspect the bedding, while Akitada went out into the service yard. There was a small kitchen building here, and in it he found the cook.

She was stirring some soup in a small pot over a small fire. It smelled appetizing but seemed totally inadequate to feed three guests.

"Who are you?" she asked, staring at his sudden appearance.

Taken aback by the rude question, Akitada snapped, "Lord Sugawara. We are guests of your master. Where is everybody?"

"Just me and the boy."

It did not sound promising. "What is that you're cooking?"

"Beans and cabbage." She added, "It's for my boy and me."

So much for food.

Or hospitality.

"Weren't you told that guests are expected?"

She shook her head. "Sanekane never came back."

The woman was in her forties, quite ugly and shapeless in her brown jacket and pants, her hair gathered in a careless knot at the back of her head. She also seemed not to be very bright. Experienced servants would never speak this way to their betters. Akitada's hopes for regular home-cooked meals faded.

"Where is Sanekane?" he asked. "Send the boy for him."

She shook her head again. "How should I know where he is. He doesn't tell me. He's always gone when nobody from the family's here."

"Are there any house servants?"

"No. Sanekane hires them when the master comes here."

"You should have been told about our coming. Lord Kosehira expected the house to be staffed."

She scowled. "Not my fault. Ask Sanekane. He's the one takes care of things."

"When did he leave?"

"Two days ago."

"What?"

"Two days ago."

"But why didn't you send for the constables?"

She gave a harsh laugh. "He wouldn't thank me for that."

Akitada gave up and went in search of Tora. He found him in the stable checking on the horses and chatting with the stable boy. The boy had done a creditable job of making the horses comfortable. Akitada explained the situation and asked, "Do you know where Sanekane might be?"

Tora said, "He might be home. He doesn't live here. Only this boy and his mother live here."

Akitada asked the boy, "Could you run and bring him? He needs to hire staff."

It crossed Akitada's mind that he would probably pay for the servants and the supplies that would be needed. Kosehira would be deeply embarrassed if he discovered what had happened, and Sanekane most likely would be out of a job. In any case, it might bring Kosehira to Nara and Akitada would find his time with Sadako spoiled by having to deal with their host.

The boy was willing and took off. Akitada and Tora returned to the main house to tell Sadako what they had learned.

She was dismayed."I'd better speak to that cook. She needs to shop for provisions. I'll need some money."

Impressed by her calm competence, Akitada gave her a portion of their funds. He hoped the matter of the missing lady could be resolved quickly because he foresaw greater expenses ahead.

"You might see about making a fire under the bath water," she said, slipping into her quilted jacket for the trip to the kitchen.

"Surely . . . ," he started to protest, then nodded meekly. It would give them something to do while they waited.

When the stable boy returned, he found Akitada and Tora watching the flames of a lusty fire heating their bath water. It would take a couple of hours and would need stoking, but they expected that Sanekane would be back by then.

But the boy brought bad news. He had drifted up and stood in amazement watching a nobleman in fine silk clothing tending the bath fire.

Akitada asked him, "Well? Where is he?"

The boy woke up from his trance. "Gone," he said. "The women said he's gone."

"Gone where?"

The boy heard the impatience in Akitada's voice and backed away a step. "He drinks," he explained.

After a stunned silence, Akitada said, "The gods give me patience. Can you find him?"

The boy shook his head.

"These women you spoke to, are they his wives?"

The boy pondered, then shook his head. "I don't think so. Ma says they're sluts."

Tora gave a snort.

"Take us to his house."

"I'll have to tell Ma."

Akitada sighed. "Go then but come right back."

He went inside to tell Sadako about the new complications. She had managed to fill a brazier with coals from the kitchen fire and had spread their bedding. After being outside, Akitada thought the room looked very cozy. His spirits lifted.

She heard his report with raised brows and shook her head. "I wonder what else can go wrong," she said with a chuckle.

Akitada's heart warmed at her good humor. He knew he was an incredibly lucky man and went to take her in his arms. Nuzzling her neck, he murmured, "I can't wait till night time, but I suppose I'd better see what's become of the cursed Sanekane. Apparently people disappear every day in this town."

"Go then," she said. "And I'll make sure we have something to eat tonight."

6

The Missing Majordomo

Akitada looked about him as they walked. The city had changed, he thought, in the twenty or more years since he had last visited. And it had not been winter then. It looked cleaner than it had then. The temples still loomed large—their huge roofs white against the blue sky— but there were more people in the streets, pilgrims most of them. Both men and women. He saw a surprising number of women.

Tora pointed. "There's Todaiji. That hall is bigger than anything I ever saw. Have you seen the giant Buddha inside?" Tora had visited more recently than Akitada. He was clearly impressed by the size and magnificence of the temples.

Akitada nodded. The history of Buddhism in his country was closely tied to Nara. It was the old capital. The wise emperor Kammu had moved the seat of government north to escape the powerful interference of the monks. In Heian-kyo, the temples had been banished outside city limits, but here in Nara, they still held enormous power and dominated the rest of the city.

"Which way is Kofukuji?" he asked, looking around.

Tora pointed. "Over there. Above those trees you can see the great pagoda. That's another big one. The pagoda is five stories. I went up. Do you want to go see it?"

"Tomorrow perhaps. It's the Fujiwara temple. They have plenty of money and power to maintain it. Hokkeji is nearby, I think."

That's where the lady nun was living?"

"Yes. Very strange for a lady of that rank to disappear. But at least she should be easy to find."

Tora laughed. "What's the matter? Too many monks and nuns for your taste?"

"And too many powerful people involved. I sometimes think the monks of Nara still pull the strings in our government."

"Stop worrying and enjoy the trip with your lady. She's excited to be here."

Akitada smiled. "Yes, Tora. You're quite right. I'm letting my bad humor spoil her enjoyment."

The stable boy had given them directions, and Akitada and Tora walked quickly to an area not far from the market. It was a good quarter, inhabited mostly by successful merchants. There, in a quiet back street, Sanekane owned a house with a garden covered in snow.

The garden was unusually generous and the path to the house wound through a landscape of trees and bushes to end up before a door with a gate rattle. Tora gave it a couple of violent assaults, and the door was opened by a large-breasted woman in a gray-and-black-patterned robe. She was perhaps fifty and wore her hair in a bun. Her face had been whitened and there was rouge on her lips. She eyed them carefully, letting her eyes rest a moment on Akitada's clothing and then studying Tora with some interest.

Akitada said, "I'm looking for Sanekane."

She raised a pudgy hand to her mouth and chuckled. "You and me both, sir. He isn't home. I don't know when he'll be back. We're all alone." She batted her eyes at him, making him wonder if it was an invitation.

Irritated, he said, "Can we come in? I'd like to talk to you."

Her eyes shifted to Tora again and she giggled . "You're both charming gentlemen, but what would people think? I'm sorry, but there are only women here at the moment."

Her smiles belied her concerns for propriety. She reminded Akitada of an auntie in a brothel, teasing a customer. Before he could say anything, Tora stepped forward and flashed her one of his devastating smiles. "Very proper, my lovely! Good-looking women must be careful. However, this is Lord Sugawara and I'm Tora. We're guests of Lord Kosehira. I assure you, madam, your reputation and those of the other ladies are quite safe from us."

She simpered, bowed to Akitada, and opened the door wider. "In that case it's a pleasure. I'm Kiyo. There's only my daughter Otoyo and me," she explained, stepping aside for them. "I apologize, but women without a man to protect them are quite helpless. People gossip so."

They slipped off their boots and followed her into a cluttered room with a few worn cushions and a small brazier in a ring of ashes. A tray with used dishes stood beside it. The daughter, a younger version of the mother, her hair loosely tied back, jumped up from one of the cushions. She was also buxom and round-faced, but more lively and more heavily painted. Akitada guessed her to be about thirty years old. She, too, eyed Tora speculatively.

The older woman introduced them to her daughter and said, "I'm sorry. You find us unprepared for company. We were doing our chores." She gestured for them to sit.

The daughter wore a somewhat stained robe patterned with rather large white chrysanthemum blossoms on a blue ground. Neither looked as though they had been working very hard. And both wore paint on their faces. Akitada wondered what sort of work she was talking about.

Meanwhile, it was Tora who had their interest. With women it was always Tora. And he still wore that silly smile on his face.

"Now then," said Akitada, frowning at Tora, "what is this about Sanekane being gone? This is his house, I think?"

They took their eyes off Tora and nodded. The mother said. "It is. It's his house."

"And you two are . . . what?" The question was blunt and insulting. Akitada regretted it immediately.

The mother laughed a little. "Sorry. I'm his housekeeper. My daughter and I live here."

That hardly reassured Akitada's suspicions.

Tora said, "Sanekane's a lucky man."

They giggled and looked at each other. Then they giggled some more. Most likely, thought Akitada, both women were kept by the majordomo. He asked, "How old is Sanekane?"

The mother answered. "Nearly seventy. He's an old gentleman, poor dear. That's why he needs looking after." More giggling from the daughter.

Akitada's frown deepened. "He is frail?"

They both laughed now. "No," said the mother. "Not frail at all. Not frail in body, I mean." They exchanged smiles and nods. "He's quite strong and healthy."

"So where is he?"

The daughter said, "We don't know. He could be anywhere. It's a big worry sometimes."

"Are you telling me that this has happened before?"

"Oh, yes." They both nodded.

After a moment, Kiyo said, "He enjoys his cup of wine. With friends. We are quite used to it. He'll come home soon."

They looked complacent about all of this, as if certain he would always return because they took such good care of him. Akitada was beginning to dislike both women.

"You mean he drinks for days? Where does he sleep when he's not here?"

They looked embarrassed. "We don't know," said the daughter. "It's very inconsiderate."

There was no more to be gained. Akitada asked them to send Sanekane as soon as he returned, and they took their leave.

Outside Tora said, "That old geezer has two cuddly females to look after him and he goes out to drink and spends his nights elsewhere? Something's wrong with that picture."

Akitada was still irritated by Tora's flirting. "You have a dirty mind. The older one is his housekeeper and the daughter lives with her mother. Maybe she's the maid. Not everyone thinks about sex all the time."

Tora laughed and winked at him.

Akitada ignored this impertinent hint at his own recent marriage but he blushed. Tora was probably right about Sanekane. A man who had two willing females at home must have run into some other problem. "I'm going back. Since you have a better understanding about how this man's mind works, I suggest you find out where he spends his drinking time."

7

On Sanekane's Trail

Tora was pleased with this assignment. He had hoped to have some free time to enjoy the Nara nightlife in any case, and here he had the perfect excuse while using his skills of detection. He started by exploring the neighborhood where Sanekane lived. Only a block from his house, he found a well-kept wine shop he thought would have appealed to a man of Sanekane's status. As majordomo to one of the great Fujiwara lords, he would be selective where to take his custom. The place, called "Peaceful Grove of Refreshment" according to its door curtain, did not disappoint him inside either. It was clean, attended by customers who seemed well-to-do and mature, and he was greeted by a neatly dressed host. As it turned out, it also served a very decent wine.

Tora tasted, smacked his lips, and complimented the host. "Will you join me in a cup?" he invited.

The host was willing and poured himself a liberal drink. "You've come to visit the great Buddha?" he asked with a smile.

"Why not?" said Tora. "Though I intended to visit an old friend. Alas, he seems to have disappeared."

"Really?"

Tora poured more wine. "Name of Sanekane. They tell me he might have come here."

The host's brows rose. "Sanekane? Nice fellow. He used to come, but I haven't seen him for a month. Meant to go ask him if I've offended him somehow. Good customer."

Tora chuckled. "Yes, I hear Sanekane likes a good cup of wine at the end of his work day. Any idea what happened?"

"None." The host was clearly regretful. "See the woman serving the customers over there?"

Tora peered. A young but plain female was placing bowls of snacks beside several guests. "What about her?"

"Her parents died, one right after the other. She had no money for their funerals and was in a terrible state. Sanekane found out and paid."

"That's very generous." Tora thought of the two women in Sanekane's house. "She isn't his girlfriend by any chance?"

His host frowned. "Of course not. She was about to be married. And Sanekane's old enough to be her grandfather. I thought you said he was a friend of yours?"

Tora bit his lip. "Well, stranger things have happened. Paying for two funerals for a total stranger is a bit unusual."

"That's Sanekane for you. He's really generous."

"He must be wealthier than I thought. He said he worked as a majordomo for a Fujiwara lord."

"And so he does. But Sanekane's got family money and owns land south of the city. In any case, he's got a soft heart. And he couldn't stand to see her cry like that."

"Would she know where he is?"

"Don't think so. You can ask her." He shouted, "Hey, Kimi, come over here!"

She came, smiling, cheerful, eager to help.

"This man's looking for Sanekane. Says he's disappeared. You know where he might be?"

Her face fell. "Oh, is something wrong? Poor Sanekane's elderly. He hasn't come in for a long time."

The host said, "See, I told you."

She asked Tora, "Did you ask at his house?"

"Yes. The women there haven't seen him for a couple of days."

She shook her head. "I hope he's all right."

Clearly she had no information and seemed genuinely worried about him. Tora began to worry a little himself. He thanked them both, paid, and rose to leave.

His host said, "If you find him, tell him Ogata and Kimi asked about him."

"Will do."

When he was at the door, Kimi ran after him and grabbed his sleeve. "Oh, please," she said, "find him. He's a good man."

Tora nodded. "I'll do my very best."

He walked out into the snowy streets thinking about what he had learned. From appearing to be no more than an irritating and unreliable servant, Sanekane was beginning to take on a different character. He was perhaps still too fond of wine, though you couldn't believe everything those two painted women said, but he was also a well-to-do old man who was very kind. Tora knew such people often became victims because they were too trusting. But why had he not been found if something had happened to him?

For a while, Tora walked the streets, checking wine shops that might have served Sanekane. In several he was known and an appreciated customer. There seemed little doubt that Sanekane was a heavy drinker. But here also nobody had seen him for a while.

It was getting dark by now and lights were coming on. Lanterns glowed and torches lit the sparkling snow. People carried lanterns. The streets had become more crowded as visitors to the holy places now sought food before finding some place to sleep for the night.

Tora was also getting hungry again and decided to have his evening rice in a place next to one of the city's small rivers. Outside it had been well-lit, but once inside, he could barely find his way to the main room. This overlooked the river, though the shutters were partially closed to keep out the chill. A brazier warmed the place he was shown to, and he was quite comfortable during his meal, which was hot and delicious. When he had eaten, he sat a while longer over a cup of warm wine and peered through the half open shutter at the river outside. In summer or fall it was probably pleasant here, but on a snowy night, the water merely flowed black and cold.

Willows grew along the banks, bare now, and a small bridge crossed in the distance. Houses lined the banks on both sides, outlined against the glow from lights in the next street. Tora leaned forward to peer around the shutter in the other direction and saw dark figures gathered near the water. Someone brought a flaming torch. Something in the water had attracted their interest. More torches arrived with more people, and then Tora saw a flash of red. Constables, if he was not mistaken. Some crime had been discovered. They seemed to be pulling something from the river.

Tora called to the waiter, paid, and ran outside. The missing Sanekane, he thought. They've found the missing majordomo. Drowned. Another drunk who had tumbled into a river.

But once outside, he saw it was not so easy to get to the spot on the other side of the river. He hurried along the street looking for the bridge he had seen, found it eventually, and followed another street in the general direction he remembered. This was by no means easy. While the city was laid out on a grid like the capital, the rivers and canals had minds of their own. And asking for directions was hampered by the fact that many of the people he encountered were visitors to Nara themselves and unfamiliar with its neighborhoods.

A lot of time had passed when he finally found the place. It could be reached only by a narrow alleyway between two houses. The constables had left and taken the victim with them, but a small clutch of people still stood about, talking.

Tora approached them with a polite greeting and asked, "What happened?"

They were three elderly men and a youngster and they eyed him suspiciously.

"What's it to you?" one of the old men asked.

A strong smell of cheap *sake* hung over the men. The boy looked to be about fourteen. When Tora's eyes met his, his ears turned red and he looked away. "I can ask the constables," Tora said. "You'd save me a walk."

"Why should we?" the belligerent geezer demanded.

Tora pulled out a piece of silver. "Bet you could use something warm after standing around out here."

They looked at each other. One of the others nodded. "Can't refuse a man who knows his manners," he said enthusiastically and snatched the coin.

The third nodded, and the ill-tempered one turned on the boy. "Home with you! Time you were in bed."

The boy slouched away but stopped at the next corner to watch. Tora said, "All right. What gives?"

They talked all at once. "They pulled out a dead one." "Not a stitch of clothes. In this weather." "The constables made jokes." "Bet it's murder. All that riffraff around. Nobody's safe."

Tora was confused. "A naked old man?"

"What old man?" demanded the irate fellow. "Nothing of the sort."

"What then?"

"A woman. Young. As naked as the day she was born."

"Killed herself, I bet," offered the first old timer.

The first man growled, "You're a fool. You think she took off her clothes first? So as not to get them wet?"

Tora, who was still digesting the fact that the corpse was not Sanekane, asked, "Did the constables say it was murder?"

"What do they know?" snapped the irate man. "Not a brain between them. Let's go. I'm getting cold."

Tora might have asked more questions, but it was late and this dead woman was none of his business. He was no closer to finding Sanekane. Well, tomorrow was another day. He looked after the three old men shuffling off toward a wine shop and was about to turn away, when he saw the boy watching him. He waved him over.

"Did you know the dead woman?" he asked.

The boy shook his head and blushed. "She was white all over. She was beautiful." Tears came to his eyes and he looked away, embarrassed.

"Ah, yes. Must've been upsetting," said Tora, who had long since lost the capacity of becoming upset by corpses of naked women. "Did you see what killed her?"

The boy shook his head.

"I wonder what the constables thought."

"Her neck was broken. I could tell something broke her neck."

"How do you know?"

"Her head flopped about when they picked her up."

"Ah," said Tora, then fished out a few coppers and handed them over. "Here. I bet your parents are worried about you."

The boy cheered up and clutched the coins to his chest as he ran off.

And Tora went home.

8

Sightseeing

Akitada and his spouse woke to another servantless day. The room was bitterly cold and the temptation to remain in each other's arms under a mountain of quilted blankets was enormous. It was Sadako who insisted on getting up to see if the cook had started a fire in the kitchen.

Akitada rose, grumbling, and wrapped himself in whatever clothes he could find before walking outside to blink at the brilliant whiteness. He could recall more pleasant experiences of sunny winter mornings.

The stable boy was making feeble progress at removing some new snow from the steps.

Akitada ran a hand over his stubbly chin and stopped him. "You can do that later. Go see if there's a fire under the bath water."

The boy left rather sullenly.

Tora joined Akitada and looked after him. "I'd better give him a hand," he said, and followed. Akitada went back inside and headed for the kitchen. There he found his wife in an argument with the cook about the way she should prepare Akitada's gruel. This cheered him and he smiled at his wife. Together they carried two braziers and some hot water to their room. There, Sadako brewed tea. She had adopted her husband's custom of preferring tea to wine first thing in the morning, and on this cold day it was especially welcome.

They sat together near the braziers, feeling more cheerful, when Tora joined them.

Akitada said, "I don't believe we can hope for wine, but will you drink some tea?"

Tora grinned. "Thanks, no. That stuff's for sick people. I came to report, sir."

"Good. I take it you didn't find the missing Sanekane."

"No, sir. But the women were right. He's a drunk. They know him well in the better wine shops."

"You don't say. I expect my friend Kosehira will be interested to hear that. So what do you think?"

"I'm worried, sir. He might have fallen down drunk in the snow and died there. Maybe the new snow covered the body."

"He's been gone for days. The new snow fell last night. Surely he would have been found before."

Tora shifted nervously with a glance at Sadako, who was all ears. "Well, they fished out a body from one of the rivers last night. He could have fallen in that river, or in a canal."

Akitada frowned. "What body? Did you find out?"

Another nervous glance. "Umm, yes. It took me a while to find the place and by then the constables had left with the body, but some old men said it was a woman."

"A woman?" Akitada and Sadako said together.

Tora looked embarrassed. "Well, clearly not Sanekane. They said she was young. Broken neck."

Akitada said, "You're aware that we've come to Nara to ask about the disappearance of one of the nuns?"

Tora nodded. "Couldn't be her, sir. The old men thought she was a street walker."

"Oh. Well, I suppose you'd better continue the search for Sanekane. I'm tired of starting the bath fire every day. The man must be somewhere."

Tora chuckled. "I'll see to the bath, sir."

Akitada and Sadako set out together to view the temples of Nara. Their first visit was, quite naturally, to Kofukuji. It was not too far, Akitada knew the way. Kofukuji was the Fujiwara temple, and Hokkeji was close to it.

As it turned out, so were the provincial headquarters with the tribunal and the police station. Nara was the capital of Yamato Province and the administration was in the former imperial palace. Akitada saw the flags marking its entrance and was tempted to pay a visit, but he said nothing. He was having second thoughts about dragging Sadako into something that might be very unpleasant. Both the unexplained disappearance of the majordomo and the woman's body fished out of the icy river reminded him of past cases that had involved him in murder.

Kofukuji was impressive. Fujiwara money had shoaled up the ancient buildings and supplied many layers of gold to embellish them and their contents. The five-story pagoda towered over a very large and open enclosure containing many halls.

In the bright winter sun and against the brilliant snow on roofs and the surrounding scene, the red pillars shone brilliantly. They entered by the south gate and were directed to the main courtyard via a middle gate. There a monk received them and asked their names. When Akitada identified himself and his lady, the monk sent a message for a guide.

This guide turned out to be an imposing, middle-aged monk in black robes. He introduced himself as Kakushin, the prior of the temple. He assured Akitada that Abbot Saison would wish to greet him personally and offered to give Lady Sadako a tour of the temple's treasures in the meantime.

Meeting the abbot was a formality Akitada had hoped to escape, but he suspected that Kosehira had notified him of Akitada's visit and asked him to be of assistance. So he parted somewhat reluctantly from his wife and followed a young monk to the abbot's residence.

This was of generous size, as befits the head of such an important and well-endowed monastery. He was taken to a medium-sized reception room where several braziers provided warmth and large candles lit the room while the shutters were closed.

The abbot was not alone. With him was an elegantly dressed gentleman in a brown court robe worn over white silk trousers. The abbot, a fat man who sat comfortably in an abbot's chair, was draped in dark robes and a brocade stole. He rose politely when Akitada entered. The other man rose also and bowed.

The abbot said, "Welcome, Lord Sugawara. You find me at work with Wakita Tsunetaka. He is our *betto*. We would not know what to do without him."

Akitada smiled and bowed also. The *betto* was thin and in his forties and was singularly ugly with his long nose and receding chin. They exchanged the usual courtesies, and Akitada found himself disliking the man's nasal voice and his sharp eyes that seemed to probe every part of his clothing as if he were adding up the cost of the items. Eventually Wakita took his leave.

Akitada said to the abbot, "It's very good of you to see me. I'm sorry to have interrupted. This is an inconvenience for you."

"Not at all. It is a great pleasure." Saison gestured with his fan to the cushion just vacated by the *betto* and seated himself again. "Forgive me for sitting in this chair. I find my old knees have lost the strength of my youth."

Akitada sat down and watched as two young novices entered, one after the other, carrying trays with dishes. These they deposited beside Akitada who saw they held something to drink and dried fruits and nuts.

When they were alone again, the abbot said, "I don't enjoy talking about income and expenses and much prefer you to Wakita. My cousin has written me about your visit and I am delighted to make your acquaintance."

Trust Kosehira to count the abbot among his relatives, thought Akitada and wondered how much Kosehira had told the abbot about the missing lady. He responded cautiously, "Thank you. I looked forward to making myself reacquainted with the wonders of Nara but did not expect this welcome."

To give him credit, the abbot did not beat about the bush. He said, "I am glad you like our ancient city, but I am told that you have special talents and are here to find a most important person we seem to have mislaid." He smiled at his joke.

"That is so. May I ask if your Reverence has any information?"

"None at all. A very disturbing story since it involves Hokkeji." He paused and asked, "You are aware that Hokkeji is our sister temple?"

Akitada nodded. "I believe Kofukuji has the administration of Hokkeji?"

"That is so. We take as much of the external problems of running the temple and the convent off our sisters' shoulders as we can. You just met the man who bears the burden of accounting for two temples."

"I'm sure he must be a great help to them. How large are the two temples?"

Abbot Saison smiled again. "Kofukuji is quite large. We have over two hundred monks. Hokkeji is comparatively small with only sixty nuns."

"Altogether that must make administration a formidable task."

"It is. Now how can I assist you, Akitada?"

"You're very kind. Do you know how Lady Hachijo came to choose Hokkeji as her convent?"

"Yes, indeed. She has family here in Nara. I talked to her, you know, when she first approached us. Shosho—that is the name she chose to have as a nun— is a Yoshido. The Yoshido family is quite old, as old as yours, I believe. Over the centuries, they have fallen on hard times and when the capital was moved to Heian-kyo, they either could not afford the move or had lost hopes that future emperors would support them again. That is why Shosho was her mother's great hope. Shosho's mother was a nurse to His Majesty. We believe He chose her daughter to serve at the palace out of gratitude for her mother's services at the time when He was ill with smallpox. Fortunately He survived, but she contracted the disease and was disfigured."

"I recall the time," Akitada said. That spring would never be forgotten. It was the time when he had lost his own first-born son to the epidemic.

"Yes. Shosho's mother died. Well, her family and His Majesty were understandably distraught when this beautiful young woman decided to leave her life at court and serve the Buddha."

"I was told the decision had something to do with her losing her child?"

The abbot looked grave and nodded. "Yes. Very sad for everyone."

"And now?"

"And now they grieve again because she left Hokkeji and no one knows where she is. That is where you come in, the prime minister tells me."

The prime minister? Then perhaps the abbot was also closely related to the prime minister. The Fujiwara family tree was large and confusing. If the abbot was the prime minister's cousin, he was also the emperor's.

Slightly shaken, Akitada asked, "How do you suggest I proceed in this matter?"

The abbot waved this away with his fan. "My dear Akitada, that must be your decision."

Akitada sighed. "I see."

A soft chuckle. "Don't despair. From all I hear, this should be well within your famous skills. After all, where could a wellborn young woman go and stay hidden for long?"

Where indeed?

Akitada took another sip of his excellent fruit drink, thanked the abbot, and took his leave.

9

The First Body

When Akitada stepped from the abbot's residence back into the chilly white world outside, he paused. All around him rose temple buildings, their red pillars and woodwork brilliant against the winter day. He had not been long with the abbot. Perhaps, he thought, he might just stop briefly at the police station in the provincial tribunal. Surely Sadako would be occupied with the temple treasures for a while longer.

He hurried away, pleased to find that the monks had kept the paths swept and that no one stopped him.

In the tribunal he asked the way. The provincial administration seemed almost sleepy after the streets which were already packed with pilgrims, visitors, and monks.

A young sergeant who was sitting at a desk making some notes, jumped up when he saw Akitada. "Yes, sir?"

Akitada gave him a nod for a greeting and said, "Your men brought in the body of a woman last night. I'd like to speak to someone about this."

"Yes, sir. You may speak to me."

"Very well. Have you identified the dead woman?"

"May I ask why you want to know?"

Akitada was not used to these difficulties. He reminded himself that he could not very well blame this sergeant who did not know him. It was awkward.

"My name is Sugawara. I used to work with Superintendent Kobe in the capital."

If he had hoped to impress the sergeant, he failed. The sergeant simply nodded and asked, "And what is your interest in this woman?"

Akitada was becoming irritated. People put aside their objections to be of service to him. He frowned. "That is my business. It seems to me that any policeman who takes his duties seriously would be only too eager to gain information in an unsolved case. For all you know, I may recognize your victim."

The sergeant raised his chin stubbornly. "The case is not unsolved. It is closed."

"You amaze me. According to my information, she was found only last night."

The man smirked. "In Nara we work fast."

Akitada gritted his teeth. "Then would you be so good as to let me know your findings?"

"That is not permitted."

"Where is your superior?"

"He rarely comes in until midday."

Akitada clamped his lips together and turned to leave. At that moment, a short man in the red coat of the police bustled in. He also wore a court hat with rank insignia. When he saw Akitada, he stopped. "Ah, we have a guest. Good morning, sir. Is all well or do you need our help?"

Akitada shot the sergeant a glance and said, "Both. Are you in command here?"

The short man grinned. "I am! For my sins. Katsuura's the name. The constables are but a backward bunch and have to be beaten into submission every day." He chuckled at his joke.

Akitada introduced himself again. Captain Katsuura responded with a gratifying show of being impressed and Akitada shot the sergeant a glance. The man was still stone-faced. The captain gushed, "What an honor, sir! We have heard of you and often wished for your expertise in difficult cases. What brings you today?"

Akitada explained that his retainer had observed the recovery of a corpse, and wondered if it might be the missing Sanekane.

"Oh, no," cried Captain Katsuura. "This one's just a prostitute. We find them often in the river."

"Drowned?"

"Yes. Suicide. It's a hard life, even for the young ones."

"Ah. This one was young?"

"Yes. About twenty I would guess."

The age was right for Lady Hachijo. Akitada felt his scalp prickle at the thought that the emperor's concubine had been murdered in the brothel quarter of Nara. He said, "I take an interest in suicides. Might I see her?"

The captain made no objections and seemed pleased to entertain the nobleman from the capital. He led the way out the back and across an open area to an outbuilding and a small room that could have been used for a cell but in this case was the repository of the dead. It held several bodies, all covered with reed mats.

"You're just in time," the captain said, pulling back one of the reed mats. "I was about to send for the monks to come get her."

Akitada saw the nude body of a young woman, well-shaped, and well-nourished. Her hair was still wet and had been pulled back from her face. Her face was pale, the eyes closed, and the mouth slightly open with her tongue just showing. Her neck was badly bruised, and the rest of her body showed scratches and bruises that she might have got falling into the river. But Akitada did not think so. He knelt and looked at her neck closely.

"Oh," said the captain, "she broke her neck when she jumped."

Akitada looked up, astonished. "She jumped? From where?"

"There's a bridge upstream. She must have jumped from there."

"Where are her clothes?"

"She was naked."

"Isn't that unusual for a suicide? In the middle of winter?"

The captain looked uneasy. "We think someone stole her clothes. It's not far from a bad part of town. Whatever she jumped in may have come off in the river."

"Hmm." Akitada felt the woman's skull. "Has the coroner seen her?"

"Just to pronounce her dead."

Akitada found only a bruise on her skull, but as he turned her head, the broken neck became obvious. And he noticed something curious about her hair. It was short. Many peasant women cut their hair because it got in the way of their chores, but prostitutes tended to keep theirs long and even augmented it. He checked her hands. They were pale and soft, the nails trimmed neatly. Looking at them closely, he saw some evidence of blood under one nail, but these were not the hands of a peasant woman or a humble housewife. Prostitutes, of course, did have smooth hands, but they tended to tint their nails and wear them longer than the dead woman. And the hands were clean, except for some black stains on one forefinger. He looked at these closely and decided it was ink. He had frequently stained his own fingers when rubbing an ink cake in water.

Then he looked at her feet. He found them covered with small cuts, and shook his head.

The captain said admiringly, "You're as thorough as a coroner. May I ask, have you studied medicine?"

Akitada got to his feet. "Not at the university, but I have read all the books I could find and I talked with many coroners. This woman was not a prostitute and she did not commit suicide. Most likely she tried to escape, but was caught and murdered and tossed into the river afterward. Not far from where she was found. I highly recommend having the coroner do a thorough examination."

The captain goggled. "But this cannot be murder, sir. The only woman reported missing is a prostitute and she fits her appearance."

"Ah, then you have an identification?"

"Not by a witness. No. But a woman from the quarter was reported missing and she was the right age and said to be unhappy." He paused, then added, "I had meant to have someone come and look at her."

"You do that, Captain. But in case she isn't recognized, you might ask if anyone is missing a nun. And have the coroner take a look at her."

10
Hokkeji

Akitada returned to Kofukuji to fetch his wife. The sight of the dead woman had disturbed him a good deal. First of all, her age fitted that of the missing Lady Hachijo, and secondly, when he had parted her hair, he found that it had been cut short in the style worn by novices before their final ordination, at which time their heads were shaved like those of the monks. He thought that the dead woman was a nun rather than a prostitute and he was curious about what the coroner would find. Lady Hachijo had given birth not long ago. A good coroner could establish if the same was true for the dead woman. He hoped not, even though this would end his uncomfortable assignment rather quickly.

Sadako was taking tea with the prior and the *betto.* Akitada searched his mind for the *betto*'s name, and she supplied it quickly.

"You must have met Wakita Tsunetaka earlier, Akitada. He's the *betto* for this temple and the Hokkeji convent. And you recall Prior Kakushin, I think."

Akitada gave her a grateful smile and bowed to both. "Forgive my delay. You are very good to keep my wife company."

They expressed their pleasure at making Lady Sugawara's acquaintance and begged him to join them. Akitada sat down and accepted a cup of tea, most welcome after his cold walk.

The prior smiled. "You had a long meeting with his Reverence. I trust it is not because you are investigating some crime in the temple?" He chuckled.

"I wouldn't dream of it. His Reverence was most kind, and his conversation was inspirational. No, I decided to look in at the police station to inquire about a body that was recovered from the river last night."

The *betto* asked, "Really? So there *is* a murder to solve. But surely it isn't what brought you to Nara?"

Clearly the man was fishing for information. Akitada said, "No. Not at all. My retainer happened to watch them pull the young woman from the water last night. I was curious, that's all."

"Ah." The prior nodded. "Professional curiosity. And did you discover what happened to the poor young woman?"

Akitada was beginning to feel uncomfortable with such persistent interest. He wondered how much these two men knew about Lady Hachijo's disappearance but could not bring up the subject. So he said merely, "It was as you say, mere professional curiosity to see how things are handled here. There was little to learn. They are still at the beginning of their investigation." When nobody commented, he looked at his wife, "Well, my dear, if you're rested, shall we continue our sightseeing with Todaiji?"

She nodded eagerly, and the prior clapped his hands. "Yes, the great Buddha! A wondrous sight. They say the artist had divine help."

Akitada rose and extended a hand to help his wife get up. "We shall be inspired," he said with a smile. They bowed to the two men and departed.

When they were outside, Sadako blinked against the blinding light and said, "You were gone a long time."

"I'm sorry. Was it very dreary talking to them?"

"Not too bad. The prior put himself out for me. Wakita joined us much later. He seemed very interested in you."

"No doubt."

She looked at him searchingly. "You don't trust them?"

He smiled a little. "I'm very distrustful early in a case."

"What happened at the tribunal?"

"They think the woman is a prostitute who committed suicide by jumping off a bridge."

"Dreadful. And what do you think?"

"I think she's a nun and was murdered."

Sadako raised a hand to her mouth. "Oh! Our missing lady?"

"I don't know. Shall we pay a visit to Hokkeji and ask a few questions?"

*

The abbess at Hokkeji received them courteously, but there was a very different atmosphere here. She was a woman of middle age, though it was difficult to be sure because her head was shaved. Since her robes resembled those of the male monks, even her gender was not obvious until she spoke. The same was true of her two companions.

Hokkeji occupied a large space but had few buildings. This hinted at the fact that it had once been lavishly supported by empresses, who frequently retired here, and had later fallen on hard times. Still, the nuns hardly lived in penury, though they made their lives as simple as their faith demanded.

Akitada found the encounter uncomfortable. Not only was he not one of the faithful, paying at best perfunctory respect to the Buddhist religion, but seeing women turned into monks revolted him. Women without hair were not a pleasing sight. Did they know this? Was that the sacrifice they made to the Buddha?

He introduced himself and was informed by the abbess that he had been expected. The two nuns in attendance were named, nodded, and then remained silent. The abbess next turned her attention to Sadako, almost as if to remind him of his manners to his spouse. This irritated him further. He fell as silent as the other two nuns while Sadako and the abbess chatted. The small talk seemed to him disrespectful of the situation. Did they not care about the missing Lady Hachijo?

So, Hokkeji, the Lotus Temple, belonged to the women who venerated the Lotus Sutra because in it women were admitted to salvation. Akitada was familiar with the legend of the dragon king's daughter. He noticed that Sadako seemed very interested. Was his new wife religious? His previous wives had not paid much attention to such things and he approved of that.

Perhaps as an explanation for the preferential treatment of his wife, Akitada next heard that the temple had been founded by an empress as the female version of Todaiji, the temple of the great Buddha. She had been moved to do so by a dream in which a beggar asked her to bathe his grotesquely and repulsively suppurating body. When she pitied him and did so, he revealed himself as the Buddha. Hokkeji had a *mandala* depicting the tale and a bathhouse. Female pilgrims came regularly to worship here.

Akitada was becoming restless. The abbess noticed and finally turned to him. "Perhaps your lady might like to see some of our treasures while we chat?"

Poor Sadako! She was being bundled off to her second sightseeing excursion among temple artifacts. She shot him a glance, but her smile was firmly in place. As soon as she had left with the two nuns who had been in attendance on the abbess, he found himself alone with her Reverence.

11

The Imperial Nun

She studied him for a moment. "They say you are good at solving puzzles," she finally said.

"Puzzles? I usually deal in murder," Akitada corrected her coldly.

That took her aback. "Murder? What murder? There has been no murder."

"Are you certain?"

She paled a little and drew herself up.. "Nonsense! Shosho merely absented herself without explanation." She added, "Or permission." Her tone showed her irritation. "It will cause no end of damage to all concerned if you bandy words like 'murder' about. I cannot imagine what His Excellency was about when he sent you."

Akitada would have none of the reprimand. He merely raised his brows. "Exactly when did Lady Hachijo leave the convent?"

"Her name is Shosho. She has taken her vows and entered the path of renunciation ."

"I see. So she has become a full-fledged member of your convent?"

"Well, she was preparing for the next step. All of this is well known. Have you not been informed?"

There was again the suggestion that he was not qualified to look for the missing nun. He repeated his question, "Exactly when did she leave?"

The abbess cast up her eyes and sighed. "Two weeks ago. On the tenth day of the frost month. As if that matters."

"Thank you. And when did she arrive here?"

"A month earlier." The abbess still glowered.

"Then she made rather rapid progress to become a novice so quickly, didn't she?"

The abbess compressed her lips. "Shosho is particularly devout and had begun her studies long before she took this step."

"I see. Do you mean that she had been a regular visitor while she still lived in the palace?"

"No, of course not. Not regular."

"Did you realize right away that she had left?"

"I did not. I was told the next day."

"She lived with the other nuns?"

"She has her own quarters. I assumed she had gone to visit her family. They live here, you know."

"Yes, I know. Did you eventually send to them to ask about her?"

"Certainly. I was told she was not there. Then her brother came and made unwarranted accusations."

"Ah. What sort?"

"He said we were responsible for her and had better produce her or he would think someone had done something to Shosho. As if any of us would do such a thing."

"He accused you of murdering her?" Akitada asked .

She rattled her beads angrily. "Of course not. I have no idea what he meant. He was most offensive. I have made a complaint to His Majesty."

"Was that when His Majesty became concerned?"

She looked down at her beads and unclenched her hands. "Is there anything else you wish to know?"

"Why do you think she left? Was she unhappy?"

"Certainly not. She was finally happy in having renounced all of her worldly attachments."

Akitada sighed. "I have something to tell you. Last night a young woman was found in the river. The police think she's a suicide. I saw her. She looks like a novice nun to me. Her hair had been cut as a first step toward becoming a nun."

The abbess turned white. "No," she gasped. "It couldn't be."

"Someone should go to look at her just in case. Will you?"

The abbess closed her eyes, then nodded slowly. "Someone will go. Is that all, sir?"

"Yes, thank you. I may want to ask more questions another time. Let me know if you recognize the dead woman. I'm staying in Lord Kosehira's residence."

Sadako awaited him in an anteroom to her Reverence's room. She smiled. "I'm very hungry," she announced. "I ate all the nuts they offered me."

Akitada's mood lifted. "Forgive me, my love. I haven't been thinking. We missed our midday rice. Let's go and treat ourselves to a good meal. There won't be anything at the house, unless the majordomo has returned. And I have a feeling he'll stay away just like Lady Hachijo."

"Shosho," Sadako corrected.

They emerged into the white, bright world of Nara and made for the main street where all the wine shops and eating places were. Akitada paused to look at his wife. "Did the two nuns tell you anything?"

"Food first. I'm nearly faint."

Akitada laughed and they walked quickly to a large eating place. Though they were late for the midday meal and too early for the evening rice, a waiter seated them quickly and recited a list of delicacies available immediately. Sadako's eyes sparkled. Akitada felt guilty. Clearly he had been inattentive to his wife, starving her while he pursued the fate of other women. He ordered quickly and abundantly.

Then he asked, "Well, what have you learned?"

But the waiter approached with their soup, and Sadako fell to, her eyes twinkling at Akitada over the rim of her bowl. He said, "Sorry, my love. I have neglected you."

She came up for breath. "Only my stomach. This is delicious. Eat!"

He ate and cursed his impatience.

When the bowl was empty, she set it down, dabbed her lips with a tissue from her sash and said, "They didn't like her much. Jealousy, I think."

He raised his brows. "Nuns are jealous?"

"Oh, goodness, Akitada. They are women living together with nothing much to occupy them but reciting sutras. Or copying them. They are starved for gossip."

Akitada thought of the ink-stained fingers of the dead woman. Had she been copying sutras?

He said, "You surprise me. What about their devotion?"

"They are devout. But that, too, can be a competition."

She amazed him. He had learned early that women could be very intelligent. Both Tamako and Yukiko had been bright, educated, and curious. But he had not expected such astonishing understanding of people from Sadako. It proved that he had much to learn yet from his new companion. He suddenly felt very proud of her, and a bit guilty that she had been a mere servant in his house for such a long time.

The rest of the food arrived. He said hopefully, "Go on!"

She sampled some shrimp and said, "Shosho was the highest ranking member of the convent. An imperial concubine! She outranked the abbess who, by the way, is related to the minister of the right."

"But surely their past doesn't matter any longer. They put their old lives behind them."

"Not quite, Akitada. They bring with them education and influence. Both are useful to the temple. Eat!"

He ate, amazed. Every day, it seemed, Sadako revealed new aspects into her character. Having been raised in the far north, though in a noble family, she could not have developed such insight into how the world worked in the center of the country, among men and women of power. How did she do it?

"Sadako," he said, between bites, "how do you come to know such things?"

She chuckled. "I read. I watch people. I watched you. I talk to your sister. Your sister is a very well informed woman. She has been at pains to prepare me for marriage to you."

Akitada set down his bowl, aghast. "Akiko has been talking about me? What did she say?"

"Don't be shocked. She loves you. She told me all about your past and your mother. Or stepmother, I should say. She has accepted that you'll never have any ambition."

"What? I have ambition. I have plenty of ambition. I have done quite well for myself. You shouldn't listen to such nonsense."

He saw that his new wife was laughing. She was laughing at him. He frowned. "Sadako!" he said in a warning tone.

"She also said that you have a bad temper when you're crossed. Are you now angry with me?"

"I do not have a bad temper," he said stiffly. "I'm very easy to get along with."

Sadako reached for the rice, her eyes laughing at him. "You mustn't blame me, Akitada. I'm still getting to know you. As a husband, I mean."

"Oh."

She lifted a bit of fish from her bowl and offered it. "Taste this. It's delicious."

He tasted. Obediently. And wondered how she had managed to diffuse his anger so easily. His righteous anger, because what husband permitted his sister to blacken his character to a new wife. To cover his confusion, he said, "We were discussing the nuns."

"Yes. The two I spoke to are senior nuns. One is the rector, and the other the prioress. The rector was born a Kii, and the prioress is a Tachibana. So both are well born and both have served the Buddha for more than twenty years. As I said, they don't like her. They think she ran away and are pleased. It proves she was not a good nun, and they are rid of her."

"Did they hate her enough to have her killed?"

Sadako looked astonished. "You think she's been murdered? That would be quite shocking, given her history."

"Yes. Well, I'm just considering all possibilities. And there is the nun they dragged from the river last night. The abbess will have to take a look."

"The abbess? I rather think she'll send someone else."

"Unless she had a hand in Shosho's disappearance. Then she may well go and say she never saw her before in her life."

"Oh, Akitada. You have a terribly suspicious mind. Now you think the sacred Hokkeji is a place for murdering people."

"So you think this impossible?"

She frowned. "For the whole convent, yes. But I wouldn't rule out a single individual with violent tendencies."

"But not the abbess?"

"No. She's surely too old. And why would she want to murder the new nun? Her rank bestows benefits on the temple. There will be rich donations from the throne and from the Fujiwara family, and the reputation of the temple will be made."

Akitada sighed. "Perhaps. So we're looking for an unwelcome nun. Any information about her?"

Sadako shook her head. "No. Shosho kept to herself. She complained a lot, apparently, and doesn't seem to have made friends."

"Well, we must await the identification of the dead nun."

"But she could be anyone. There's not just Hokkeji, but there are all the pilgrims. A lot of them are women."

"I know."

12
Another Body

The next morning Akitada decided to hire two servants. He was tired of firing up the bath water every day. Cook and her son were nearly useless. At best, the boy looked after the horses and swept snow from the steps to the house. It had snowed again overnight, and both Akitada and Sadako woke shivering to face the day without a brazier of hot coals, warm gruel, tea, or water warm enough to wash in.

Tora, he discovered, had returned late the night before and had already left again. It did not promise well for locating the majordomo.

At least the cook provided information about people hired by Sanekane. Akitada told her to send for a strong young male and a young woman who could act as maid for his wife. He would pay them himself. Satisfied that their lives would soon become more comfortable, he left Sadako to instruct the new servants in their duties and set out for the tribunal.

The police captain greeted him politely. Akitada asked about progress and was told that the abbess of Hokkeji had sent two nuns to have a look at the dead woman.

"They didn't know her, sir," he announced with satisfaction.

Akitada nodded. It answered nothing. If the dead woman was the missing Lady Hachijo, the nuns might well have denied the fact to protect the temple. They would have thought that an unknown corpse would soon enough be given over to the funeral pyre and the whole business would go away.

As if to confirm this, the captain said, "Hokkeji asked to be allowed to handle the funeral. Very proper, I thought it. We promised to release the body as soon as the coroner's done."

"Ah. He's still here?"

"Yes. I cannot imagine he'll find anything." The captain sounded aggrieved that Akitada had insisted on an unnecessary procedure.

"I'd like to talk to him."

With a sigh, the captain started for the door when it opened and a short elderly man in a plain grey gown came in. His sparse white hair was tied into a topknot above tired eyes and a drooping white mustache.

The captain said, "Here he is himself. Doctor Hayashi, our coroner. Well, Doc, what news?"

The old man ignored him and bowed to Akitada.

Akitada said, "I'm Sugawara. From the capital. I came to ask about the dead woman."

The old doctor cocked his head. "Not the Sugawara from the Justice Ministry?" he asked.

Akitada, hugely pleased, nodded. "The very same."

The old man bowed again, more deeply this time. "You're interested, sir?"

"Yes. A woman has disappeared. I wondered."

"Ah. Well, this poor thing was murdered."

The captain cried, "Murdered? Are you sure?"

The doctor gave him a disdainful look. "Quite sure. Her neck was broken. Your constables must have noticed the fact."

"From the fall, surely."

"No. From someone strangling her and snapping her neck."

Akitada said, "Ah! I thought so. What else could you discover?"

"She was raped first."

"Raped?"

The captain grunted. "What? Are you mad? Who rapes a whore?"

There was a pause. The doctor looked down at his hands. "She wasn't a whore, Captain."

"Are you saying she was a virgin?" the captain asked, becoming excited.

The doctor sighed. "No, Captain. Not that either."

"Then how can you be sure she wasn't a whore?" The captain glared at his coroner.

This time the doctor did not answer. He turned to Akitada. "Is there anything specific you wondered about, sir?"

"Yes. Was there any sign that she had given birth not long ago?"

"No."

"Thank you, doctor." Akitada turned to the captain. "I believe the young woman is a nun, a novice. Even if the nuns from Hokkeji did not recognize her, you might ask about missing visitors. I understand quite a few religious women visit Nara."

The captain scowled. It would require a lot of work, and Akitada did not promise himself much of an effort from the man. He took his leave, with a bow to the doctor and a nod to the captain, and returned to the Fujiwara house to see if Sadako was ready for more sight-seeing.

But when he walked into the courtyard, where little had been done about snow removal, he found visitors. Two women seemed to be in a loud discussion with the cook and her son. He decided it was high time that they got more servants and that cook was reminded of her duties.

He strode up to the group and recognized the two women from Sanekane's house. They recognized him also and immediately turned their attention to him.

"Sir," cried the mother, "you must come and do something. We are just two poor women. We cannot cope. Such a horrible thing! How could he do this to us?"

Akitada glared. "What happened? Did your master return?"

"Master?" wailed the mother. "More like husband and father. Oh, what will we do?"

"Really? You didn't mention this when I spoke to you last."

"Well . . ." She glanced at her daughter who said nothing. "Perhaps not precisely a husband. And my daughter's my own. Her father's dead. Died in battle. He was a brave man. But Sanekane took us in and we lived as a family."

Akitada snapped, "Get on with it. What happened?"

"He came home, sir."

Akitada looked about. "Where is he? He's supposed to be here. This is insufferable behavior. You said he was off somewhere drinking."

"And so he was. But he came home last night, drunk out of his head, and he fell down dead on his doorstep. What're we to do now?"

"He is dead? When did he die?"

"Must've been in the night some time. We were asleep. We always lock the door and we sleep in the back of the house. When we got up this morning, I looked out and there he was, lying on the step, covered with snow, dead and frozen stiff."

At this point, Sadako appeared on the veranda, saw the gathering and quickly descended. "Has something happened?" she asked, tiptoeing through the snow.

Even while his mind tried to deal with the news of another body, Akitada noted with pride how pretty and lively his wife looked in the green robe over layers of red and gold underrobes. He said, "It's about Sanekane. It appears he came back to die."

The two women and the cook stared at Sadako. The younger one said, "What pretty clothes! See, Mother, I could have used those colors. Let's go and buy that silk I saw. It would suit me well." She crept closer and extended her hand to feel the fabric.

Sadako stepped back. "Thank you, but surely you will need to wear mourning now."

The two women looked at each other, and Cook said, "Of course you will." And chuckled.

A man was dead and no one seemed to mourn him. Akitada frowned at them and said, "I'll have a look. Sadako, you'd better go inside. It's cold out here and the snow will ruin your slippers." He shot the boy a stern glance the boy ignored.

Sadako asked, "Will you be long?"

"I'll come back as soon as the police have had a look."

This caused an outcry from the two women. "Police? No." The mother said, "He just fell down and died. We need no police. We'll send for the monks. But the funeral. Who's going to pay for the funeral?"

Akitada ignored her and told the boy to run to the police and take the constables to Sanekane's house.

When he turned to walk away, the two women wailed and ran after him, entreating him, begging, arguing. He did not respond and eventually they fell silent and trudged along behind him.

At the gate of the Sanekane house, Akitada stopped the women. "Stay off the path so you don't destroy the footprints," he told them.

The daughter gave a hysterical laugh. "We've already been over it, coming to your place."

"I know. But it may still be possible to make out his footprints."

They looked at each other, then followed him as he walked well over to the side. He saw that the new snow had partially obscured some prints, while the women's tracks were sharply defined. He looked for other prints, but could only see one set of the older ones. There was however a new, sharp set of prints made by feet much larger than the women's. Someone had arrived after the women left. He turned the corner and saw the house.

To his surprise, Akitada found Tora standing guard over the majordomo's body. "Ah, there you are, sir," he greeted Akitada. "I just got here and found him. He seems to be dead." His eyes moved past Akitada. "So there you are! I wondered where you'd got to," he said to the two women.

Akitada told him, "They came to tell us. I've sent for the police."

Tora nodded. "Good. He's dead. I can't tell what was wrong with him. There's no blood. He did vomit though."

Akitada went closer and bent to look at the body. Sanekane lay on his stomach, his arms flung out and clutching at snow, his legs rigid. Under his face was a pool of vomit partially covered by snow. Akitada knelt and sniffed. It smelled of food and wine. Sanekane had consumed a meal not too long before his death.

He straightened and looked along the path. Sanekane's tracks wobbled this way and that. "He seems to have been alone."

Tora nodded. "He was old, he ate, and he drank too much. Then he walked home through the snow and died."

The mother snapped. "There! I told you so. The old fool finally killed himself."

13

The Comforts of Home

The police arrived: first three constables with the cook's son, then the captain himself with another constable and the coroner.

Akitada had gone back to meet them and point out the significance of the tracks in the snow.

The captain looked and nodded, then went to look at the body. "So," he said, straightening up, "he came home alone and died alone. No sign of foul play, as you say. And no problem for us then." He glanced at the two women curiously, but did not speak to them.

"I would not say that." Akitada nodded toward Dr. Hayashi. "Perhaps the doctor could make sure?"

Hayashi walked to the body and set down his box of medical tools in the snow. Then he felt the body at several points, the side of the neck, the back of the skull, the wrists and the legs. He frowned. Lifting the head by its topknot, he looked at the dead man's face. Akitada could see that the face was puffy, the lips drawn back as if he were gasping for breath or crying out, and the eyes bulged. In death, the majordomo was not attractive.

Apparently the daughter shared that view because she gave a shudder and said, "Ugh!" The mother elbowed her, but she, too, was watching avidly.

Akitada asked them, "Did you hear him last night? He may have cried out for help."

The mother said, "No. We sleep in the back. We heard nothing."

"Was the door locked?"

The mother looked a little uneasy. "Yes. We were afraid. Two women alone . . ." She let her voice trail away.

The doctor said, "A pity." He did not look kindly at the women.

During all of this the captain had been shuffling his feet impatiently. To be sure, it was chilly and standing in the snow was unpleasant. Now he said, "Well, Doc? What do you say?"

"I cannot be sure. He died before the hour of the rat. Before he died, he vomited. There is no sign of a wound, though one may reveal itself once I have his clothes off, and he wasn't bludgeoned. Have your men carry him back to the tribunal. I'll take a better look at him there."

The captain was not pleased, but he gave his orders. Being irritated, he snapped at the women, "You will stay in the house. We may need to question you."

The daughter protested, "I have to go to the market. You cannot keep us trapped here."

"I can do just that. If either of you leaves, you'll both go to jail where we can keep an eye on you."

Then he nodded to Akitada and Tora and followed his constables who had rolled the body onto the garden gate and were carrying Sanekane away.

The coroner paused a moment. "I wonder where he had his last meal," he said, looking at the two women. Then he, too, walked away.

Akitada gestured to the door. "Let's go inside and talk about this," he said.

They looked angry, but submitted without more than a muttered protest. Akitada and Tora followed them inside. The house was, if anything, dirtier than the last time. A glance into the kitchen revealed unwashed bowls and cooking vessels caked with old food. A rat scurried away from a bit of boiled rice that had fallen on the stone floor. Tora muttered, "Messy!" and shook his head.

In the main room, matters were no better. The women's bedding lay tumbled on the floor. Ashes had spilled from an overturned brazier, and women's garments hung over racks or lay about on the floor. Akitada wondered why Sanekane would keep two such slovenly servants around. They did nothing for him but expected to be kept in food and pay.

But then, perhaps their services were of another kind. He looked at them with a distinct feeling of revulsion. Both were fat, both were painted, and neither would have made a very successful harlot.

He asked, "Has it occurred to either of you that Sanekane may have called for help or knocked on the door?"

They looked at each other. The mother raised her chin. "I told you, we were fast asleep. We didn't hear anything."

"Oh, the poor man," moaned her daughter and started weeping.

The mother snapped, "Stop that." Then she added to Akitada, "She has a very soft heart. He was like a father to her."

Tora snorted.

The daughter gulped and cried, "He was not my father. And he was not your husband."

They glared at each other.

Tora asked, "Then what exactly are you doing in his house?"

There was a moment's silence. Then the mother said, "We kept his house. He was majordomo for the Fujiwara lord and he needed someone to look after his property. We've lived here for four years now and he'd grown fond of us."

Tora snorted again and said, "I bet."

Akitada gestured at the messy room. "Is this how you kept his house? And is that why he went out to get drunk?"

The mother protested, "We were upset. And there hasn't been time to pick up things after we found him. We didn't want him to go out, but he was a stubborn man."

"He wasn't married?"

The daughter said, "She died. He took it hard. I tried to make it up to him." She smiled a little and shot her mother a look.

Tora grinned at her. "He must've been very grateful." She gave him a coquettish look.

The mother said, "We both did. He was happy to have us here."

Akitada glanced around the room, which was surely the main room of the house. "You both slept with him?"

They did not answer. The mother chewed her lip and the daughter flirted with Tora.

"Well? Was that the nature of your relationship with him?" Akitada persisted.

The daughter said, "Yes, and why not? The poor man was so alone. There's no harm in it. It made him feel better. More alive. We both gave him comfort."

Tora said, "You must've been worried when he started leaving home for days and nights to drink elsewhere. You must've thought he'd found another woman and you two would be out on the street."

The daughter cried, "I wasn't worried. He'd never prefer some slut to me."

The mother added, "He'd never send us away. He was a kind man. He made a will, leaving this house to us."

The daughter burst into tears again. "Oh, poor, dear, kind Sanekane."

Tora and Akitada looked at each other. Akitada said, "Well, you heard the captain. Stay here."

They left the house. Akitada shaking his head, and Tora chortling.

14
Sanekane

On the street outside Sanekane's house, Akitada said, "It's not funny. They may have killed him."

Tora stopped chortling. "How? He was found outside the house. Mind you, they shouldn't have locked him out. It's his house."

"Yes, and now they claim he left it to them in their will. I'd like to know more about those two."

"Shall I go back and ask them?"

"No. They would tell you lies. The cook at the house might know. I'll talk to her. By the way, what did you learn yesterday? I was surprised to find you at Sanekane's house."

"Oh. Yes. Not much, but when I traced his way through the local wine shops to the outskirts of town, I ran into a man who thought he'd taken his custom to a noodle shop."

"A noodle shop? I thought the man drank."

"Well, he eats sometimes. Anyway, the woman who runs the noodle shop makes an outstanding bowl of soup. She makes the noodles herself and she uses cabbage and various roots and some local fish –"

"Tora! What about Sanekane?"

Tora grinned. "You have to chat a little to get the information. Sometimes I make sacrifices."

Akitada glared.

"Anyway, the shop was closed. I thought he'd probably left to go home. So I went to his house, but it was closed up and nobody answered. I figured he'd stopped for a drink and the women were elsewhere and I came home to sleep. This morning I went back and found him."

"I see. Well, we must wait for the coroner. I'll speak to Cook and you might ask the neighbors some questions about the two women."

Sanekane was a complication Akitada did not relish. He wanted to get on with the search for the missing Lady Hachijo, or Shosho as the nuns called her. But he was staying in his friend's house, and he owed Kosehira an explanation of what had happened to his majordomo. He hoped the coroner would call the death accidental, due to sleeping drunk in the snow. But meanwhile, the two women troubled him enough to pursue the matter with the cook.

He found Sadako interviewing or instructing the new servants, eyed them briefly, a sturdy young male and a woman in her thirties, both looking healthy and clean, and then went to the kitchen.

The cook was washing the breakfast bowls and pots in the scullery. In the kitchen a fire burned under the stove and rice cooker. When she saw Akitada, she wiped her hands on her skirt and, looking aggrieved, said, "Anything wrong with the service?"

He wanted to say "Yes, Let me count the ways," but refrained. Instead he said, "Sanekane is dead. He died last night."

She gaped at him, then sat down on a covered barrel. "Dead? How can he be dead? Who's gonna see about getting me some help?"

Akitada frowned. "Lady Sugawara has hired a young man and a maid. You'll meet them shortly."

She was not appeased. "No kitchen staff and more mouths to feed. And who's gonna pay?"

"I am. Is this all you can say about Sanekane's death? Did you hate him so much?"

This surprised her. "Hate Sanekane? No. He was what he was. A drunk. And he was old. Old people die. It's that way with all people."

"Aren't you at all curious about how he died?"

"No. Who's gonna pay for the funeral food? And for the monks?"

Akitada had not considered the effect of Sanekane's death on his own finances beyond the food they ate and the two servants he had just hired. Funeral costs tended to be significant. He asked, "What about his family?"

She pondered for a moment. "He has a son."

"Good. Where does this son live?"

"In the capital. He's a clerk or something. Never came to see him. Didn't get along with his father."

"His name?"

"Sanekata, I think."

"Do you know where he lives?"

"No."

Akitada wondered about the dead man again. Perhaps the strange household with the two women was explained by the aging man's loneliness. He was widowed and had only the one son who seemed to be less than filial. He asked, "How old was Sanekane?"

"Seventy. Maybe older. I told you he was old."

That confirmed what the woman Kiyo had said. "Are there other children?"

"There was a daughter, but she died in childbirth. No children and her husband won't lift a finger."

"What do you know about the two women who are keeping house for him."

"What, Kiyo and Otoyo? I found them for him. Kiyo's a widow. Her husband was a soldier and died in a war. They're good women."

"How well do you know them?"

"Kiyo's my cousin. Older than me. He was lucky to get her and her daughter. They work for their room and board." She was emphatic about this. Perhaps out of nervousness? Did she know how the two women had kept house and treated Sanekane?

"Did they share his bed?"

Cook glared. "None of my business and none of yours."

"Keep a civil tongue. I'm about to write to Lord Kosehira about this."

That shocked her. He could see the slow realization that she might be in trouble pass across her face. She hung her head. "Beggin' your pardon, your honor. It's the shock. I couldn't say what goes on in that house."

"Your cousin claims Sanekane left her his house."

"I'm happy to hear it. Life's hard for widows. Their men go off to war and don't come back and there's nothing for them but to go out and beg."

It was true for too many, and Akitada thought about the desperate situation of women like Kiyo and Otoyo if they found themselves out on the street. Was such need a motive for murder? He had not completely accepted the women's claim that they had not heard their master coming home. He had staggered to his door, found it locked, and no one had come to let him in. He was old and perhaps they thought he would die in the snow, as he had. Even if they had just been too lazy to get up, it would be unforgivable.

Akitada left the cook to her work and checked on his horses. The boy, snoring on a straw bale, came awake with a start. Akitada looked over each horse, found them well cared for, and saw food and water standing ready. He thanked the boy and gave him a small silver coin.

"Sanekane has died, but I've hired a man to help with the outside work and a maid for the house."

The boy gaped. "How'd he die?"

"He probably froze to death in the snow."

The boy nodded. "He drinks," he said. "Mother's always said it would kill him."

Akitada retreated to the house to share a light meal with Sadako, and then unwrapped his writing box to tell Kosehira about his dead majordomo. Then he went out again to see the coroner.

15
A Philosophical Coroner

This time, neither the captain nor the sergeant made any objections when Akitada came to see the coroner. They directed him to the back of the courtyard behind the tribunal.

Doctor Hayashi was again in the room that served as the place for the dead bodies collected by the constables. They were kept here for examination and to be identified before being turned over to their families, or, if there was no family, to be buried outside the city.

It was bitterly cold in the small room. The windows were wide open. Today Akitada saw seven or eight figures deposited next to one another on top of reed mats and covered with more reed mats. Only one body lay uncovered, and Hayashi, wearing a thick quilted garment, was crouched beside it, his nose almost touching the dead man's nose. He used a small silver probe to open the dead man's mouth. The dead man was Sanekane.

"What are you doing?" Akitada asked.

The small doctor jumped and looked up at him. "Oh," he said, "it's you, sir. I expected Constable Miyada. I thought I smelled something in his vomit earlier. I was trying to see if it would come to me."

"You mentioned almonds."

"Yes, but that's not it. There was something else."

"Something he ate? Would that matter?"

"Something he shouldn't have eaten." The little doctor got up. "Oh, well, it'll come to me."

"You think he was poisoned?" Akitada thought again of the two women and their inheritance.

"Oh, no." The doctor pondered his answer, then said, "Or rather it may have been an accident. When a man is old, he may not be able to take certain medicines." He stopped and looked distracted again, pursing his lips and staring down at the dead man.

"I take it, there are no wounds? Nothing to suggest an attack?"

"No. Nothing like that. And yet . . ."

Akitada was becoming impatient. "What about that smell?"

Hayashi, still abstracted, waved his hand, perhaps to wave away the question. Akitada gave up. He went to sniff the dead man's half open mouth. A mix of sour vomit and rancid wine met his nose. Perfectly normal for a man who had drunk himself senseless. He got up. "What about the young woman?"

"Ah, the broken neck? No question, she was murdered."

"If she's not identified, what happens next?"

"It's up to the police and the judge. If it were summer, she'd already be buried, but this time of year, we keep them longer."He looked around. "It's getting crowded."

"Eight bodies? Is there much crime here?"

"Oh, no. The occasional drunken brawls. The young woman is unusual. Want to have a look?"

Akitada did not mind another look. The case nagged at him. He nodded and followed Hayashi to one of the mounds of reed mats. The coroner took it off in a strangely gentle manner, revealing the body, its nakedness now covered with a bit of unbleached hemp. The hemp was unusual in a morgue and had not been there last time. Akitada wondered who had covered her nakedness. For a moment, they stood looking at the young, soft face and the bruises on her neck.

"A pity," said Hayashi. "Such a girl should warm her husband's bed and raise his children. She should have had time to find pleasure and pain and to know that life is full of wonderful things. Instead, some brute found her, raped her, and then it was all over. I wonder why her parents allowed it."

Startled, Akitada asked, "Allowed what?"

The coroner looked at him. "Let her be a nun, what else?"

"You think she was killed because she was a nun?"

"I don't know. That's your business. I just look at them to discover the reason for their death. And sometimes I think about them."

He turned and lifted the mat off the neighboring corpse. It was a burly male, deeply tanned except about the hips, his arms tattooed, and his face battered into pulp. "He's a laborer and an ex-convict who got into a fight. His wife has claimed him, but she has no money for a funeral. She asked me to keep him for a while. She's trying to sell some things." He sighed. "She came in with a black eye he'd given her the night before he died, and she wept when she saw him. Women have a great capacity for love."

The coroner amazed Akitada. He no longer wondered who had covered the young nun so tenderly. He said, "Have those responsible been arrested?"

"I doubt it. Nobody talks after one of those fights. You'd make enemies."

"But that is wrong."

"Perhaps. But it is the way of the common people. We all try to do the best we can with what we're given. In this, there's a certain justice."

Akitada pondered his notion. It was surely wrong to let the killer or killers of this brute go free; on the other hand, if he had not been killed, his wife might be lying here now. "What will the police do?"

The doctor raised his brows. "They ask questions, they threaten, they may even try to beat it out of a witness. In the end, there's another murder and they forget." He wandered on to a small mound and raised the mat. A child, a boy of about nine or ten, lay there. His body was bruised and mangled.

"What happened to him?"

"He fell under a heavily laden wagon while leading the ox downhill. The father was on the wagon."

"A tragic accident."

"Perhaps."

"What do you mean, 'perhaps'?"

The doctor bent and turned the small, thin body.. Black and blue bruises ran up to his buttocks. "Not from the accident," he said. "They say the wasp stings the crying face. At least his pain is over."

"You mean the father beat him?"

The coroner nodded.

Akitada could not find words. Too many, far too many never found justice. Or found it too late.

But Hayashi was already uncovering another. This one was a woman in her forties, rail thin but with the swollen belly of recent pregnancy. Hayashi shook his head. "She gave her husband ten children and worked every day in the fields. The last birth was too much for her." He covered the body quickly and moved on to another corpse.

Sickened and hoping to make him stop, Akitada said, "So most of these are natural deaths?"

The coroner stopped to look at him. "Natural? What is natural? They were murdered in one way or another, and your fine laws have done nothing to protect them." He turned and removed the mat. It was a middle-aged male, well-built and well-nourished. His face was smooth-shaven and he wore his hair in a top-knot. Hayashi said, "We don't know who he is. His clothes were good. Like yours." He looked over his shoulder at Akitada. "He looks a bit like you and may have been in the same profession. Do you know him?"

Akitada stepped closer. "No. How did he die?"

"Shot with an arrow. Found in a ditch beside the highway a few miles outside town."

"Did they find the killer?"

"No. Most likely it was highwaymen. He had no papers on him." Akitada bent to examine the man's feet. He wore soft slippers of the type often worn with boots. "He didn't walk," he said. "What about his horse?"

"No doubt it's already been sold on the market. There are robbers in every country and rats in every house."

"That hardly helps." Akitada was becoming irritated with Hayashi.

At that moment, Hayashi said, "Apricots!"

Akitada stared at him.

The little coroner smiled broadly and nodded his head once or twice. "Your majordomo. I smelled apricots."

Thinking the coroner must be mad, Akitada said, "I didn't smell apricots. Just vomit and wine. And why apricots? They are not in season."

"Apricot kernels. They smell a bit like almonds."

"But why eat those?" Akitada paused. "Do you mean he was poisoned with them?"

Hayashi nodded again. "He could have been. He was old and the wine would've hidden the taste."

"It doesn't sound practical."

The coroner smiled a little. "We sell them ground up as medicine. The Chinese call it *xing ren.* Depends on how much you eat."

"Oh. Can you prove it? I mean can you prove someone murdered him?"

"No."

"How do you explain his death then?"

"He may have doctored himself. Or someone may have played a trick on him. It causes nausea and diarrhea. Or he committed suicide. Or it was all a stupid mistake."

Akitada shook his head. "That's not much help."

Hayashi said cheerfully, "None at all. Just an observation by an old coroner. I've seen many bodies that may have been murdered. I leave it to the police to check into the case."

"How long does it take to die after you eat a sufficient dose?"

"You'd get sick within an hour, I think. He was old. And he drank. He may have choked to death on his vomit."

Akitada said, "Don't you care that a man may have died at the hands of another and you cannot make it right?"

"Make it right? How? He's dead, one way or another. Catching the killer merely pleases us because it's tidy. We're scared that we might be next and try to make sure it cannot happen to us. And for having frightened us, we punish the killer with the utmost severity."

Akitada snapped, "What severity? Executions are against the law. That's why murderers run about free."

The coroner regarded him calmly. "The Chinese perfected the concept of punishment. Their public executions were drawn-out spectacles. Would you like to return to the ancient ways?"

Akitada bit his lip, turned around, and walked out. What good was a coroner who lacked all sense of justice?

16

An Ancient Family

A very frustrated Akitada returned to the Fujiwara residence. Not only was he shocked that a coroner, a man who was paid to help solve crimes and on whom police and judges depended, had such a lackadaisical attitude toward justice, but Hayashi did not seem to care. In both cases where Akitada had taken an interest, the fate of the majordomo and the death of the unknown nun, the coroner had been unable or unwilling to make a decision about what had killed them. True, he had certified that the nun had a broken neck, but since she appeared to be a visitor and therefore someone else's problem, Hayashi had seemed uninterested in her murder and had instead complained about the waste of sending young women to nunneries. And what of the well-dressed man–the one Hayashi insisted on comparing to Akitada? The victims of the random violence of murderous bandit gangs clearly did not concern the doctor. He left such things as stopping them to others.

And then there was the matter of time. It was very cold, but even in this temperature, the bodies in Hayashi's morgue could not last. In fact, the coroner was eager to get them buried as soon as possible.

Sadako saw instantly that her husband was angry. "What happened?" she asked and came to help him off with his outer robe. "You look frozen. Come closer to the braziers."

There were two of these, and candles lit an area where cushions had been placed away from the inevitable drafts from the shuttered windows. She had had a desk placed close by, and a tea kettle simmered on one brazier.

Her care embraced him, soothed away his troubled thoughts of death, and warmed his soul. He took her warm hands into his cold ones and drew her close. "I have been looking too closely at death, my love. I almost forgot I left life here with you."

She pulled him to her and buried her head against his chest. "Your heart still beats," she said. "That means you're alive. Very much alive. Don't stray again, my husband. I have need of you."

After a moment of holding her, he let her go, reluctantly, to sit down and watch her make tea for both of them. "I'm very glad you also like tea," he said. "I have some very odd habits, I'm afraid."

"I've always liked tea, though we only got it when we were sick. With honey. Children like that, unless the herbs are very bitter." She came to sit with him. "Tell me about it."

He shuddered at the thought of bringing death into this small, warm place of happiness, and shook his head.

"I want to share your life. Please don't shut me out."

Akitada looked at her a long time, then he nodded and told her. When he was done, she said, "It's very dreadful what you have seen and what you must have seen often in your life. I was raised to avoid death. We did not go to houses where someone had died, even if he was a good friend. How did you ever manage to break all those taboos? How do you keep yourself clean to worship the gods?"

This made him smile. The onerous taboos associated with reverence for their gods had long since been discarded except for a few. He said, "I bathe and wash myself a lot. What about you?"

She did not smile. "There were so many wars where I grew up. Death was commonplace. In the face of disaster, you put some things aside to cope with survival."

He nodded. "For me, there was always the need to find a murderer, to give the soul of the victim peace or to help console a family. But this coroner, he doesn't care about bringing killers to justice. He merely accepts dying as an escape from the ugliness of life."

"You know," she said, "you're probably more alike than you think. You must remember that he communicates only with the dead. You deal with the living. But both of you have great pity for suffering."

Akitada was embarrassed that she knew him so well, and a little ashamed that he had revealed so much. "Not at all," he said firmly. "I shall always serve justice."

"Of course. It is quite admirable." She smiled.

He looked at her uncertainly. "You're making fun of me."

"Oh, Akitada! I love you. Just the way you are."

He melted, blinked a few times, and squeezed her hand.

She patted his and said briskly, "And what is your next step now?"

He gathered his thoughts, sadly scattered by thoughts of love. "Umm, yes. The Hachijo lady. That's why we came after all. I suppose we'd better pay a visit to her family. I would like to know more about her. Perhaps there are answers in her background and upbringing."

She gave him a sidelong glance. "We?"

"Oh. Do you mind? Would you rather look at more temples?"

"No more temples for a while. I look forward to meeting Lady Yoshido." She jumped up and sorted through her clothes. "Will I need to be very fine? I only brought ordinary gowns."

Akitada watched her, smiling. He had been smiling a lot lately when around Sadako. "You'll look lovely. Keep in mind, we are here on business."

She held up two robes looking from one to the other. "Yes, but on the emperor's business." She selected a deep green, shimmering outer robe and frowned at her dark red and lighter red present attire.

"They will look well together," her husband said. "And the colors are subdued enough if they are in mourning."

"Mourning? Would they mourn when they haven't found her dead body?"

"I don't know. It's been a long time. And it's winter."

Her face fell. "Yes. Sanekane died in the snow."

"Sanekane may have been poisoned."

She sighed and put on her green robe. Akitada went to help her, sorry that his words had broken her happy mood.

The Yoshido mansion was not far from the provincial headquarters which occupied the former imperial palace, and the Yoshido family used to be powerful. It was a large property, spreading over two acres, but it was in poor repair. The tall walls had lost patches of plaster and many of the tiles on top, and the great gate was leaning, though it was still massive and impressive with its ornamentation. A tattered flag flew from the roof. A few tracks led to it through the new snow.

Sadako eyed it and asked why they would fly flags.

"It's the family crest. Old habits die hard." Akitada pushed at one side of the gate, expecting little, but the gate slowly swung open, creaking loudly. Beyond lay a huge courtyard, mostly pristine under its snow cover. He said, "I suppose they used to exercise their soldiers and guards here. They must have fallen on dire poverty. You would have thought they could have sold the property to a temple and bought themselves smaller but better quarters elsewhere. But there again, their pride stands in their way."

They looked across at another gallery with a second gateway. The tracks led that way, and they followed them. The second gate had once been ornamented with red lacquer and gold. Little of either was left. Beyond lay another courtyard, smaller but more formal. The tracks led to the main house and climbed an imposingly wide staircase. Here, too, the lacquer had worn off the railings. The house was huge, but all its windows were shuttered. The front door stood open.

They climbed the steps, finding one broken, and walked inside.

It was dark. They were in some large reception room but could not make out anything. A corridor led toward daylight and another door to the outside.

Akitada called out, "Ho! Anybody? The Yoshido family? Where are you?" His voice echoed around them. Sadako jumped and clutched her husband's arm. "Something touched my foot," she gasped.

"Mice?"

"Bigger," she said. "Come, let's go on. I don't like it here."

They entered the long corridor. The walls were covered with strange shapes that revealed themselves as collections of banners and weapons as they got closer to the open door. Just before they reached it, a black shadow crossed before them and disappeared outside.

"What was that?" Sadako clutched her husband again.

He chuckled and patted her hand. He enjoyed being clutched. "A cat. Nothing to be afraid of."

"Oh." She released him.

"You can hold on to me again," he suggested.

"Nonsense. How would it look if we arrived embracing each other?"

He pictured it and burst into laughter.

An irritated voice called out, "Who's there? What are you doing? Get out of the house or I'll call the constables."

Akitada stepped forward and found himself on another gallery, temporarily blinded by the sun and snow as he looked down into what must be a large garden.

"Who the devil are you? What are you doing in my house?"

Eyes adjusted, Akitada made out the figure of a gaunt old man wearing a short patterned brocade robe so old it hung in tatters around his skinny legs. There were old boots on his feet, but the gap between them and the robe left his bony knees exposed to the cold. A long white beard hung to the middle of his chest, and angry eyes squinted up at Akitada.

"I beg your pardon, sir. There was no one to announce us. The name is Sugawara."

The old man's eyes shifted to Sadako who had stepped up beside her husband. The old man blinked and shaded his eyes. "Masako? Is that you, child?" He limped forward a few paces.

"My wife, Lady Sadako," said Akitada quickly.

The old man stopped. His shoulders sagged. "What do you want?" he asked harshly.

"His Majesty sent me. Are you Yoshido Akihira?"

The old man nodded. "Didn't expect anyone." He looked down at himself and added irritably, "Well, come along then," turned, and hobbled off toward another wing of the house where he climbed the steps painfully to the gallery.

Akitada and Sadako followed the gallery around until they met him. He looked them over carefully, acknowledging their bows with a nod. Akitada suppressed a smile. Such regal manners in someone dressed in rags!

Lord Yoshido let his eyes rest appreciatively on Sadako. "No, you're not my granddaughter, but you're very pretty. If I were a bit younger, I'd take you away from him." He grinned, revealing yellow teeth.

Sadako murmured, "Thank you, sir."

The old lord cackled. "You'd like that, eh? I'd show you a good time." He moved closer and extended a shriveled hand to touch her face. Sadako froze.

Akitada snapped, "Behave yourself, old man!"

The hand dropped, and Yoshido turned to glare at him. "How dare you? You dog! A Sugawara, did you say? They're nothing. You think I'm afraid of you?"

Akitada was still angry, but the situation struck him as comical and a little sad. "I mean no disrespect, sir, but I will not have you insult my wife."

Yoshido sagged again. "Quite right. Sorry. She's a tempting little morsel. Come in, come in. No point standing about in the cold." He turned and entered the house.

They followed and found themselves in a large room with low carved beams overhead, a large number of damaged screens standing about, and an old lady seated on the dais wrapped in many-colored quilts. On one side stood a lovely old candle stick with a single candle, and on the other a brazier with glowing coals. Her eyes glittered darkly in the light cast by the candle and her face looked flushed from the heat of the coals.

"My dear," said the old lord, "we have company. Sugawara and his wife. He just walked in. No announcements and no mounted escort."

Akitada said, "My apologies, Lady Yoshido," and regretted it. The old man was rude. True, his family was ancient, but so was the Sugawara clan. More so, in fact. And in view of the pitiful condition of the house and its inhabitants, it was a bit much. But such spirit in view of the abject poverty was impressive.

The old lord hmphd and sat down beside his wife. He gestured to some faded cushions on the dusty floor. Sitting on them would put them on a lower level. Akitada shook his head and remained standing.

The old woman said in a cracked voice, "Call the maid. We shall have some spiced wine. I think spiced wine is very pleasant on a winter day." She raised a painted fan and quoted, "The snow falls deeper in the mountain village; what loneliness it brings to those who dwell amid the drifts that bury all."

Her husband shot her an irritated look and said, "What do you want, Sugawara?"

"Shall I call the servant?" Akitada offered maliciously.

Lord Yoshido stared at him. "There's no servant," he snapped. "There's no wine. Pay no attention to her. State your business."

"No servant? You live here alone? Surely not."

"We're not dead yet, and what business is it of yours?"

The old lady said, "My grandson has come. Soon the house will be full again." She hid a happy smile behind her fan.

Akitada felt a wave of pity. How was it that this family, in such desperate straits, had managed to place a granddaughter in an emperor's bed? He said, "I'm here about Lady Hachijo. She is your granddaughter, I think?"

"What about her?" demanded Lord Yoshido.

"If you choose to love," quoted his wife, "never let it show where it will catch people's eyes like silk dyed with purple moor grass."

He turned on her and shouted, "Shut up, old woman!"

Ashamed, she hid behind her fan.

Akitada said, "Lady Hachijo has disappeared. His Majesty is concerned. That's why I am here. What can you tell me?"

His wife dropped her fan and stared at him. "The emperor? He wants her to come back?"

Akitada said nothing. Lord Yoshido also seemed startled. Then he looked at his wife, "She's a nun. What are you talking about, foolish woman?" Her face fell and she began to weep silently.

At this awkward moment, the door behind the two old people opened and a handsome young man stepped in.

17
The Yoshido Heir

"Masatada!" said Lord Yoshido. "There you are. How was your journey?"

Lady Yoshido murmured, "Dear Masatada."

The young man stared at Akitada and his wife, still standing before the dais like a couple of servants who expected a reprimand from their master. Akitada was losing his patience. Reverence for old age be damned, he thought. These people don't deserve reverence.

He said, "Who is this? Please observe customary manners and introduce him."

The old man ignored him, but the young one snapped, "Yoshido Masatada. And you?"

"Sugawara. First secretary in the Ministry of Justice. This is my wife. Your grandparents have not seen fit to receive us properly, but I am here at the request of His Majesty."

Masatada blinked at this and looked at his grandfather who said nothing. "Erh, my grandparents are old and there are no servants. I've only just returned from military service in the north and have not had time to hire people." He bowed to Akitada and Sadako.

"Very well," said Akitada. "Be good enough to join us,"—he gestured to the cushions—"since your grandparents aren't interested in speaking with us." He proceeded to lead Sadako to one of the cushions, seated himself with his back to the old couple, and pointed to another cushion across from himself.

Masatada hesitated. Then he went to his grandfather and whispered in his ear. The old lord got up with a helping hand from the grandson and both helped Lady Yoshido and led her from the room. When the door had closed behind his grandparents, Masatada returned and seated himself. He said, "My apologies. I think you must have had a very poor welcome. Allow me to explain."

Akitada nodded.

"As I said, I have only just returned and found things as you see them. The servants have run away. My sister has disappeared. There seems to be no money. And my grandparents are at a loss how to explain all this."

"That must be very unpleasant," said Akitada noncommittally. It seemed a rather odd combination of disasters. "What are you going to do about it?"

The young man waved a dismissive hand. "What you might expect. Hire someone to look after the old ones and then find out where the money and the rice went. My guess is the servants absconded with them."

"And your sister?"

The young Yoshido heir compressed his lips. "She has deserted her family."

"I understood that she was one of His Majesty's favorites and gave him a son. Surely that must have propped up your family amazingly."

Masatada said bitterly, "I wasn't here then. It seems extraordinary. But the child was born dead and so His Majesty abandoned her."

"Surely not. Her title was Lady Hachijo in recognition of her status."

He shook his head. "Perhaps so, but then she decided to go into a nunnery. I still have to find out how my grandfather could permit such a thing." His voice shook a little with suppressed anger.

And indeed the effect of Hachijo's decision must have been profound on this family which clearly had been poor for several generations. Akitada knew very well about families that had fallen into disfavor. His own family was one such because his ancestor had opposed the powerful Fujiwara clan.

"What happened to your parents? Uncles, cousins, friends?"

He said bitterly, "The Yoshido family did not make the move to the new capital. Thus they had no more access to power. We lost most of our possessions.

My parents died in the last epidemic. I had an uncle and two cousins but they died in wars. Military service was the only option for a Yoshido male. Eventually there were just my grandparents and my sister and I."

Akitada said sympathetically, "And so you volunteered for military service and your sister went to serve at court? You were quite likely to die also."

He nodded. "I almost did. When my parents died I asked to come back. It took two years to get permission." He made a face. "Bureaucrats! I hate them."

Akitada belonged to this group. He said nothing. He knew well enough how paperwork got lost or passed to the wrong department. And the northern front was a long way from the capital.

He said, "I'm sorry about your troubles. His Majesty has asked me to make sure all is well with Lady Hachijo. Do you have any information about why she left the convent or where she might have gone?"

Masatada brushed a tired hand across his face. "I don't know and I don't care. I have more important things to do."

"You sound angry."

Masatada got to his feet. "Of course, I'm angry. She held her family's future in her hands and threw it away. She cared nothing for us. It doesn't matter if she's dead or alive. To me she is dead. That's all I have to say."

It was a dismissal. Akitada and Sadako rose also. Sadako said softly, "You have our best wishes for the future. Soon it will be the New Year. Your fortune must change for the better."

Masatada looked at her for the first time and gave a hollow laugh. "Not likely. I cannot pay our debts."

They left then. It had been an unpleasant and futile visit. Outside Sadako said, "Such misery! It was quite shocking. Those two old people, so proud and so poor. I wonder when they ate last."

Akitada nodded. "You would think he'd be desperate to find his sister. Surely she could intercede with the emperor. She's entitled to a small fortune for her upkeep."

"The temple will have taken whatever His Majesty pays her."

"Then Masatada should demand it back from the nuns."

His wife gasped. "You cannot take back what you have donated to a temple, Akitada. It's impossible."

"Yes. More's the pity. They take and take and never give back. Maybe they killed her. Her income must have been substantial."

Sadako frowned. "Perhaps someone did. It would help to know what the financial arrangements were. We should talk to those nuns again."

"Why didn't she make sure her grandparents had enough to live on? Did she go to see them when she left the palace? We'll have to talk to the Yoshido family again. I should have asked more questions in the capital." He looked at his wife as she walked cautiously on the slippery roadway. The sky was clouding over. It had warmed a little, but the cloud bank was the dense grayish white that promised more snow. He said, "Perhaps we should just go back. Things are not very comfortable here with the majordomo dead and the inadequate staff. I'm sorry this hasn't been a better trip for you."

"Oh, Akitada, don't be. I've been so happy. We have seen such wonderful things, and most of all, there have been just the two of us and you have let me into your life."

He was astonished. "But you *are* in my life. You'll always be in my life wherever we are." He saw her eyes fill with tears and her hand, small and icy cold, squeezed his. "Come," he said. "You're freezing. Let's go back and see if that big lout of a new servant has heated the bath water. There will be more snow. I have a good mind to keep you with me tomorrow, warm inside our bedding."

She blushed and giggled. "You would forget your duty so quickly, my husband?"

"To the devil with my duty. I'm entitled to love my wife. Come along now. I'm becoming impatient."

But a surprise awaited them at the house. The courtyard was full of men moving about shoveling snow and running back and forth between the house and the service yard. They paused, startled. An older man approached them. He looked vaguely familiar to Akitada.

"My lord, my lady! Lord Kosehira has sent out to find you. He's inside."

Kosehira had come with a small army. The letter about Sanekane's death had sent him post-haste to make sure they were properly looked after. And Akitada wished him to the devil. He wanted his hot bath with his wife and then to make love to her under a mountain of silken quilts while the snow fell silently outside.

18

Tora Eats Well

Tora had set out obediently to ask questions of Sanekane's neighbors. It was midmorning and he took his way through the market. Food at the Fujiwara residence had been a disappointment, and, following his nose, Tora found a vendor of those delicious grilled eels. These he ate while strolling about to familiarize himself with Nara merchandise. It offered few surprises, though there seemed to be a lot of places selling Buddhist religious objects. One store was given over completely to items one expected to find in temples.

The eel was covered with a sweet and sticky sauce, mouthwatering but messy. After cleaning his hands with snow, Tora set off for Sanekane's neighborhood. The majordomo's street was short. There were five houses on each side. Tora started at one end on Sanekane's side.

A maid was sweeping the front steps. Tora observed her approvingly. She was in her twenties and slender, and she wielded the broom firmly. He leaned on the gate and whistled. When she stopped to look, he gave her a big smile.

She stared for a moment, then tossed her head. "What do you want?"

"Just admiring the view."

"Go away! You're too old. Bet you're married."

Tora had the grace to blush. "You guessed it. And I have a nearly grown son. But I'll never forget to give a pretty woman her due, especially when she's such a good worker."

She mellowed a little. "I have no time to chat, if that's what you have in mind."

"I did want to ask you about your neighbor, Sanekane. He worked for my master." This was not strictly correct, but Tora had no wish to go into lengthy explanations.

She leaned her broom against the wall and came to the fence. "The old man who died? I know him. What about him?"

"Well, it's just that it was odd. I wondered how he could've died in the snow. He didn't seem that old."

"Sanekane was a drunk. He was always drinking. And the two witches he lives with locked him out. It's murder, if you ask me. I hope your master sets the police on them."

Tora raised his brows. "You don't say. That's terrible. They hated him that much?"

"Don't be silly. Those two do what they do for the money."

Tora gaped. "Somebody paid them to kill Sanekane?"

She laughed. "No, silly. He had money and he was getting tired of them. They were about to be thrown out, the lazy bitches."

"Really? How do you know?"

"I've got eyes. He's been staying away for days. Found himself another woman, I bet."

Tora shook his head, thanked her, and walked to the next house. There the snow lay undisturbed and nobody answered when he knocked. The maid peered after him and called out, "Gone. On a pilgrimage to Ise."

He thanked her again. The Sanekane house was next. The snow was trampled from all the people who had visited recently. There was no sign that the women had tried to improve on matters. A bit of smoke curled from the back of the house. Tora went on.

At the next neighbor's the snow also lay undisturbed. Tora was about to pass by, when the door opened and a voice called, "Young man?"

Tora responded eagerly, trudging through the snow drifts, and climbed the steps. A tiny old woman peered up at him from a round, deeply wrinkled face. She was wrapped in a patched quilt, and leaned on a cane.

Tora smiled down at her and said, "Good Morning, Grandmother." It was the polite greeting, and she had flattered him with that "young man."

She grinned toothlessly. "You look strong and very handsome."

Tora laughed. "Thank you. How can I be of service?"

"Oh, that's very good of you. Thank you. The shovel is right here. Would you clear my path? I'm past it, and I need to go to the market." And with this, she closed the door.

With a sigh, Tora set to work. It was a long walk and served to remind him not to believe women when they called him "young" and "strong" and "handsome." When he was done, he had worked up a sweat and his hands were frozen. He knocked on the door.

She opened quickly, seized his hand with a clawlike grip and pulled him inside. He thought she was about to put him to more work, but she took him into her kitchen where a fire burned in the stove. There she made him sit on an upturned bucket. "Warm yourself," she ordered. Then she filled a bowl with steaming rice gruel so delicately scented that his mouth watered, added an egg and a dollop of honey, stirred, and passed it to him. "Eat," she said. "It's good."

It was. Very good! And it would never do to disrespect an old lady's wishes. She watched him, nodding happily. When he was done, he thanked her and asked if he could do anything else for her.

"Well, maybe you could bring in a bit more wood. The shed is out back." He went out and found the wood needed splitting, so he worked some more and brought her a neat stack of firewood.

She thanked him, and he finally remembered his purpose there. "Did you know about Sanekane?" he asked.

"I know he's dead."

"Yes. I found him."

She nodded, smiling. "I know. I saw you."

A woman who was watchful! Tora's heart beat a little faster. "Oh. Do you know what happened?"

"No. My hearing's not so good. What happened?"

Disappointed, Tora explained.

She nodded. "Poor man. He drank a lot, you know."

"Do you know the two women, Kiyo and Otoyo?"

"A little. Lazy. And they wear paint. Decent women don't wear paint. He hired the mother after his wife died. To look after the house. The daughter came later. Seeing that he was gone all day at his place of work, they made themselves at home." She sniffed.

"The mother claims he left her the house."

She chuckled. "The son won't like that."

Tora wondered where the son was. Surely the police had sent for him. He asked, "What sort of man was Sanekane?"

"He was all right until his wife died. Then he started drinking."

"The women said he stayed away for days."

She nodded. "Maybe. I wouldn't know."

Tora gave up. She had probably told him all she knew, and seemed to be casting about for something else for him to do. He thanked her for the food, and crossed to the other side of the street. But here his luck was not good. In one house, the people were new and did not know Sanekane. In another, there was only a barking dog tied up to keep watch on an empty house. Two housewives, busy with their chores, had nothing to tell him except what he already knew. Only in one house he found a garrulous old man who, like the old lady with the gruel, welcomed him eagerly. There was no gruel here, however, but there were some excellent nuts and a cup of decent wine. The old-timer was lonely and wanted someone to talk to.

Sanekane, he said, was a former drinking companion. Tora had to listen to a long list of memorable excesses which also included visits to prostitutes. Their excursions had been terminated by this old man's ill health and Sanekane's hiring of Kiyo. The old man was bitter about this.

"Don't know what he saw in her," he grumbled. "She's fat and common. But Sanekane always liked his women big." He shook his head. "And old. I joked about it, and he said the more mature, the better. They knew all the tricks and were grateful for a man." He cackled. "You gotta admit he had something there." More cackling and a poke at Tora's arm. Then he got serious. "Poor bastard! I guess they did him in in the end. Locked him out in the cold. How about that? Women are mean."

Tora nodded. "Some are," he said judiciously. "You think they did it on purpose?"

"Of course. Two of them. The daughter moved in, too. The better to bleed him dry." The old man's mouth worked as if he were gnashing his teeth. He was angry and spit a little as he talked. "Poor bastard!" he said again, clenching his bony hands and falling into a state of melancholy.

"The mother says he left them his house."

The old man perked up. "Never. Sanekane's got a son."

"People claim he was a kind and generous man who liked to help poor people. That he took the two women in out of pity."

"Well, he was a fool. Gave away good money. There was this woman working in a wine shop. He gave her money to bury her parents. A lot of money!"

"Yes. I talked to her. Were there others?"

"Probably. Women mostly." The old man chuckled suddenly. "Maybe he was paying for favors. Costly, but he liked women. Too much, if you ask me. Look what happened."

And that seemed to be the consensus. Tora left the old man to walk across town to the noodle shop. He hoped to learn a bit more there. Besides, it was nearly sundown by now, and he was hungry again. He had heard that this woman's noodle soup was something special and he intended to sample it.

19
The Noodle Shop

The noodle shop operated out of an old farmhouse on the outskirts of the city. It was not on any major road and its success seemed quite unlikely, but Tora saw right away that it was attracting a large number of customers. A broad path to its door had been swept and even as he watched, two women made their way to it. It had no name painted on its door curtain, but delightful smells wafted out when the two women ducked inside. Tora followed.

It was a good-sized establishment, the owner having turned the raised main room over to guests while the cooking was being done in an open kitchen behind it. And it was crowded. Tora sniffed and looked. The smells were mouth-watering. The guests appeared a mixed crowd. Many were practically in rags, others wore the clothing of clerks or well-to-do merchants. Tora saw a number of painted women, prostitutes filling their bellies for a night on the cold streets selling their bodies, or entertainers working in some brothel.

Attracted by the delicious smell, Tora walked closer to the kitchen and almost collided with a fat man carrying two bowls of steaming soup.

Tora reached. "For me?"

The fat man glared at him. "Wait your turn. A bowl costs twenty coppers. With fried dough on top, it's thirty."

Tora looked and smacked his lips. "I'll have one. With fried stuff."

"Sit down and get out of my way."

The customers whose soup it was cursed him for a greedy oaf, and Tora stepped aside. He looked into the kitchen and saw he had attracted the attention of a fat woman with a sullen, pock-marked face and untidy graying hair. She was stirring the soup kettle, a large iron one suspended over the fire. Beside her leaned a stack of bowls. And behind her, in the scullery, a thin young woman bent over a vat filled with water. She was rinsing used bowls.

A smoothly running business.

Tora gave the cook one of his grins and called out to her, "It smells delicious. What's in it?"

Her glum look eased a little. "Buy a bowl and find out!"

Tora looked around, found a couple of decently dressed and sober men near the kitchen and went to join them. He bowed politely, wishing them a "good evening," and they invited him to sit.

"Stranger in town?" the one with the neat beard and bushy eyebrows asked.

"From the capital. You're both locals?"

"Mostly only locals come here," said his companion, who wore a blue robe something like Tora's own. "Our secret. How'd you find out about Sachiko?"

Tora glanced at the cook. "She's Sachiko?"

They nodded. The bearded fellow said, "Best cook in Nara."

The other man added, "Best cook anywhere!" He shouted to the cook, "You hear me, Sachiko? You're the best cook in the whole world."

She cracked a smile. "Flattery won't get you free soup."

The fat man arrived beside Tora and handed him a steaming bowl. "That'll be twenty coppers," he said. "Introductory price."

Tora took the bowl and paid. "Not cheap," he said, sniffing the aroma.

"Shut up and eat," snapped the fat man.

Tora ate. It was heaven! The bits of fish that melted on your tongue, the succulent noodles, the crunchy, flavorful vegetables, and, oh, the broth! He ate and drank it all, sighed, and met the watching eyes of the cook. She smirked and ladled out the next bowl.

Tora's neighbors laughed. "Another convert, Sachiko!" the bearded man called out. There was a smattering of applause and then the slurping continued. Tora looked at his empty bowl. Then he glanced toward the kitchen. "How come that girl back there stays so thin? I'd have thought anyone eating here would end up fat."

The man in the blue robe said, "That's Midori. She doesn't eat much. Life on the street tends to turn your stomach."

"She's a whore? Why is she working here?"

"She's one Sachiko's taken in. The guy who hands out the bowls and collects the money is Ushimatsu. He's a gambler. They caught him cheating and now he's afraid to leave the house."

"You mean he lives here?"

His companions nodded. "They all live here."

The bearded man said, "Sachiko takes them in until they find their feet. They pay her back by helping out."

The fat man arrived with more bowls of soup. This time, Tora paid happily. After a few bites, he asked the two men, "You happen to know a guy called Sanekane?"

They grinned and nodded. "He's not here today," the bearded man said. "Must've gone home," the other added.

Tora looked from one to the other. He thought about their response and asked, "You mean he stays here sometimes?"

They chuckled. "Oh, Sanekane's her favorite," said the man in the blue robe with a nod toward the cook. "Mind you, he's not poor. He came, liked the noodle soup, and stayed. He's generous with his money."

Tora, his heart beating faster, asked, "He was here last night?"

"Sure," said the bearded man. "He's been here the whole week."

"Did either of you see him leave?"

They shook their heads. The bearded man frowned, "Why do you ask?"

"Because I found Sanekane dead early this morning."

They gasped and looked at each other. The man in blue said, "Are you sure? Sanekane's dead?"

The fat man was passing on his way back for more bowls of soup. He stopped. "What?"

The bearded man told him, "He says Sanekane's dead."

Tora explained, "I found him this morning. Dead and frozen stiff in the snow."

The fat man shouted to the cook, "Sachiko! He says Sanekane's dead." There were gasps all around. She dropped her ladle, and the thin girl let loose a piercing wail.

Sachiko stopped serving her guests and shooed them out. Tora stayed, and when the room was empty, she came to him and sat on one of the cushions. The fat man and the thin girl joined them, their faces strained. The thin girl was weeping.

"Now tell me!" Sachiko said.

Tora told his story about the missing major-domo and his search for him.

"You talk to those two women in his house?" Sachiko asked.

"Yes. They claim they didn't hear him."

Sachiko said, "You mean, he got all the way home and they wouldn't let him in?"

"Well, they may not have heard him."

Sachiko snorted. "Those two!"

The thin girl whispered, "He died all alone. He was out there with nobody to help him. And he helped everybody." Sobs shook her frail body.

"May all the devils in hell punish those evil women," muttered the fat man.

"What was he doing here in the first place?" Tora asked. "They say he's been staying here."

Sachiko blushed a little and nodded. "Sanekane liked it here. He was lonely. He was the loneliest man I ever met."

The other two nodded their heads. The thin girl wiped her eyes and sniffled. "He came to eat. They all come to eat. The noodle soup is wonderful, and Sachiko is good to people. He was good to people, too. So he stayed. He said he liked to be someplace where people were happy for a little while."

Sachiko sighed deeply. "He'd go home sometimes. Said he had his work to do, but he wasn't needed all the time, so he'd come back here as soon as he could."

She added sadly, "He always came back to me."

Tora asked, "Did he eat here before he left?"

She shook her head. "No. Midori needed some help. He went with her."

The thin girl shivered. "I'd been having trouble with some rowdy boys. He walked me to the brothel. He was always kind like that." She gave another small sob.

Tora stared at her. On closer inspection, she was in her late twenties and might have been pretty once. Now she would hardly be attractive to a man who looked for a warm, sensuous embrace. She was pale and haggard.

Sachiko saw his surprise and said, "Midori's working at night when she can get work. They sent for her."

Midori gave him a tremulous smile and nodded.

So Midori worked in a brothel. She was not only frail and thin; she looked sick. Tora guessed she was worn out by the hard life on the streets. Her clothes, while showy and colorful, were cotton and stained, proving she was not successful at her work, and so did the fact that she had found refuge with Sachiko.

At this point they were joined by a crippled boy of about sixteen or seventeen who carried a heavy bundle. His back was malformed and he shuffled in, asking in a querulous voice, "Where's everybody? What's going on, Mother Sachiko?"

"Come in, Kosuke. Sanekane's dead."

The boy dropped his bundle. "How? Where?"

The story was told again, and Kosuke started sniveling also. It seemed that, whatever the two women in his house were to Sanekane, he had found more loving companions here.

Sachiko interrupted the general grief. "Midori, you'll have to go now or you'll be late. I packed your dinner for you."

Midori ran back to the kitchen, and Tora looked after her. "I'll walk with her. Make sure she's all right."

Sachiko nodded. "Good. She's had a hard time."

And so Tora left the noodle shop with Midori. As they walked through the dark, snowy streets toward the brothel quarter, Tora asked her what had happened after she and Sanekane had left Sachiko's place the night before.

Midori started to cry again. "Those boys," she mumbled through tears. "They were waiting for me. They put stones in snow and throw them at me. He went to them and talked, and they ran away. He told me they wouldn't bother me again."

"Ah. That was good. And then what did you do?"

"He walked me all the way to my work and then he left."

"To go home?"

She thought. "He said, he'd have some warm wine on the way."

Outside the brothel, Midori stopped and looked up at him. "Thank you. You're a good man. Like Sanekane."

And that was that. Sanekane was gone and nobody knew what had happened to him.

20
Kosehira's Visit

Kosehira was full of apologies and commiserations when none was due. Akitada and Sadako tried to reassure him that it was not his fault and that they had managed very well, that it had all been an adventure.

In retrospect, it had been. Both were sorry that they had lost the privacy of their togetherness. Such a blissful state was practically unknown in their own home or in the great houses of their equals. There were always servants everywhere. And the servants knew precisely what they were doing, and discussed among each other the occasions when they slept together. Tora was not the only one who would meet his master with a knowing grin on his face.

Their evening was quickly organized by Kosehira who sent out for hot food and personally inspected sleeping arrangements and bathing facilities. He went to the kitchen, where he terrorized the cook into frenzied activity, and to the stable to shout at her son. Sadako retreated to their room. Willy-nilly, Akitada trailed along with Kosehira, muttering reassurances.

When the food arrived, the two men ate together and Kosehira asked for particulars about Sanekane's death. Akitada told him what he knew.

"He was a good man," said Kosehira. "I'm sorry for it. Though, mind you, he seems to have been absent from his job a great deal lately. I didn't know. You put your trust in people because there are so many things to look after."

Akitada nodded. He knew it well enough from his own life, and Kosehira's, given his wealth and influence must be a great deal more complex. He said, "Do you think he had changed?"

"Yes. I think so. After his wife died and his son moved away, he must have been lonely. Strange, to get old and suddenly find you have no one left."

This was unlikely to happen to Kosehira with three healthy wives, nearly ten children, and heavens knew how many grandchildren. But Akitada knew what loneliness was, so he nodded again.

"So he died from falling asleep in the snow?" Kosehira asked.

"Perhaps, but he did reach home and he vomited before he died. Something he ate or drank did not agree with him."

"But he'd been drinking. Sanekane drank, you know. I knew it, but I made allowances. There was little enough in his life."

Akitada did not comment. "You knew about the two women he took in?"

"Yes. It made sense. Someone to take care of his household while he worked at my place. Only he seems to have left them, too."

"Tora has been checking into this."

"Good. I would not dream to ask you to waste your time. What news of Lady Hachijo?"

"None. I've spoken to the abbess of Hokkeji and to Hachijo's family. I drew blanks from both, and that is curious."

"How so?"

"Well, the abbess seemed detached. Unnaturally so."

"That's the way they are. They become nuns and nothing matters anymore."

"Perhaps, but it struck me as strange. She must at least be concerned for the reputation of her convent."

Kosehira nodded. "Yes. You'd think so. What about the family?"

"Grandparents. In their dotage. And an angry brother."

"Ah, yes. I recall she lost both of her parents during the epidemic. His Majesty sent for the boy to come home. He was with the imperial army up north. So he's back?"

"Yes. And it seems to have taken him long enough. He says he just returned. I thought he'd come because of his sister, but apparently not. I'm puzzled by his anger."

"Oh, well. Hachijo was his family's fortune. They don't have anything else. Dreadfully poor!"

"He blames her? For what? She lost her child. That seems to have brought about the change in fortune." That and the fickle affections of the emperor or the maneuvers of the Fujiwara clan to promote one of their own daughters to His affections.

Kosehira looked uncomfortable. "There was some foolish talk."

"There always is," Akitada said sarcastically. "What precisely?"

"Some maids said she wanted to lose the child."

Akitada swallowed. "Surely that seems unbelievable."

"Yes. His Majesty eventually forgave her when he learned how ill and distraught she was. But she did not forgive Him, I think."

They fell silent, pondering the strange tensions of the imperial bedchamber and the efforts of others to control it.

Then Kosehira said, "It would explain her family's behavior toward her as well as her decision to enter the convent rather than return to them."

"Yes."

Another silence. Akitada thought of Hachijo, doubly rejected. Would she have found a better welcome from the nuns? Apparently not, if Sadako was right. So had she merely run away again? And who was the dead woman at the jail?

Kosehira heaved a deep sigh. "Come," he said, "I have kept you long enough from your wife. Let's go to bed and see what tomorrow brings."

21
Another Nun Dies

The next morning, Tora reported what he had learned about Sanekane and the noodle shop. Akitada listened attentively. "Did you check any of the wine shops on Sanekane's way home? He must have stopped somewhere to drink."

"I did. Nobody remembered him. It doesn't mean he didn't, though."

"But it's a dead end," Akitada said. "The coroner thinks he's eaten apricot kernels. They seem to be in some medicines and may have made him sick. He says he would have got sick an hour after eating them."

Tora frowned as he thought about it. "He was at the noodle shop. He could have eaten the stuff there. But they seemed really shocked by his death. They liked him a lot. Maybe he stopped somewhere on the way home. Or those two women in his house poisoned him and threw him outside to die."

The thought made Akitada shudder. "Perhaps we can get a little closer to what happened, if you ask some more questions. Meanwhile, Lord Kosehira has arrived and there's the matter of what happened to Lady Hachijo."

"Did you learn anything from her family?"

"The son is very angry at his sister. He blames her for destroying his family."

Tora raised his brows. "That's pretty selfish. Doesn't he care about her at all? She may be dead."

"I know. It's hard to understand, but the Yoshido family has fallen on desperate times, and they're very proud of their past. They had pinned their hopes on Hachijo to save them when she became empress."

"Empress? She was going to be an empress?"

"Probably not. The Fujiwara clique would not have permitted her to be elevated above one of their own. They had started a campaign against her already."

"You think they killed her?"

Akitada did not answer that. His opinion of court morality was low, but he hoped they would not resort to murder. Could such a thing be hushed up? It was unlikely. Too many people would know or suspect. But his appointment to find Lady Hachijo was beginning to make more sense. There was talk already, and the emperor as well as the Fujiwara officials wished to stop it. The best way to do that would be to locate the missing lady. If something had happened to her, then other measures could be taken.

And if he failed?

Yes, that was the trouble. There would be retribution. He could only protect himself by solving the case.

He said, "I shall be busy with the Hachijo case. You can try to get more information about Sanekane's friends. And we still don't know where he ate the apricot kernels. I know Lord Kosehira would like to be reassured that the death was natural or accidental."

Akitada was prevented from going to see the coroner when a monk arrived with a message from the abbess of Hokkeji to come right away. He was a little resentful of such highhandedness, but as he was curious about the nuns at Hokkeji, he went.

To his surprise he found red-coated constables at the temple gate. He was expected and one of them took him to the abbess.

She received him in the company of the police captain and the same two nuns as before.

Greetings exchanged, Akitada asked, "What has happened?"

The abbess, who looked shaken, said, "One of our nuns has been found . . . dead."

The captain cleared his throat. "Murdered, to be precise. We are investigating, but her reverence insisted in consulting you." He paused and added, "As a courtesy, sir."

Akitada ignored this and asked the abbess, "Is it the lady I asked about?"

She started. "Oh, no. No, not at all. It is Enchi. It is only Enchi." She blushed. Her rosary clinked in her hands. "I don't mean it like that. Your concern for Shosho was on my mind. No this is old Enchi who's been here as long as I can remember. It is very upsetting to all of us. We all loved Enchi." She glanced at the other two nuns, who nodded. "I felt you should be informed because of the . . . other matter."

"Yes. Thank you."

The captain stared at Akitada. He asked, "You were concerned for one of the nuns, sir?"

"Not precisely concerned, Captain. I carried a message from her friends, but she seems to have gone on a retreat without leaving directions."

The captain frowned, "When was that?"

The abbess answered quickly. "On the second day of the frost month." One of her companions added, "Two weeks ago."

The captain was satisfied. "Oh. Well, the old one hasn't been dead that long. A day at most."

Akitada was still trying to absorb the news. "Where was she found?"

It was again the abbess who answered. "We have a storehouse in the back of the temple compound. It is rarely used. I cannot imagine what made her go there. When she was found by one of the male lay workers who noticed the open door, I thought at first she had succumbed to old age. But the nuns reported that she had been struck on the head." She compressed her lips. "Who would raise their hand against a harmless old woman who has given her life to Buddha?"

The captain assured her, "We shall find the murderer. You may leave it to me." He glanced at Akitada.

Akitada knew he was being warned off. He asked, "Have you made any progress with the other body, Captain? You recall, the young woman who may also have been a nun?"

The captain looked pained. "Since you insisted, we are continuing that investigation."

The abbess moved impatiently. "I won't keep you, Captain Katsuura. You are a busy man."

The captain rose, bowed, and left. Akitada made a move to follow him. He very badly wanted to see the body and the place where it had been found, but the abbess said, "A few more minutes of your time, Lord Sugawara."

Akitada sat back down.

The abbess waited a moment, fidgeting with her rosary, "Have you made any progress with your search, sir?"

"Very little."

She sighed."I sent Shosho's closest friends to look at the body you told me about. I thought they would recognize her. I'm afraid they were so shocked by the dead woman's nakedness that they did not look very closely."

"Oh? Then you think it may be her after all?"

"Not really. I hope not. But I thought you should know. You must understand that Shosho kept company with women of her own background. I'm afraid they aren't accustomed to approaching dead bodies."

The abbess's companions looked grave and nodded.

Akitada said, "Ah! The Shinto prohibition of contacting death in any form?"

"Precisely. Our teachings are meant to overcome this, but old habits are strong." The abbess bit her lip. "I blame myself. After you came and asked about her and . . . and suggested the dead woman might be Shosho, I thought her friends would recognize her. They did not, of course, but also they were frightened. You see, some of the women who come to join us have led very different lives."

Her companions nodded again.

"Because they came from noble families?"

All three nodded.

"I want to speak to them."

She flinched at his peremptory tone. "If they wish it."

"Even if they don't. Arrange it, please. And now I must see about this murder." He got up, noting the strained expressions on the three elderly faces, and left.

He asked one of the constables the way to the storehouse. Once again he was amazed how much land Hokkeji occupied. It looked as though once there had been many more halls and buildings. Now there were open spaces, small groves of trees, a vegetable plot, a strolling garden, and a large number of graveled courtyards. The storehouse was in one of these, an area enclosed with a wooden fence and containing five or six smaller buildings. It seemed to serve the temple as a general storage area with buildings devoted to specific purposes.

The nun Enchi lay in the middle of the wooden floor in the building storing temple furnishings and utensils used in services. She was face down, and her shaved head was a mass of blood and splintered bone. Next to her lay the object that had killed her, a *vajra*, or thunderbolt. It was made of heavy bronze and had five prongs. The prongs were covered with blood.

Strewn about the body and the room were other objects of Buddhist ceremonial and life. There were *kongo* bells, wheels, ewers, conch shells, whisks, candle sticks, censers, sutra boxes, alms bowls and staffs, and prayer beads. On shelves rested Buddha figures, inlaid lacquer utensils, and assorted ivory carvings. Someone had ransacked the entire storehouse, leaving the floor covered with objects.

Captain Katsuura stood over the victim and watched Akitada. He said, "She surprised a robber."

"It looks that way. Was anything taken?"

"Still trying to find out. These nuns are scatterbrained. I doubt they kept an inventory."

"What about the other dead nun?"

The captain scowled. "Nobody recognized her. I bet she was on a pilgrimage and strayed into a bad part of town. Someone attacked and murdered her. We'll never find out who she is or what happened."

"Where is this bad part of town?"

The captain frowned. "It was a manner of speaking. There are always drunks and vagrants about at night. They see a woman and they go crazy."

"Do you have many rapes here?"

Katsuura looked angry. "No more than in the capital. She was naked. That means her attackers caught her, stripped her, and raped her. The coroner says she fought. There were marks on her body. During that fight, the killer or killers accidentally broke her neck. That's when they panicked and dumped her in the river."

Akitada remembered the bruises on her body, the blood under a fingernail. He said reluctantly, "Yes. It could have happened that way."

"It did. Anything else, sir?"

Akitada looked around him one more time and shook his head. "No. Thank you."

22
The Coroner's Opinion

It was a thoughtful Akitada who returned to the house. The fact that the three nuns sent to identify the dead woman had probably been too terrified or appalled to look closely put the captain's theory in doubt again. Akitada, in any case, had never believed that the woman was a prostitute, but it was possible that she was a nun visiting the Nara temples to worship. Nuns were a frequent sight on the roads and highways. They seemed to be traveling a great deal and rather fearlessly. Of course women like Lady Hachijo would scarcely travel on foot and without an escort, but ordinary nuns shunned expense and show. Their devotion forbade fear of death. In fact, their faith taught them to anticipate eagerly being translated into a better state of being.

The other murder victim was most likely an unknown woman. Unless her family or temple searched for her, she would soon be forgotten. But what if she were, in fact, Lady Hachijo, and her companions had failed to realize this? He planned to speak to them as soon as possible.

At the house, he found Kosehira preparing to depart again. He had hired a new majordomo, a pleasant elderly man called Akazoma, who had been a schoolmaster and hoped to earn a small salary by looking after a house that was mostly empty. He was an educated man and promised to live in the residence and keep his eyes on the staff.

Akitada was content and secretly glad that Kosehira had decided to leave so soon. He had disliked the interruption of his work in Nara almost as much as his friend's presence when he hoped to be alone with his wife.

When he told Kosehira about the murdered nun at Hokkeji, his friend looked grave. "I'm afraid something terrible is going on," he said. "You will be very careful?"

"Yes. Thank you, Kosehira. It looks like a robbery, but you never know. I plan to speak to three nuns who were close to Lady Hachijo. Perhaps they know something."

Kosehira was doubtful. "Hachijo did not make friends easily. Certainly not at court. By the way, once the court hears about this murder at Hokkeji, they'll send someone down here. Or maybe they'll call you back to explain."

Akitada made a face. "There has been very little time. Three days. And yet already there are three people dead."

"You think Sanekane was involved?"

"No. Not really."

"I feel responsible for old Sanekane. Let me know if Tora finds out what happened."

Akitada promised and so they saw Kosehira off. Sadako also looked relieved and thanked him for his thoughtfulness. As soon as he was gone, they retreated to their room for the midday meal. Akitada reported what had happened at Hokkeji and asked if she would be willing to accompany him when he went to speak to the three nuns about Hachijo. She was eager.

"You honor me with your interest in my work," he said, taking her hand and kissing her palm. "Aren't you afraid of death? I'm always dealing with the dead, it seems."

She smiled. "I'm not afraid of anything when I'm with you. And you honor me with your confidence."

Loving another and being loved in return was the most exquisite experience in the world. He would never know anything better or greater. His eyes filled with tears. "Oh, my dear," he said softly, "I cannot lose you. Not ever. I could not bear it."

She squeezed his hand, then took hers back. "Don't think such things. Eat, and tell me what your plans are."

He laughed a little, embarrassed by his emotion. "I shall have to see that coroner again, but afterward I'll come for you and we'll go together to Hokkeji. And after that, what would you most like to do?"

"Nothing. With you."

He leaned over to kiss her.

Akitada did not relish the prospect of seeing the coroner again. The man held some peculiar views of justice and tended to be unhelpful in his diagnosis. In fact, his attitude amounted to obstructionism.

He found Doctor Hayashi busy washing the new corpse. The elderly nun was no pretty sight. Life's ravages had left her with drooping breasts and age spots on her face and arms. Her legs were swollen and purple veins crisscrossed them. Unlike the young nun, this woman had work-worn hands and feet that had clearly gone barefoot all of her life. Her head was shaved, showing that she had been fully ordained.

He asked, "Can you tell when she was killed?"

"Not long ago. The body is still quite fresh. No flies either."

"Isn't it too cold for flies?"

"Perhaps, but even in cold weather the body changes."

"So overnight?"

"Well, perhaps late the day before. " Hayashi looked up. "You might ask when she was last seen."

"I will. I'm afraid neither the abbess nor the captain is cooperative."

Hayashi looked thoughtful and said. "Ah."

Akitada saw that the wound to the victim's skull had also been cleaned. The bronze *vajra* had left deep lacerations. He asked, "Do you think she was hit more than once?"

"Yes. Twice. With great force. They brought the weapon with the body. Sacrilege to use the Buddha's thunderbolt to kill a nun. But she didn't care, I suppose. At least not at the time." He gave a dry chuckle. "I wonder what the rest of them make of it."

"The rest of them?"

"The nuns. Are they very shocked?"

Akitada said, "I expect they grieve the death of one of their own."

Hayashi chuckled. "Not if their mind is on the Buddha."

"You don't believe?"

The coroner finished his ablutions and examinations and sat up. "I believe what I see. No more."

They looked at each other in mutual understanding. Akitada nodded. He said, "The police are treating it as the work of a robber. No doubt they are scouring the city looking for some poor devil who was caught stealing on other occasions."

The coroner got to his feet. "And what do *you* think?"

"I don't know. I was hoping you could help me. Two nuns killed in less than three days."

"You think someone hates nuns?"

"No, surely not. But the abbess of Hokkeji thinks the nuns she sent to look at the young one didn't look closely. She is sending someone else."

The coroner nodded. He bent and covered the aged body carefully. Then he stood and looked down at it thoughtfully. "I wonder if she was happy."

"Happy? As a nun? Content perhaps. They give up all the things that make the rest of us happy."

Hayashi looked at him. "She was a woman. What do we know of the happiness of women? We think it's fine silk clothes, pretty fans, music, and love. If a woman is poor, she won't have any of those things. Instead she'll have hard labor and painful and often fatal births. The nuns are at least free of those. And of cruel husbands and selfish children." He sounded bitter.

Akitada was rapidly becoming depressed again. What about Sadako? She had not had an easy life, and he knew she cared little about what his wealth could buy her. He said nothing.

Hayashi studied him, then smiled suddenly. "Forgive me. I'm alone in the world, I see too much of death, and I have too much time to think about life."

Akitada touched his shoulder. "I understand. We don't want to think such thoughts, but we see too much that . . ." He broke off and cleared his throat. "Is there any new information on Sanekane and the young nun?"

"No. I wish I could be more helpful."

Akitada thanked him and returned home.

23
More Heirs

The noodle shop was already busy when Tora arrived. Ushimatsu was sweeping, several men were eating their morning meal, Midori was chopping vegetables, and Sachiko was busy making noodles for the next batch. She greeted him with a smile. "You're back for more?"

"Thanks, Sachiko, but I just ate. Later maybe. It's about the last time Sanekane was here. I wondered if he ate before he left?"

She stopped her work. "No, he didn't. He left hungry. We'd been very busy and there was no time. Midori was late and he wanted to walk her to her work-place. Oh, the poor, dear man!"

She had avoided calling Midori's place of work a brothel. Kindheartedness was a way of life here. Tora asked, "Any idea where he might've stopped for a bite?"

"Sanekane, bless him, would've stopped for wine. Those women at his house wouldn't let him drink. Mean bitches."

Tora agreed with her. He liked the idea of those two women having poisoned him and then put him outside in the snow to make it look as if he had never made it inside. He thanked her, waved to Ushimatsu and Midori, who gave him a big smile, and left.

He walked to the brothel and from there to Sanekane's house, asking his questions anywhere the majordomo might have stopped that night. He got nothing, as expected. There was no point in it. Even if anybody had remembered him, it was unlikely that strangers would have had murderous intentions. At best, if he had eaten what killed him, it had been by accident. No, Tora's money was on Sanekane's housemates.

And so he went to pay the two women another visit.

To his surprise, he found they had a visitor already, a neatly-dressed younger man who eyed Tora with a frown.

The women wore their best clothes and were smiling, and the room was much neater than it had been last time.

"Who's this?" Tora asked the women somewhat rudely. His pointless search had left him resentful and his conviction that he was looking at two murderesses did not help his disposition. How dare they start entertaining men so soon after Sanekane's death?

"This is *Taireishi* Sanekata," said the mother. "He's come to see about his father's funeral."

So this was Sanekane's son, and he was a senior clerk in one of the government offices. Tora, impressed, adjusted his attitude and bowed. "Sashima Kamatari," he said, using his official name. "I go by Tora and am a retainer of Lord Sugawara. My condolences on your loss."

Sanekata nodded. "The ladies have mentioned you and your master. May I ask what interest Lord Sugawara has in my father's death?"

The mother said quickly, "Lord Sugawara and his wife are staying at the Fujiwara place. They were inconvenienced by your honored father's absence."

Sanekata's face froze. "Indeed? Surely some respect was due to my father who served Lord Fujiwara and his family for as long as I can remember. Or to you ladies."

Tora was becoming irritated again. "Lord Kosehira has charged my master with looking into your father's death."

"Why?" Sanekata looked utterly astonished. "Kiyo says Father had been drinking too much and fell the night he died."

Tora snapped, "He may have had something to drink, but he died on his doorstep."

The majordomo's son blinked and turned to the women. "What is this? He died outside his door?"

The daughter cried, "We didn't know. We sleep back here. That's a long way from the front. And we sleep very hard. We didn't hear him."

Sanekata looked around the room. "This is the reception room. You've been sleeping here?"

The mother blushed and looked down. "It was your father's wish," she murmured.

There was a moment's silence, then Sanekata grimaced. "Both of you slept here?"

Now they both blushed. The daughter said defiantly, "Your dear father was very fond of us."

As the son appeared speechless, Tora said, "Then he was a fool. You locked him out on a cold winter night, and the police have some other questions as to the cause of his death."

Sanekane's son cried, "What?"

"You may wish to speak to the coroner, sir."

There were loud protests from the women. The daughter began to weep again. The mother was very angry. She waved the document at Tora. "How dare you? He'd never have signed over his house to us, if he hadn't trusted and loved us. We were like family."

Tora snorted.

"You bastard!" shrieked Kiyo, lumbering to her feet. "I'll lay charges against you. There are laws against lying about people. I'll see you and your master in jail and before a judge."

Tora laughed. "Don't be silly, woman. The house belongs to his son who'll get rid of both of you soon enough."

Sanekata finally raised a hand to interrupt. "Quiet! You, Kiyo and your daughter will stay here for the time being while I see about my father's funeral. Later we'll look into who gets the property." He turned to Tora. "And you, sir, must moderate your tone. This is a family in mourning. As for your accusations about my father's death, I believe we'll let the police do their duty."

The son's anger was clear. Tora blinked, realized he had overstepped the bounds of decent behavior, and decided to withdraw. He bowed to Sanekata and turned to leave.

Kiyo had the last word, "I'm not forgetting what you said. I'll lay charges today."

Tora and Akitada arrived home within moments of each other. Both looked dejected.

Akitada asked first, "What's wrong?"

"Those women, sir. They're vicious. And now they've found a protector."

"What do you mean, 'They're vicious'? Irritating perhaps, but not really aggressive. What happened? And what were you doing there? I thought you were finding out where Sanekane had his last meal."

"I asked everywhere. He must've gone straight home. So I went to his house. Which isn't his house, it appears."

Akitada frowned. "You're not making much sense. Let's go inside and talk."

They climbed the stairs to the veranda and took off their snow boots, then went inside. The house was dark and quiet. It was also cold, though after the outside it was less bone-chilling. In the room Akitada shared with his wife, they were welcomed by light, warmth, and comforts. Sadako jumped up, crying, "There you finally are. And Tora, too. There's hot wine waiting for you. Are you quite frozen? Sit down near the brazier."

They smiled and sat obediently. Tora heaved an envious sigh. "What a lucky man you are, sir!"

"I am indeed. But so are you."

"Hanae stopped spoiling me years ago. Now she tells me to stay out of her way because she's busy."

Sadako clicked her tongue. "Surely you exaggerate, Tora." She brought them their hot wine and sat down again. "Hanae dotes on you."

Tora drank and said, "There's nothing like new love, Lady Sadako. Later, wives learn all our faults and it's all over then."

Akitada was taken aback by the thought. In retrospect, and he had two marriages to consider, there was much to what Tora was saying. He looked at Sadako and said sadly, "I have many faults."

She smiled. "No doubt. Drink your wine. You'll feel better."

He drank and let his eyes love her.

Tora cleared his throat. "Maybe we can talk later," he offered, looking from one to the other.

Akitada blushed. "Erh, no. I want to hear what you have to say. And you both will want to know what I've learned."

Tora plunged into his account of Sanekane's son and the fact that the two women seemed to have gained ownership of Sanekane's property. "And when I told him that they must've killed his father, he took their side."

"You told him they killed his father?" Akitada asked.

"Well, nothing else is possible. You always say to check out all the suspects and if you can clear all but one, he must be guilty."

"Two," corrected Sadako. "You think the two women plotted from the start to get Sanekane's house?"

Tora said firmly, "Yes, I do. Sanekane came straight home from the noodle shop. He didn't eat anything anywhere. That leaves only the two women."

Sadako asked, "But why did they kill him, if they already had the house?"

Silence.

Then Tora said, "Because he was a nuisance. He was a drunk. They wanted to be rid of him. I tell you they are vicious."

Akitada nodded slowly. "Yes. If that's the case, they are indeed vicious."

Tora cheered up a little. "Surely nobody would pay attention if they complained about what I said?"

Akitada's brows shot up. "Is there any chance they might?"

"I don't know. I tell you, they're evil."

"What about his son? What did he say?"

"What does he know? He just goes by what his father thought of them."

"Hmm."

Sadako asked, "Is Tora in trouble?"

Her husband glowered at Tora. "He may be. He should have known better than to make unsubstantiated accusations. He had no proof."

Tora protested weakly, "But there's nobody else. I searched and searched. They must've done it. If I could get into that house, I'd probably find the poison."

"But you can't. I may have to send you home."

This shocked Tora. "No, please. You and your lady will have no one then. I don't like what's going on in Nara. I won't go home."

Akitada sighed. "Well, let's hope that nothing comes of it. Now let me fill you in on my case."

24

The Abbess Has News

Both Sadako and Tora were shocked by the nun's murder in Hokkeji.

Tora said, "You've stirred up a wasps' nest, sir. Now we shall finally get some answers."

Sadako looked at him. "What makes you say that, Tora?"

He gave her one of his grins. "Happens every time your husband starts sniffing around a murder: someone else gets killed. It means the killer's getting nervous and trying to protect himself."

"Or herself?" Sadako corrected.

Tora, perhaps reminded of his recent encounter with the two women, nodded. "Yes, quite right, Lady Sadako. Women have been known to be far more evil than men."

Akitada saw Sadako's astonishment and said with a smile, "Tora thinks the two women living with Sanekane killed him for his house."

Tora plunged into explaining the logic of his argument.

Sadako listened, then said, "That would indeed have been evil. But can you be sure that he didn't eat something someplace else?"

Akitada stopped the conversation about Sanekane. "We were talking about this poor old nun. Enchi. She was surely a harmless woman. Why would someone murder her?"

"If the robber was afraid she'd raise an alarm?" Tora suggested.

Akitada shook his head. "The storehouses are a good distance from the rest of the temple, which is not, in any case, heavily populated. He could have escaped."

"Perhaps she recognized him?" Sadako said.

"Possibly, though you wonder how an elderly nun would be familiar with the sort of man who robs temples."

A silence fell. Akitada sighed. "I cannot think of anything either, but it's in the hands of the police. My responsibility is to find Lady Hachijo. Are you ready to visit the abbess again, my love?"

Sadako jumped up to get her quilted cloak and her boots.

"What about me?" Tora looked hopeful.

"You stay here and do nothing. And hope the women forget about you."

The sun was low when they reached Hokkeji. It gilded the snowy roofs and sparkled on the snowy ground. Its particularly golden light made the temple buildings an enchanting sight.

Akitada felt grim. The red-coated police were gone, but he had an ominous feeling about the temple. Outside the abbess's house they encountered the *betto* from Kofukuji. Apparently he had been discussing temple finances with the Hokkeji nuns. Life went on, even after a murder.

The abbess was alone and looked very grave when they walked in. She invited them to sit and then plunged right into her bad news.

"As I told you, I sent two other nuns to have a look at the body in the morgue. It turns out, she is one of us after all. We have lost two of our small community." She closed her eyes and worked her beads for a moment.

Akitada and Sadako remained respectfully silent.

After a while the abbess opened her eyes again and looked at Akitada. "I promise you my utmost support in your investigation, my lord."

Akitada exhaled a breath. "Then the novice in the morgue was indeed Lady Hachijo?"

The abbess's eyes widened in shock. "Oh, no! Not that. No, the young one is Chozen. Chozen has been with us only a short while. She came from another convent. We knew she was unhappy here. It is my hope that she did not take her own life."

Akitada felt relief and then guilt. It was not the imperial lady, but it was another young woman with as much right to her life. He said harshly, "No. She was murdered."

The abbess shrank from his tone. "She may have run away. Or more likely, she decided to return to the other convent."

"Without telling you?"

She bit her lip. "I had had reason to reprimand her."

Sadako asked, "What had she done?"

The abbess ignored her. She said to Akitada, "The young women are not always ready to make sacrifices. This one was a schoolmaster's daughter. It is good for women to learn about our faith and history, and it is also helpful if they can read and write, but this man raised Chozen as if she were a son. It made her quite unmanageable. She was too proud of her skills. I put her to keeping accounts, but I think she resented that also."

Akitada frowned. "As my wife asked earlier, what had she done to win your disapproval?"

The abbess drew herself up and glowered. "I do not discuss the shortcomings of my fellow nuns. Let it suffice that she had not done her work diligently and I told her so."

Akitada bit his lip. "Did she have any particular friends here who might know more about her state of mind?"

"Not really. She had not been here long enough."

"What about her family and the convent she came from."

"I have given that information to Captain Katsuura. It is his investigation. You are here on another matter."

Another rebuff. And Katsuura had also changed his pleasant manner to one of jealously guarding the details of his investigation. What was going on here?

Akitada raised his brows and said in his most authoritative manner, "I must remind you that I have instructions from His Majesty himself to find Lady Hachijo. It is you who have misplaced her and now I find that your nuns are being murdered. I assure you that the deaths of the nuns Enchi and Chozen are very much my business."

The abbess gaped at him, then bristled, "I resent being blamed for Shosho's absence. Neither I nor my nuns have anything to do with it. She is not lost, or misplaced as you say, but rather on a pilgrimage. Her status allows her a certain freedom of movement and she chose to gain deeper insight into our faith by traveling to the great temples of Mount Koya and others."

"Mount Koya? You did not mention this before."

The abbess's eyes shifted. "I was not sure. But it seems she had mentioned an intention of making it her destination."

"I see. To return to Chozen. What was her relationship to Shosho?"

"There was none. They lived in different buildings and only met during services."

"And meals?"

"Shosho and her companions had their meals in their own place."

So the segregation between nobility and commoners continued in this convent. Akitada asked, "Isn't that unusual?"

"Perhaps in some areas, but we are so close to the court that it seems a reasonable arrangement to allow noble women to grow accustomed to our ways."

"And you? Did you see Shosho or Chozen frequently?"

"Not Chozen. She worked on our accounts since she could write. Shosho received instruction from me and from the two nuns you've met. The senior officers of the convent."

"I'd like to speak to those who worked with Chozen after speaking with Shosho's companions."

"Tomorrow. Between services. Now you must excuse me. Prayer service is about to start."

Akitada and Sadako bowed and rose obediently. One of the abbess's servants came in and helped her rise. It became apparent that the abbess was nearly crippled by her age. Leaning on the servant, she hobbled out.

25
The Noodle Shop Family

Tora was upset with the way things had turned out. He was still certain that those two females had poisoned Sanekane and then locked him out of the house to freeze to death if the poison did not do its job.

A very strange character, that Sanekane, taking people into his house and handing out money to total strangers. He wanted to know more about him, but since he was absolutely forbidden to show his face at Sanekane's place, he dared not return to the neighborhood.

In the end, he spent several hours with the stable boy, exercising their horses. They took them in relays out of the city, enjoying the perfect weather with its deep blue sky against the shimmering whiteness of the snow. This snow had come suddenly and abundantly this year. But soon it would be the New Year and Tora looked forward to the festivities. He hoped they would be back in the capital by then.

"Tell me, Yuki," he said to the stable boy, "what sort of man was Sanekane?"

The boy frowned. "How do you mean, Tora? He was very old."

"Well, not so very old," Tora said, stung. Sanekane had been seventy. Tora was getting closer to fifty himself.

The boy grinned. "Well, too old to be doing it with two women."

"Ah. You mean those two at his house?"

Yuki grinned. "Mother said so. Two whores, she called them. Why does an old man need two whores?"

"Well, maybe he only slept with one."

The boy shook his head. "That would be stupid. The young one isn't bad looking and the old one is hot for it."

Tora raised his brows. "Where did you learn such language? How old are you?"

"Fifteen. And I've done it. Many times."

Tora suppressed a laugh. "Really? Does your mother know that?"

Alarmed, the boy said, "You won't tell her?"

"No. But about Sanekane, he left his two women in the end."

Yuki grinned. "Sanekane had money. There are many women in Nara. Bet he got bored with all the fussing. He didn't like fussing."

A thought crossed Tora's mind. "Fussing? Like your mother?"

A guffaw. "She tried. I could've told her it wouldn't work. But she tried. Cooked him all sorts of dainty dishes and sewed him a pair of fine trousers."

"Hmm. Bet that was a disappointment."

A glum expression. "Life wasn't worth living."

Tora laughed, but he was thoughtful. The cook had a grudge against Sanekane. And also against the two women in his house.

"People say, Sanekane was generous. Did he give you presents?"

Yuki nodded. "Sometimes. He wasn't a bad guy. He gave Mother money, too. But she wanted him."

In the end, Tora was not much wiser about Sanekane. He was still a very strange character who gave money away and took up with unsuitable women. By midday, they were done with the horses and Akitada had not returned. Tora decided to satisfy his hunger at the noodle shop.

He found them all busy again. He lent a hand with serving and collecting money, then settled down with a special bowl of the delicious soup. He was joined by Ushimatsu when the cripple Kosuke took over serving.

Ushimatsu said, "She likes you."

"Who? Sachiko?"

"Yes. She's been down since Sanekane's died. Cried her eyes out at night. But when you come in, she gets that look again."

Tora paused slurping broth. "What look?"

Ushimatsu gave a low, rumbling laugh. "That hungry look women get. Midori's the same. They'll try to get you to move in. Then they'll get you in their beds."

Tora stopped eating. He swallowed hard as he looked over at Sachiko, fat, pock-marked, and frizzle-haired. There was quite a bit of gray in that hair, too. Tora brushed a hand over his own head. They could be the same age, though he would have taken Sachiko for older. And well past sleeping with men—even if she could still find one willing. And Midori wasn't much better, sickly pale and scrawny. She did smile at him a lot.

He asked, "Sanekane slept with Sachiko?"

His tone of disbelief angered Ushimatsu. "And why not? Sachiko's all woman. Warm, soft, and loving. A man could do far worse."

Not in Tora's opinion, but he now gave Ushimatsu another look. The gambler with his fat belly and pudgy face was no beauty himself. Had he been jealous of Sanekane?

He asked, "How do you know they slept together?"

Ushimatsu pointed at the ceiling. "We all sleep upstairs."

Tora glanced up. Narrow steps led to the loft above the big room. These old farmhouses had ample storage up there for feed for their cattle. It made sense that Sachiko should have used the space for sleeping. And she could in this way provide shelter for the men and women she took in. Did they all live and sleep together?

He asked, "What about you, Ushimatsu? You get lucky, too?"

Ushimatsu grimaced. "Not after Sanekane came." He looked at Tora sadly. "And now you."

"Not me!" Tora said it too emphatically and added quickly, "Tempting, but I haven't got the time. Besides I have a wife in the capital."

Ushimatsu said "Oh."

At that moment, Sachiko called, "Tora? Can you give Midori a hand?"

Tora saw that Midori was struggling to carry the large basin full of dirty water and jumped up to take it from her. She followed him outside where he emptied it into the snow.

She pointed to the well. "Just half full."

He saw that she looked very ill. "What's wrong with you, Midori?" he asked. She shook her head and started coughing. She coughed long and hard, bent double, and when she spat, he saw that she was spitting blood.

"Oh, Midori. Come," he said, dropping the basin, and putting his arm around her shoulders. "You must go inside and lie down. I'll get the doctor."

She shook her head, but let him walk her inside.

Sachiko saw them. Tora said, "She's sick. She needs to lie down."

Sachiko put down her ladle and came to look at Midori. "Is it bad again?" she asked.

Midori nodded. She seemed past speech.

"Kosuke," Sachiko called. "Go up and bring down some bedding. We'll make Midori a bed here near the fire."

Midori murmured, "The water."

Tora ran outside, filled the basin at the well with water and carried it in. Midori was coughing again. There was more blood.

Sachiko saw him. "Just set it down,Tora. Then run to Horyuji and ask Myoson to come. Tell him, she's worse."

Tora hesitated. "You're sending for a monk?"

"He has medicine. It makes her feel better. Now hurry!"

Midori started another coughing fit, and Tora ran.

Horyuji was not far. It was another of the great old temples, and Tora ran up to the gatekeeper, asking for Myoson. The gatekeeper directed him to the monks' quarters where a monk took him to a room that was fragrant with herbs. A thin monk with weathered skin and a deeply lined face was grinding some medicine.

Tora, out of breath and tense, gasped, "You must come. Quickly." He seized the monk's thin, sinewy arm and pulled.

"Wait! Who is it? What's wrong?"

"No time! Come!"

With surprising strength the monk shook Tora off. "You cannot use a boat without oars!" he snapped.

Tora gaped. "Boat? There's no river. It's only to Sachiko's noodle shop."

The monk's eyes widened. "Midori?"

"Yes. She's spitting blood."

"I shall need my medicines."

Ashamed, Tora waited. Myoson turned away and reached for a twist of paper in a basket. Then he added an assortment of pills. All of this he put into a small lacquer box that was attached to his sash. Only then did he make for the door.

Myoson walked quickly. Tora ran beside him. "What's wrong with her?"

"Her breath is infected. It's slowly killing her."

"You can't save her?"

Myoson turned his head to look at him. He had strangely calm and clear eyes. "A living body is a dying body. Why fight a useless battle?"

Outraged, Tora cried, "Then why do you pretend to be a healer?"

"I only ease the pain."

Tora fell silent.

Sachiko received the monk gratefully. The shop was empty of customers. Midori rested beside the fire, surrounded by Kosuke and Ushimatsu. A pale child, a boy of eight or nine, had also come and sat beside her, holding her hand.

26

The Nun Shosho

They went back the next day as instructed by the abbess. Sadako was eager to hear what Lady Hachijo's companions would have to say about her. Her husband was glum. He was still angry that the abbess had refused to discuss the nun Chozen with him. He had no faith in Captain Katsuura and was increasingly convinced that someone was killing nuns and that Hachijo might also be a victim and they just had not found her body yet.

They were taken to a small hall nearby but separate from the nun's quarters. Here they found three nuns in the usual dark robes. Two had the shaven heads of fully ordained nuns, and the third had the short, shoulder-length hair of the novices. They were seated on cushions and rose to bow and offer them also cushions to sit on. The bowing was unusual. Monks and nuns did not recognize status, but these former noblewomen had not forgotten their training. In any case, the abbess was not there to reproach them.

They were no longer young. Two were in their early thirties, Akitada guessed, and the third must be close to fifty. He wondered what had brought them to this place in their lives, not the least because he also wanted to understand Lady Hachijo's decision.

The oldest of the three was Shinnyo. The other ordained nun gave her name as Jizen, and the novice was Kanren. Akitada was uncomfortable with the names, as well as with the shaven heads of two of the nuns. There was something mannish about them, he thought. They looked too much like monks.

He introduced himself and Sadako, assuring them, that his wife had been eager to meet them.

He saw that they were pleased. Shinnyo smiled at her. "We, too, had another life, Sadako," she said in a warm voice, "I used to be Fujiwara Takako, and Jizen, who is our rector, was Taira Masako. Kanren is our newest member. She was Ono Nobuko and came to us from her home. And you, Sadako?"

"My family is in the North Country. I grew up there but the wars brought me south."

They thought this fascinating and wanted to know about the North Country, but Akitada was afraid that talking about her past would sadden his wife and changed the subject. "Her Reverence, the abbess, will have told you that I'm here to find the former Lady Hachijo. You know her as Shosho."

They nodded, looking grave.

"I'm told she left on a pilgrimage a month ago and has not returned or been heard from since. I think the three of you knew her well?"

"Yes," said Kanren. "Shosho was an imperial lady in her past life. None of the rest of us ever rose so high."

Akitada thought he heard a slight note of envy. He said with a smile, "But apparently she preferred your life here."

Jizen frowned at Kanren. "Indeed. There is no better life than service to the Buddha."

Kanren hung her head. "I know. Forgive me, Jizen. It's just that she did not always think so."

Akitada asked quickly, "How do you know?"

Kanren said softly, "Please don't think badly of her. She was very sad because she lost her child. It must have been terribly hard for her."

Jizen said firmly, 'But this is precisely why she came to us. She had learned that life in the world is painful. And she was making excellent progress in her lessons and looked forward to her ordination. She was studying the Lotus Sutra with great interest."

"The Lotus Sutra is full of hope for women," Sadako said. "She must have found that very uplifting."

Jizen nodded. "Exactly." She smiled at Sadako. "Shosho was very happy here."

Kanren looked unconvinced but nodded reluctantly.

The Lotus Sutra was just about the only piece of Buddhist scripture that offered women a chance of salvation. Akitada knew that the ladies at court would all have been familiar with it and so he did not attach much significance to this information.

"Perhaps you could tell me a little about her daily life here," he suggested.

They looked at each other. Jizen said, "Well, there are the daily services. I think she spent much time here studying with the abbess, and with reading, and sutra copying."

Kanren said, "Shosho did go out sometimes."

Akitada decided that Kanren was a fount of interesting information. "Is that permitted?"

They all nodded. Shinnyo said, "We have no restrictions. It's not at all like our former lives. We are nuns now, not daughters or wives. But most nuns stay in the convent. We have our duties."

Kanren said, "She hadn't been here long. Her Reverence had not yet assigned her duties."

Sadako asked, "Did you enjoy her company? Did you talk much to each other?"

Kanren hesitated. Shinnyo said, "I think Shosho was closer to Kanren than to me or Jizen. They were both recent arrivals, you see."

Kanren nodded. "We talked a little, but she was so sad in the beginning. And later she spent most of her time studying."

Sadako asked, "You said she went out. Where did she go, do you know?"

Akitada knew that this was the most important question and he hoped for an answer.

Kanren said, "Once, in the beginning, she went to visit her grandparents. She came back, very upset and cried all night."

A brief silence fell while everyone considered the significance of this information. Then Shinnyo cleared her throat. "It is sometimes difficult for families to accept a daughter's decision to become a nun."

Akitada nodded. "Yes. I've spoken to her family. They were very upset by the recent events of Lady Hachijo's life. Were there also other journeys before she set out on her pilgrimage?"

But Kanren was becoming more uncertain. "No. Nothing longer than a visit in the city. She didn't always say what she was doing. She may have visited the temples and the shrine. Such visits seemed to be good for her. She was in much better spirits when she came back."

"Thank you." Akitada addressed all three. "Now my last question. Can any of you suggest where she may have gone on her pilgrimage and why she hasn't returned by this time?"

"She said she hoped to visit Mount Koya, to study at Kongobuji," Jizen said. "It was an enormous undertaking for a woman alone, but she insisted it would be her penance and her sacrifice. And she hoped for enlightenment and ease from her grief from the teachings of Kobo-Daishi. We could not stop her."

Kobo-Daishi was the name given to the monk Kukai who had founded a temple on top of a remote mountain in order to teach people far from the distractions of cities and courts. His teachings were intended to help the suffering. Akitada knew that life was never easy in his world, and clearly it had not been easy for Lady Hachijo. He accepted her wish for this pilgrimage. He thanked the three nuns and they prepared to leave. On the point of walking out, it struck him that no one had mentioned the murdered nuns. He turned and said, "It grieves me that you have lost two of your number, the nuns Enchi and Chozen. This must have come as a great shock."

Jizen nodded. "We do not grieve for those who have found a better life. And we should not grieve for our loss, but we're human, I'm afraid."

"Did Shosho know these two nuns?"

They looked at each other, then shook their heads.

And that was that. He did not dare question them about the two murdered nuns, though he wanted to very badly. But he had been warned off, both by the abbess and the captain. And he still knew too little to claim any connection to Lady Hachijo's disappearance. He was about to nod and leave, when Kanren said brightly, "At least poor Enchi didn't have to hear about Chozen. She'd grown so fond of her."

Sadako said politely, "Sometimes there are small mercies in bad things. Chozen was quite young and new here, I think. And Enchi, being older, perhaps befriended her?"

Kanren nodded. "Yes, you guessed it. Her Reverence sent Chozen to help old Enchi with the accounts. Enchi's eyes were failing badly."

Jizen shook her head and smiled a little. "Kanren, you're such a chatterbox. Do let them leave."

Outside, Sadako said, "Poor Kanren. I fear she's having a very hard time letting go of the world."

Akitada chuckled. "Thank the gods. At least we learned something from her."

That evening, he wrote to Kosehira to report. In particular, he asked if anyone had sent to the Mount Koya monasteries to ask about Lady Hachijo.

27
Another Death

Tora sat beside Midori, holding her hand, watching anxiously her labored breathing. He was in a quandary. He should long since have reported back. There was already trouble because the women in Sanekane's house were filing a complaint against him. It did not do to ignore his duties this way. But this poor young woman's suffering twisted his heart.

On Midori's other side sat the little boy. His eyes were on her face and now and then his lower lip quivered. Tora had asked Sachiko earlier who he was and been told he was Midori's.

"What does that mean?" he had asked.

Sachiko had sighed. "She isn't saying. He belongs to her because she brought him and she looks after him."

Tora tried to trace the boy's features in Midori's. He failed. The boy was only about five, his face still soft and round, his eyes bright, his mouth tender and moist. Midori's face was haggard, the eyes ringed with dark circles, and her cracked lips parted as she gasped for every breath. But it was clear the boy loved her.

His own presence was not so easily explained. He did not know why she had grasped his hand when he had come to kneel beside her to ask how she was doing. He had hoped the monk's medicine was working, that she was better and just resting. That was when she had seized his hand as one of her coughing fits seized her again. She had grasped it painfully in the paroxysm and she had not let go of him after it was over. The boy had held her other hand and whimpered. Perhaps her grip had hurt him, but he had borne it manfully, though tears spilled from his eyes, and he was still holding her hand.

And so they sat, both caught, as night fell. The boy had not said a word all evening. Sachiko had brought him some soup earlier, but he had not touched it. She had also brought Tora some, but the boy's grief had taken his appetite away.

This odd group of people! They were all looking after each other. Tora found this very moving. They had so little themselves, but what they had, they shared. Midori had long since been too sick to work regularly as a prostitute, but she had worked as long as she could, bringing the earnings to Sachiko who had used them for the family, which also apparently included this child, who might or might not be Midori's.

Sometime toward the middle of the night, Tora saw that the boy had fallen asleep with his head on Midori's shoulder. She seemed to breathe a little easier and her eyes were closed. Sachiko had gone up to her bed, and so had Ushimatsu. Only Kosuke still sat in his corner, snoring.

Tora tried to slip his hand from Midori's, thinking of going home long enough to explain his absence, but her fingers tightened, and her eyes opened. She turned her head to look at him.

Her lips moved, and he bent closer. "Sanekane was so good to me," she whispered, and tears slid from the corners of her eyes.

He said softly, "He's gone to paradise. He's happy now."

She looked at him sadly. "He didn't want me." Her face contracted painfully and she closed her eyes again. "I wanted him, but . . ."

Tora was embarrassed by this. Midori was a whore while Sanekane was an old man. Perhaps she had loved him for his goodness. Tora wished that goodness had extended to making this poor woman happy for a little while.

She squeezed his hand. "I killed him, Tora," she said, her voice suddenly strong and loud. The boy stirred and Kosuke stopped snoring.

Tora stared at her, "What?"

She labored to speak, her breathing ragged, and said again, hoarsely, "I killed him. It's my fault . . ."

And then the cough was back, harder and longer than ever. Her lips drew back as she gasped for breath, her back arching, and then the blood poured from her mouth. Tora jumped up and cried out. The boy screamed and flung himself on her. Kosuke shouted something unintelligible, and Sachiko and Ushimatsu tumbled down the steep steps so fast that they almost fell.

But by then it was too late.

Midori was dead, and Tora was trying to make sense of her confession of murder and her pitiful life and death. He was profoundly shocked and disturbed. Midori had become someone who appealed to his instinct to protect the weak and suffering. In fact, this was why he had first embraced the noodle shop family. They were people who were both abjectly poor and yet full of love for others like themselves. Surely Sanekane had felt the same way and had come here and been made welcome. Sanekane was not poor in the worldly sense, but he had been poor in the matter of love. Those two women he had taken in, hoping for a family of his own, had betrayed him and he had gone out to find love elsewhere.

But he had found death instead. Because those who had welcomed him had also killed him. Midori, the young woman he had walked to her work to protect her, she had killed him.

Why? Why, in the name of all that was holy, had she done it?

There was a possible answer. It was not an explanation Tora wanted to accept: she had killed Sanekane because he had rejected her. That much, at least, might explain her final, painful words.

She had offered Sanekane her body, and he had turned her down.

Tora said nothing to the others about her confession. He left them to their grief and walked home through the cold winter night.

28
A Lesson in Temple Politics

Tora reported the morning after Midori's death. He had not slept after he returned home. It was too close to sunrise by then, and he had spent time mulling over the Sanekane case.

Its sudden and shocking solution was altogether unsatisfactory. Not only were those two lazy sluts in Sanekane's house apparently innocent of the murder, but their heartlessness of locking a dying man out would go unpunished.

Instead poor, abused Midori had confessed her guilt.

If she had not confessed, nobody would have been the wiser. But apparently she had felt the burden of the murder weighing on her soul, no doubt all the more so because Sanekane had been good to her.

There was no justice in any of these events.

He finally got up and dressed and went to tell Akitada what he had learned, hoping against hope that his master would have a better understanding of the situation.

Akitada and Sadako were sipping their morning tea when Tora walked in. Tea drinking was a custom Tora had never embraced. He thought that warm wine did a great deal more for his well-being than the watery, bitter brew. Akitada, on the other hand, had learned to savor tea from old Seimei, who had been a great believer in all sorts of herbal concoctions. His wife's adoption of the custom pleased her husband.

Akitada kept his face bland. "You look tired. Some tea?"

Lady Sadako smiled at Tora. "We have wine," she said and busied herself warming some on the brazier.

Akitada eyed Tora more closely. "I think he's had far too much of that. Been drinking all night, no doubt."

Tora was in no mood for teasing. "I have not," he growled.

"Ah! Then it's something else that put you in that bad mood?"

Tora sat down—uninvited, but they did not observe many rules in private—and said, "I know who killed Sanekane."

"Not the two women you've been accusing?"

"No. I was wrong."

"Ah!"

"It was Midori. She confessed. Last night. Oh, it was just before dawn, I guess." Tora brushed a hand over his bleary eyes. "She died. Back in that noodle shop. I was sitting beside her, holding her hand for hours. Or she was holding mine. She was lying there and the boy was sleeping beside her. There was only the light of an oil lamp. Everyone else had gone to bed." He sighed deeply.

Akitada regretted his teasing. "Who is Midori?" he asked when Tora seemed to have run out of words.

Tora looked at him blankly. "Just a sick prostitute. She told me she killed Sanekane, and then she died. It was terrible. She couldn't breathe and then she choked on her own blood."

Sadako gave a little gasp and pressed a cup of warm wine in Tora's hand. "Drink this," she said. "I'm so sorry."

Akitada frowned. "You're not making much sense, Tora. This woman confessed and then died? How?"

Tora drank. Lowering the cup, he said impatiently, "I told you she was sick. She was spitting up blood."

"Hmm. Why did she kill Sanekane?"

"I don't know. She didn't say. You're right, it doesn't make sense. She was grateful to him. They were all grateful to him. He'd been helping them."

Akitada said dryly, "Sanekane seems to have made a habit out of helping people. In my experience, people do this only if they expect something in return. Was he paying this Midori for sexual pleasures?"

"No. That's just it. She offered. He turned her down. It must've hurt her feelings." Tora paused, then added, "She wasn't very attractive. She rarely got work at the brothel. Only when they expected extra business or someone was sick. She was sick herself. You could see it. She shouldn't have been working, but they all try to help."

"So many helpful people. I shall have to visit that noodle shop."

Tora glared. "Don't mock them. They have more kindness than those people you associate with."

"Sorry. No doubt you're right. But did you believe her confession?"

"Of course. She was dying. People don't lie when they are dying."

"What exactly did she say?"

Tora thought. "She talked about how good Sanekane was. And then she said there was nothing between them. She sounded sad about it. And then she said 'I killed him'."

"Perhaps she just felt guilty. Felt responsible?"

Tora thought about that and cheered up a little. "You think so? Maybe because he was going back to those murderous bitches? Maybe she thought she should have stopped him?"

Akitada sighed. "I don't know, Tora. The confession sounds a bit strange. There doesn't seem to be a motive. Maybe you'd better ask some more questions at the noodle shop. And did you speak to all of Sanekane's neighbors?"

"Some weren't home."

"You might as well go back there, too. I promised Kosehira we'd find out what happened to Sanekane."

Sometime after this conversation with Tora, Akitada went back to Kofukuji to speak with its abbot. He felt uneasy about Hokkeji's abbess who had so readily turned over the murders to Captain Katsuura. Hokkeji, while to all appearances independent, was under the protection of Kofukuji, the assumption being that men had more experience administering temples and communities of religious people than women. Perhaps this was so. Certainly monks had been active longer than nuns, and in far greater numbers. They occupied the largest temples and monasteries. In any case, Akitada hoped to get support and perhaps some answers.

Kofukuji was making preparations for the reading of the Buddha's names. This always happened at the end of the year. Akitada blamed himself for forgetting all about this mandatory holiday. But it was still early and perhaps the abbot was free.

As he arrived outside the abbot's chamber, the *betto* Wakita came out. The man certainly seemed busy with his duties, managing the business of Kofukuji as well as that of Hokkeji. Wakita was not ordained. He was one of the many laymen working for the temple, the highest in position and importance.

He saw Akitada, nodded, and hurried to the door to the outside.

"Umm, Wakita?" Akitada called after him. "Do you have a moment?"

Wakita turned back reluctantly. "My Lord?"

"You handle the accounts for Hokkeji, don't you?"

"I wouldn't say 'handle' exactly. I consult with the nuns every month and note their reports."

"And have you been satisfied?"

This question clearly threw Wakita. "Satisfied? How do you mean? They do their work diligently, as far as I can tell."

"And is their financial situation sound?"

"Yes." Wakita was giving signs of becoming very uncomfortable.

"I assume you were closely acquainted with the two nuns who were murdered?"

Wakita shook his head violently. "Closely acquainted? No. Not at all. What do you mean?"

Akitada almost laughed. "Oh. I beg your pardon. I merely meant that you knew them well because you approved their accounts every month."

The *betto* relaxed. "I knew Enchi. The other one was a novice. I must have seen her, I suppose."

"I see. Did your duties at Hokkeji also involve an inventory of the storehouse?"

"Yes. We have a copy of the inventory. And I have made another copy of it for the police."

"Do you know if anything is missing?"

"I do not. Now, if you'll forgive me, sir, I have an urgent appointment."

"Thank you for your time."

Akitada looked after him thoughtfully.

A monk touched his arm to remind him that the abbot would see him.

Saison was seated on his chair again. He wore a particularly gorgeous brocade stole and his robe was made of a shimmering brown silk. It was after all an important day, and one could not expect a close relative of emperors and prime ministers to wear rough hemp and go barefoot in public. The abbot wore embroidered black silk slippers over white silk socks. His expression was bland.

"Ah, Sugawara. Please sit. You are aware what day this is?"

This time Akitada sat. There was no point in establishing his position any longer. The murder of the nuns was none of his business. His assignment only involved Lady Hachijo's disappearance. But he had decided to regain some status, if possible, to get Saison's cooperation.

He said, "Yes. It is very good of you to see me again when you must be troubled with your duties and the murders."

Saison looked grave. "I'm never troubled. Life is merely a dream."

"Perhaps, but some dreams are nightmares. It is because of the murders of those two nuns that I'm here."

Saison raised his brows. "Thank you, but our police force is quite adequate."

"I'm gratified to hear it, but there is still the matter of Lady Hachijo ."

"How is that involved in this?"

"Since we have been unable to locate the lady and since she was a member of the Hokkeji community of nuns, it may be that she, too, is dead."

The abbot looked shocked. "Are you suggesting she was murdered?"

Akitada said blandly, "May the saints and their disciples forbid such a thing, but it occurred to me and I want to be certain that it is not the case."

The abbot narrowed his eyes. "And how will you do this?"

"By talking to people until I find someone who has seen her and sends me in a new direction. At the moment, the last time she was seen was in Hokkeji. I will start there. It would help me if you were to explain to me how Hokkeji is run and who is likely to have been in contact with her."

"But," said the abbot, "the fact that she has not been seen may simply be because she left Nara. Have you spoken to her family?"

"Yes. They claim she did not come to them."

The abbot said nothing.

"You suspect someone in her own family is hiding her?"

"Not at all. I simply do not know."

Akitada was frustrated. Saison was playing this game to protect his temple, and probably also Hokkeji. The Nara police could be counted on to keep the bad news about the dead nuns contained. The abbot considered him a threat.

Akitada said, "The two murdered nuns knew each other. In fact, they both worked on Hokkeji's accounts. What can you tell me about the administration of the temple? Especially its financial operation?"

The abbot threw up his hands. "But what does this have to do with the missing lady? She was not at all involved in that."

"Perhaps nothing. Humor me, please."

They stared at each other. The abbot capitulated first. He did so, making a face. "This is all very disturbing and I'm very busy. I hope you will be content after this conversation. I have other duties."

Akitada said nothing.

"Well, the temples are funded by donations. Some are large and may be from His Majesty or from high-ranking nobles. Some are smaller and come from various devout followers. In addition to these funds, we receive goods, like fabric for monks' and nuns' habits, or food, or sometimes labor and building supplies. We also receive occasionally precious objects. But the most reliable and steady income comes from the efforts of the monks and nuns themselves. They raise many small donations through their services and prayers."

Akitada said, "Yes. Thank you. That makes sense. Do I take it that each of the temples keeps its own accounts?"

"That is so."

"But Kofukuji supervises the Hokkeji account keeping?"

The abbot nodded.

"Are the temple treasures, the items kept in the storehouse, involved in this account keeping?"

The abbot frowned. "Only as a notation when a gift is given. After that such items are put on display for worshippers to see."

"Ah, yes. You were kind to allow my wife to admire some of the precious possessions of Kofukuji."

The abbot smiled a little. "We find that our visitors are grateful."

Akitada said stiffly, "Allow me to express my own gratitude," and reached into his sash for some gold pieces.

The abbot smiled more broadly and waved the offer away. "Not at all, my Lord. You are on duty, as it were. You cannot be expected to come prepared for such generosity."

Clearly a few gold pieces would not suffice. Akitada withdrew his hand. "I shall make suitable arrangements when I return home." He was furious, but he bowed and rose. "I'm doubly grateful for your instruction, your Reverence."

29
The Son's Dilemma

Tora returned to the noodle shop. To his surprise, he found it open and business going on as usual. Sachiko stood over her kettle of soup, ladling out portions for the hungry men of the neighborhood.

She gave him a smile when she saw him. "Hungry?" she asked.

As if nothing had happened.

As if Midori had never been.

In her place, the cripple Kosuke was rinsing bowls.

Tora growled, "You don't care? Is that it? She's dead, and nobody cares? What have you done with her body? Thrown it out with the garbage?"

"Sssh!" Sachiko nodded toward the customers slurping their noodles. "We have to live and they are hungry. If I close my shop, they'll go elsewhere, and they'll be angry with me. Midori wouldn't want that." She filled another bowl and handed it to him.

Tora refused it. "You expect me to eat? After I watched her die?"

She said. "Yes. You need the food. Midori would want you to eat."

He hesitated, then accepted the bowl. "Where is she?"

"The monks came for her. They are kind. She'll have a fine funeral. We all paid for that. You're invited."

"Oh." Tora fumbled for his money.

"Later," Sachiko said. "When we have time to talk."

And so he went to sit down and eat. The soup was very good, as usual, and he did feel better after eating.

Midori would have wanted that.

The thought brought tears to his eyes. He wiped them away and looked around. He remembered her, bent over her chores, smiling at him shyly, whispering something to a crying child. He did not see the boy. Was he her child? How hard her life must have been on the streets. How grateful she must have been to Sachiko for taking her in with her small child. Just like the others.

Sachiko was the center of this household, of this odd family.

Ushimatsu passed back and forth with bowls. Kosuke hobbled out to dump the dirty water and get more, and Sachiko started chopping vegetables for the next batch of soup. They all worked, and together they were more than they had been apart. They were the noodle shop. Soon someone would take Midori's place.

Ushimatsu stopped beside him. "Tora? You're finished? Here take those back to Kosuke and see about some more wood for the fire."

Tora rose obediently, then paused.

No, he thought, not me. I've got to make that clear. I've got other things to do today. But he went out for the wood, and then split some logs, since the supply seemed to be shrinking.

He was stacking the last piece when Sachiko joined him. "So, Tora, have you decided to stay?"

Tora straightened and stared at her.

She smiled. "I've talked to the others. They like you. And also for Midori's sake."

"For Midori?"

"Yes. She liked you, too. Better than any man she'd ever met, she said." Sachiko chuckled. "I thought she was crazy about Sanekane, but he was too old for her. She told you, didn't she? Before she died. But you, she was in love with you, Tora. She was dreaming about making a family with you and the boy."

Tora was aghast. "No," he said. "I'm married. I have a son who's almost grown."

Her face fell. "Ah. The good ones always are. But what are you doing here?"

Tora explained and she nodded and sighed. "Never mind. We'll find someone."

He returned reluctantly to Sanekane's street. He supposed he should really go and apologize to the two women, but he was still so angry that they left the majordomo outside to die that he could not bring himself to do it. Then he saw Sanekane's son coming from the house and decided to tell him that the women had not poisoned his father. He was not quite sure how to do this without bringing Midori into it and hesitated.

Sanekane's son saw him and came over quickly. "Tora, isn't it?"

"Yes. How are you today, Sanekata?"

Sanekata sighed. "It's all so involved. I hardly know where to begin. Would you by chance have time for a cup of wine and a chat?"

"Of course. I'm at your service." Tora was curious what had happened to make Sanekata so friendly.

They walked a few blocks to the main street and there entered a wine shop and ordered hot spiced wine to warm themselves.

When Sanekata had said nothing for a while and simply stared down at his hands, Tora said, "It looks like your father ate something that disagreed with him. The women at his house had nothing to do with it."

Sanekata nodded glumly.

"So, what seems to be the trouble?"

Sanekata heaved a sigh. "Those two women—I got the impression you didn't like them much."

Tora laughed bitterly. "After I accused them of killing your father and they threatened to make a public accusation against me? Yes. You might say that."

The other man gave him a weak smile. "Well, yes. They aren't very pleasant, are they?"

This surprised and gratified Tora. "Are you having problems with them?"

"Not really, but my conscience bothers me. You said they left my father to die outside his own house. Did you mean that?"

"Yes. They did. But they claim they didn't hear him."

The other man sighed deeply. "That's my problem: do I believe them?"

A brief silence fell. Tora drank more of his wine and thought. Then he asked, "If you found they intended your father to die, what would you do?"

"I'm not sure. You know he left them his house, don't you?"

"I wondered if that was true, or if they lied about it."

"It's true. I had the documents verified."

"Oh." Tora was disappointed—and a bit angry at a man who so lightly gave away a valuable property to such undeserving whores—for to his mind, those two, even though they claimed respectability, had seduced an elderly man and sold their sexual favors for his house. Whores!

Sanekata said, "You see, my father was a generous man. I knew it, and all his neighbors said the same. I say, I knew it, but when I still lived at home, it wasn't as pronounced as later. My mother was still alive then and she curbed his giving. After her death, when I was already living in the capital with my own family, he was alone. That's when he started giving away quite a lot of money. And then the two women came. Things improved a little, but he was very generous with them. I wondered at his taking them in, but I couldn't interfere. I thought perhaps he'd married the older woman."

Tora said, "I don't think so. Was your father interested in older women?"

"Maybe. He missed my mother so, you see."

"When did she die?"

"Three years ago. My father was inconsolable."

Tora said, "Until the two women came."

Sanekata blushed. "Precisely."

"But a house is a valuable property and should go to a man's children."

"Well, in this case, there's only me, and I'm well provided for from my mother's family. And I will still get my father's farm. It seems greedy to take the house also. I don't need it."

The generosity of this family impressed Tora. He said, "I suppose there's also your father's word to the women."

Sanekata brightened. "Yes. Exactly. That's it! It's my duty to honor my father's wishes. Thank you, Tora. You've helped me immensely."

They had finished their wine and parted then, Sanekata walking away with a firmer stride, and Tora muttering glumly to himself.

30
A Nun's Tale

Akitada was both angry and frustrated. The abbot had been as dismissive as Abbess Kunyo. He could only get information by approaching the problem from the missing court lady's case. The murders had been declared off-limits. No doubt, Captain Katsuura cooperated with the temples in every way.

Hokkeji was also celebrating the holiday of the reading of the Buddha's names, but not every nun was engaged in this continuously. The gatekeeper nun directed him to a reception hall and sent for Kanren.

Being a novice, Kanren was not participating in the readings and chantings, though she was supposed to attend. Akitada hoped to lure her away. Kanren had struck him as a young woman who had a mind of her own and would find much of the ritual difficult.

She arrived quickly enough and with a cheerful look that suggested he had guessed correctly.

"My lord," she said, smiling, "I hope you are well. And your lady, too." She looked around.

Akitada said, "My wife is not with me today. Do you mind?" Kanren, who had shared living quarters with Lady Hachijo, clearly belonged to a noble family and, being a novice, might still worry about meeting a man alone.

"Not at all," she said, "though I liked your lady very much. How can I be of assistance?"

"I'm here again about Lady Hachijo. You seemed to have known her better than the other two."

"Oh. Shinnyo and Jizen? They're more advanced in the doctrine." Her face fell. "I'm afraid I'll make a very bad nun."

Astonished, Akitada said, "Then why are you here?" He flushed at this insensitivity and added quickly, "Forgive me. I should not have asked. Please do not answer." He knew well enough that many young women took this drastic step after disastrous love affairs or the death of the man they had loved—though Kanren seemed too cheerful for this.

She smiled at him. "I have no secrets. My father dedicated me to serve the Buddha. He'd made a vow, you see."

"Oh, was he ill?"

"No. He hoped for an appointment." She added dryly, "He has many daughters."

Akitada's dismay increased. Such behavior by a father seemed to him intolerable. Kanren was perhaps no great beauty, but she was intelligent, lively, and well educated. Had the man simply decided she would lack suitors and was therefore expendable in his marriage politics?

He said lamely, "I see," and fell silent with pity.

She looked uncomfortable. "I was agreeable. A good daughter should be. And it relieved me from court duty. I didn't care for that."

"I thought all young women dream of serving at court."

"Not all. Here I can read and write and make music and have discussions with other nuns. All my wants are taken care of. All I have to do is participate in services that are quite beautiful and give me great peace."

"I'm glad. Was Lady Hachijo of the same mind?"

Kanren hesitated. "Shosho seemed to be, but I think her mind was still occupied with her past. I wasn't surprised. Imagine having been chosen by His Majesty! She is very beautiful and talented, of course. That explains it, I think."

He must remember to use Hachijo's new name. The trouble was he had a hard time imagining someone of her position in these surroundings. Kanren's answer revealed a good deal, but much of it was about Kanren herself. She was very forthright, an unusual thing for a young woman of her background. And her answer revealed her longing to be also very beautiful and desirable. So he had been right to think that she was unhappy here, even if she had denied it earlier. We don't always reveal feelings we are ashamed of.

He regarded her thoughtfully and asked, "Did Shosho talk about her life in the palace?"

Kanren blushed. "No. Of course not. How can you ask?"

He liked the fact that she reproached him for asking a forbidden question. "Forgive me. I don't know what women talk about among themselves. Her Reverence indicated that you and the others were housed together because you come from similar backgrounds. It seemed natural to assume you might have talked about your past lives. I merely wondered if her past could have caused her to leave Hokkeji."

Kanren nodded. "I don't know. Shosho seemed . . . reserved. She outranks everybody here, even the abbess."

"But past rank should not matter."

That made her smile. "I think you must know that people never quite lose their identity."

Yes, Kanren was very bright. No doubt she would rise to become an abbess herself one day. Or else, she would return to her former life. He hoped the latter.

He quoted, "Never forget, though white cloud upon cloud come between us."

She answered, "The Buddha's sun shall rise behind the clouds and shine its blissful light."

It was a perfect line, original, and spontaneous. Yes, Kanren had a very fine mind. He smiled and asked, "Do you believe that Shosho went on this extended pilgrimage?"

Kanren twisted the beads in her hands and frowned. "I don't know. It's what she said, so she must have gone to Mount Koya."

"But she has not returned. That's the problem."

"I know. Something must have happened."

He was very much afraid she was right. Whatever Lady Hachijo's attitude toward the monastic life was, she should have returned. Either to Hokkeji, or to the palace, or to her parental home. She had not, and two Hokkeji nuns were dead.

"Do you think something has happened to her?"

Kanren looked him in the eye. "You mean that she was murdered like Enchi and Chozen? I hope not. That would be shocking. Who would dare touch someone like her?"

Akitada shook his head. "Even imperial concubines are merely human. We can all be murdered. Besides, once she became a nun, she no longer had the protection she enjoyed in the palace."

"Yes. You're right. But Shosho did not much enjoy the restrictions of the palace. She seemed to be grateful to be able to walk among ordinary people."

Akitada's interest was piqued by this. "Did she often go out?"

"She was only here for some weeks and we were living together only the last three weeks. I don't know how often she went out. We are sent on errands. But she spoke of enjoying seeing the city and all the people. I know she visited the other temples here and Kasuga Shrine."

"Did she go to see her family?"

"I suppose so. But she never talked about them. Her brother came to see her once."

Akitada thought this interesting. Given the brother's anger at his sister's decision, that must have been an uncomfortable meeting. He asked, "Did she mention the visit?"

"Not to me. But I asked her once about seeing her family again and the home where she'd been raised. She said she'd left that world behind a long time ago. I wondered about that."

"Well, she had gone to court years earlier."

"I know, but it sounded as if she didn't want to talk about her family. It made her unhappy." Kanren paused. "I miss my family and that makes me sad sometimes, but it seemed Shosho was more bitter than sad."

Yes, Akitada thought, looking at this plain young girl with her serious eyes and her mouth still given to smiling, there must be moments when these women wished there had been more to their lives than this. He thought of the coroner's words.

He thanked Kanren and went home, puzzling over Lady Hachijo's personality. Finding no answers, he thought it best to consult with his wife.

31

The Maker of Shrines

Tora felt much relieved in his mind. Sanekane's son clearly also suspected the two women. Too bad that facts had proved them both wrong. Too bad that those two shrews would get the major-domo's house.

Not that there was anything he could do about it.

He returned to Sanekane's street, not because he expected to find something to charge the two females with, but because he had been told to ask more questions.

He surveyed the street. The house where the dog had barked the last time now had a man sweeping the walk. He decided to stop there first, hoping the old lady across the street would not see him and add more chores.

The man turned out to be a young servant. He paused when Tora stopped beside him and waited.

"Morning," said Tora. "Do you live here?"

The young man was unimpressed. He gave Tora a cynical look and said, "I *work* here!"

"Right. You know the neighbors though, don't you?"

"Why?"

Tora said coldly. "Because I'm interested. That house down there,"—Tora pointed at Sanekane's house on the other side—"you know those people?"

"Yes. Why?"

"I'd like to know about them."

The youth cocked his head and smiled. "How much is it worth to you?"

Bastard, Tora thought, and fishing out a small silver coin, held it up. "Better make it worth it," he snapped.

The young man leaned on his broom and grinned. "How would I know what you want? The old guy's dead, they say. Died in the blizzard. He was a drunk. So there's only the women now." He chuckled.

The chuckle seemed inappropriate. Tora narrowed his eyes. "I know all that. Tell me about the women."

That got him a laugh. "You got your eyes on them? Not very particular, are you? The maid over there, now she's a fine piece of warm flesh. Those two women, not so much. One is old and fat. She's the mother. The daughter's fat and past her prime. Which one are you planning to waste your money on?"

"Neither. I'm investigating Sanekane's death," Tora said sternly. "Stop joking around and start talking."

The young man stared. "You police?"

"No. I'm looking into the situation for the son." It was a lie, but a permissible one. Sanekata had asked him for information.

"Ah!" The youth was finally interested. "Bet he didn't like the way they treated his father. Bet he's trying to get them out of the house."

"Something like that."

The youth nodded. "Well, I happen to know that they sold their favors when old Sanekane wasn't around. You talk to the old one, you can lie with the young one for a couple of pieces of silver."

"And how could you know that?"

The youth grinned more broadly. "Guess!"

"I thought you said she wasn't worth the money."

"Oh, I didn't pay."

Tora was becoming disgusted. "Is your master home?"

"No. He's a pharmacist."

"What about your mistress?"

"New baby. She won't see you."

"Ah!" Tora tossed the silver piece and pursed his lips.

The youth said quickly, "What else do you want to know?"

Tora looked at the house behind the youth. "He's a pharmacist?"

"Yes. Big store near the old palace."

"Those two women, did they shop there?"

"Everybody shops there. They made me get them stuff sometimes."

"Ah. What stuff?"

But there Tora's luck ran out. The youth could not read and they had written their order on a piece of paper.

Tora paid the enterprising servant, and headed for the house next to the chatty maid's place.

A bent old woman opened the door. "He's in the back," she said without waiting for Tora's question. She passed him on the doorstep, carrying a market basket.

Tora looked after her, then went inside, following a dark corridor to a well-lighted area in the back. Small scratching noises were coming from there as if some very industrious rats were busy dismantling the walls.

Tora called out, and the noises stopped. A quavering voice answered, "Yes? What do you want?"

Tora walked forward, turned a corner and found himself in a small room that was lit by a number of lamps and candles. A wizened old man with bushy white hair and beard glared up at him. He sat on the floor in the middle of assorted sticks of bamboo, slices of wood, and various small metal tools. His hands were occupied with a miniature building, a tiny shrine that looked perfect in every detail.

The old man growled, "Well? Answer or get out."

Tora's face broke into a smile. "You make spirit houses! That's wonderful! I'm Tora." His eyes now moved around the room. On shelves in the shadow stood other houses, temples, gates, pagodas, all different.

The old man said, "Congratulations on your perception. I take it you didn't come to buy one. I'm not interested in anything else you might want from me. So 'Good Bye.'"

Tora laughed. He was enchanted and squatted to see the old man's work more closely. He saw now that it was not quite finished. "That looks like Ise," he said in wonder, "Have you been there to study it?"

"Of course."

Tora stretched out a finger to touch, and the old man slapped his hand away. "Never touch! Wood workers use lacquer. It's poisonous and burns your skin away."

Tora snatched back his hand. "But you're touching it," he protested.

"I know what I'm doing."

For all his rudeness, the old man seemed to be softening a bit. Tora got up and went to look at the other miniatures around the walls, .exclaiming from time to time at the details of carvings, the thatch on roofs, the perfect little stairs and doors.

"They are beautiful," he said. "I don't see any nails."

"I don't use nails."

"Oh, glue?"

"No glue."

"But how . . . ?"

"Go ahead, pick one up."

Tora did and gently turned it this way and that, peering. Finally he said, "They are magical."

The old man chuckled. "Fit for a spirit or a god, would you say?"

"Oh, yes!"

Another chuckle. "Thanks. Now what did you come for?"

Tora had finished his tour of the shelves and turned back to his host, a more willing host now. "My master has a family altar where he keeps a Buddha figure. But he really prefers Shinto. I shall tell him about you. He'll like your work."

"Thanks again. Sit down, Tora."

Tora sat. "Your neighbor, Sanekane. He died a few days ago."

The old man nodded. "So I was told. A pity. He was a good man."

"Yes, but someone murdered him. Poisoned him."

The old man stared at him. Then he said, "You know, Sanekane drank too much wine. I expect that's what did him in."

Tora said, "No. The coroner says poison."

"What? But who would do such a thing? Do they know?"

This was difficult to answer. Tora hesitated, but there was no point in lying. "A woman confessed."

"Ah." The old man nodded sadly and set the partial little shrine carefully on the straw mat before him. "He loved women too, you know. Maybe too much. Mind you, that didn't start until after his wife died. Poor Sanekane. I saw him weep once. We were on the street. He was just coming home and he looked at his empty, dark house, and the tears ran down his face."

Tora said heavily, "That's probably why he took those two in. The empty house."

"Yes. I wondered at it. But the mother was just his type. She was a lot like his wife."

"Really? I'd have thought he'd prefer the younger one."

"Oh, no. He liked the motherly type. Lost his own mother when he was very small, he told me once. Said it was terrible growing up without that sort of love and care."

There was nothing else to say or ask about. Tora sighed deeply and shook his head. Sanekane had been a strange man.

32
Family Council

Life had become considerably more comfortable since Kosehira's visit to supply his house with adequate staff. Akitada woke in a room that was no longer frigid, since a number of braziers had kept the chill out overnight. The warm body of his wife was beside him, touching his back, and again happiness flooded his mind. Here was everything he had ever wished for.

He moved cautiously, trying not to wake her, then thinking that perhaps waking her, while selfish, might not be wrong. Sadako was more passionate in the early mornings than at bedtime.

But something struck him as different. It was the light. It seemed much darker than on previous mornings. And there was an annoying small sound of dripping. He slipped from his covers and opened the shutters a crack.

It was raining. The sky was pitch black and the snow looked gray in the darkness. Overnight warm weather had come, as it often did in late winter, and quickly the brilliant, shimmering snow cover would disappear for the depressing brown world of mud and dirt. He sighed and decided not to disturb his wife. Closing the shutter softly, he tiptoed out in search of hot water and tea.

Several hours later, a watery daylight filled their room. The shutters were partially open, and the dripping and splashing sounds proved that the rain had decided to stay and turn the snowy city into puddles.

They had eaten their morning gruel and were considering unenthusiastically their program for the day when Tora arrived.

"Ah, news!" said Akitada.

Tora bowed to Sadako. "Not much, I'm afraid." He said glumly. "What about you?"

"Not much either. Sit down, have some wine, and report."

"Well," said Tora after drinking and wiping his mouth with his hand, "I went back to the noodle shop to say 'good bye' and maybe have a last bowl of that soup. I wish you could try it. It's the most amazing soup, sir. Sachiko makes the noodles the day before and simmers the vegetables and fish overnight. Then, in the morning, she adds the noodles."

Akitada frowned and Tora stopped, looking puzzled. Akitada said, "I don't want to hear about all the meals you've consumed. I expect you'll be getting fat here in Nara. If this is the best you can do, stop right there."

"It's not the best I can do. I was just leading into it. And I'm not getting fat. My point was that all was the same as if nothing had happened. Nobody seemed to care that Midori had died. It seemed . . . cold."

"People have to earn a living. Did anything else happen?"

"No, sir."

"Then we still have to accept the fact that this Midori killed Sanekane."

Tora did not comment on this. He continued his report. "I next went back to Sanekane's street as you told me to."

"Good. Were the missing people home?"

Tora nodded. "Well, the pharmacist was at his shop and his wife just had a child, but I talked to their servant."

"And?"

"He knew all about the women at Sanekane's house. He said the mother's been busy procuring men for her daughter in Sanekane's absence. He claims he enjoyed the daughter's charms for nothing."

Sadako murmured, "Are they very poor?"

"Nonsense," Akitada said firmly. "More likely they are greedy."

Tora agreed eagerly. "Very greedy. I still think they killed him."

"I thought you said this Midori woman confessed to the murder."

"Yes, but there was something odd about that. She was dying. Maybe she wasn't in her right mind."

Akitada was becoming increasingly irritable. He snapped, "Make up your mind. You cannot have it both ways."

"I don't know what to think, sir. Maybe I overlooked something."

"Hmm. Was there anything else?"

"I wondered about the pharmacist, sir. He could have sold them the poison."

Akitada thought about it. "Well, check it out. Is that it?"

"No. The old shrine maker was back. He'd been to Ise. In the middle of winter."

"Shrine maker?"

"Yes, he makes small shrines. You know, the ones people have in their houses and along streets. For the gods. He calls them spirit houses. You should see what fine work he does, sir. He doesn't use nails or glue. He just carves the wood perfectly so it all fits together. I thought you'd really like to have one of those."

Akitada said, "Aren't you getting off your subject again?"

"Oh. Well, there wasn't much new, sir. He'd liked Sanekane and was sad about his death. He confirmed that Sanekane took in the two women. It happened after Sanekane's wife died. The old man said Sanekane was very lonely after losing her. He thought

Sanekane really took them in because of the mother, because he missed his wife and wanted someone like her near him."

"Hmm. Not very helpful."

A little desperately, Tora said, "I think he meant Sanekane took the older woman as his lover. I thought it strange, but it does explain why he would leave her his house."

"Yes. That could be. Well, if that's all, I suppose you'd better speak to that pharmacist."

"I will. What about you, sir? Did you learn anything?"

Sadako cleared her throat.

They looked at her in surprise.

She said, "If you don't mind, Tora, what exactly did Midori say about Sanekane's death?"

"You mean when she was dying?"

"Yes. Forgive me for asking you to remember. I know you feel her death strongly. I wondered if you could have misunderstood."

"No, Lady Sadako. I wish I had misheard. I did like her. Not the way one is attracted to a woman but rather because she was so shy and quiet, and she worked so hard to help Sachiko."

"She also helped herself," Akitada pointed out. He was by no means taken with the noodle shop inhabitants who struck him as people who did not much care what they did as long as there was something to gain.

Sadako said softly, "I think of it as the weak helping each other to survive."

"That's it exactly," Tora said, nodding gratefully. "Anyway, let me think. She was having a hard time catching her breath without choking and coughing. We were alone by then. Well, the little boy was there, asleep beside her. He may be her son. I thought she'd fallen asleep and I tried to get up, but she held on to my hand and opened her eyes. And then she said how good Sanekane had been and how . . .." Tora paused and blushed. He shot a glance at Akitada.

Akitada said, "Go on!"

"Well, she seems to have been fond of Sanekane, but he wouldn't . . . she said she was willing, but he didn't want her." He stopped, embarrassed, and glanced at Sadako.

Sadako said, "How sad!"

Tora nodded. "And then she said 'I killed him.' She said it twice. And she started to say something else. And then she died before I could ask her what she meant by it."

Silence fell.

At last Akitada said, "You mean he rejected her and so she killed him? Because he hurt her feelings?"

Tora shook his head. "No. I don't believe that. She wasn't like that. And how did she do it? She was late for work and he walked her to her brothel. She didn't have the time or the opportunity."

Akitada grimaced. "Yes. I suppose we'll never know. It's very unsatisfactory."

Sadako was thoughtful. "Since we never met her, we have to rely on Tora's impression of her. He is a good observer and he knows people. I wonder if she meant she did something that caused someone else to kill Sanekane."

Both men stared at her. Tora said, "It could be. It could be like you say, Lady Sadako. But who?"

Sadako looked down at her hands with a little smile. "I don't know. You two are the ones who solve the murders."

Akitada said, "There's not much to go on. And this is just a guess. Best stick with the pharmacist, Tora."

Tora sighed. "I'll go today," he said with a nod, and started to get up.

Akitada detained him. "Wait. Let me fill you in on what we have learned in the matter of Lady Hachijo."

33

More Family Council

Akitada poured himself another cup of tea as he sorted his thoughts. Tora, impatient, asked, "Any trace of her yet?"

"No. However, I'm becoming very concerned since the two nuns from Hokkeji have been murdered."

"You think, she's dead, too?"

"No, Tora. Not really. I just don't know. Let me tell it my way."

Tora grinned. "Sorry. Go ahead."

"Thank you. I went back to Kofukuji to speak to the abbot again. To my surprise, he suddenly turned uncooperative. It was only by mentioning a possible connection between Hachijo and the two nuns that I could get him to listen to my questions. But I got no answers about the two dead nuns. The abbot insists that the police handle that matter. And he suggested I turn my attention elsewhere. To her family, for example."

"Well, the murder of the nuns *is* a case for their police."

"Yes, and they are uncooperative also. I had a quick word with the *betto.* He claims to know nothing about the matter and is barely acquainted with the older one. He says he only checks the accounts once a month and that's it."

Tora raised his brows. "Sounds careless to me."

"Yes. I wondered at it. So I asked Saison about the income of both temples. This is fairly complicated but seems to involve a good deal of money, rice, and other donations. The property of a temple also includes gifts of precious religious items, which brings me to the store house where Enchi died."

"A robbery?"

"It looks that way, but of course nobody is telling me much about it. And it doesn't explain the earlier murder of the novice."

Tora frowned. "They could be unconnected. There are some rough types living in this city. I wouldn't put it past one of them to attack a nun. She was young?"

"Not so very young, but I think she was pretty before she was strangled and had her neck broken."

Sadako gasped, "Poor Chozen. It must have been terrible."

Akitada gave his wife a look and said, "You shouldn't be here. This is upsetting for a woman."

She looked back quite calmly. "Imagining what another person must have suffered may be upsetting but it is what makes us human. Surely even men feel someone else's pain."

Akitada grimaced. "Sorry. You're right. I'm afraid my work has inured me to some aspects of violent death. But you . . . and this young woman was raped first."

"I'm aware of it." She studied his expression, then her face softened. "Not all men are like that, Akitada. I know that." She slipped her hand in his. He felt himself blush and returned quickly to his report.

"It would be a great coincidence if there were two people murdering nuns, Tora, but you are right. We must keep the possibility in mind. In any case, I left the unhelpful Saison and went to Hokkeji. There I had the good fortune to run into another novice, this one called Kanren."

Tora interrupted, "You haven't mentioned her."

"Oh. Well, the missing court lady shared quarters with two other nuns. Both are high-born. Apparently, the 'good' people are housed separately from the other nuns and given more privileges."

"Not surprising, sir. It's always been that way with privilege. Though I would've thought the service to the Buddha didn't permit them to claim rank advantage."

Tora was of peasant stock. These days his resentment of the nobility, the "good" people, who were responsible for the starvation death of his family, rarely surfaced.

Akitada nodded. "Yes. It struck me as odd also, but remember, the temple and the nunnery depend on support from wealthy and powerful families. They cannot afford to alienate someone in Hachijo's position."

"No. The emperor would cut off his gifts if she took offense and ran away."

"Ah. And she has run away. At least that's what everyone claims."

"Has she really?"

"Well, they say she must have left on an extended pilgrimage, but apparently she had no permission. Anyway, this Kanren thinks so. Mind you, they weren't very close. No one gets to be very close with someone who was an imperial concubine. Kanren said Hachijo, or Shosho as she's now called, left the convent frequently because she liked to see the city and the ordinary people. I asked her if she went to see her family on those occasions, and Kanren said she didn't think so. That she went there only once and came back very unhappy. She also said Hachijo's brother came to see her at Hokkeji and left her in tears."

"Maybe she didn't want to stay and her family wouldn't take her in," Tora suggested.

Akitada nodded. "But what then?"

"She could be anywhere."

"Thank you, Tora. That doesn't help."

"I mean, maybe she isn't dead."

"She's been gone a long time. At the moment, murder looks a good deal more likely, what with two other nuns dead. I think if we can find out who killed Enchi and Chozen, we may get our answer."

Sadako looked anxious. "Then you do think the emperor's lady has been murdered?"

"I regret it very much, but it's possible. Mind you, given the story of how she became the emperor's lady and left the palace may explain why she put herself in danger in the first place. Remember, Kanren said she was forever leaving Hokkeji to go into the city. Clearly that wasn't safe. And Hachijo was said to be beautiful."

Sadako objected, "Surely not in a nun's clothes."

"Well, the dead nun was attractive enough to cause some rough man to rape her."

Sadako winced, and Akitada regretted having reminded her again of the brutal ordeal the other nun had suffered before her death, He tried to distract her by saying, "She seems to have tried to escape him. Her feet had cuts from running in the snow."

"Oh!" Sadako covered her face in horror. "I wish you hadn't told me."

Akitada bit his lip. "I'm sorry. This is not a story for your ears. Tora, you might have found a better time for this."

Sadako lowered her hands. "No. It's not his fault. Or yours either. I'm glad you included me. This is your life. I want to be part of it."

A brief silence fell, then Akitada reached for her hand, and Tora departed to speak to the pharmacist.

34
The Pharmacist

The weather was dismal. The rain had finally stopped, and the clouds were clearing, but a fitful sun simply served to reveal dirty snow, mud, and large puddles. In the city streets, melting snow has slid off the roofs and was blocking the entrances to houses and shops. Everywhere, people were shoveling and digging to resume their lives and bring visitors back to their shops.

Tora made his way to the pharmacist's shop with some difficulty and in a bad mood. His report had not been well received, and only Lady Sadako seemed to understand his feelings for Midori. Besides, he had skipped his morning gruel and would normally have stopped to buy a bean paste dumpling or some fried tofu, but the usual street vendors were not around.

When he found Otomo's Pharmacy, he saw that no one had cleared the way to the door and he had to climb a small mountain of wet snow. He pounded on the door with more than his usual vigor.

It was opened cautiously by an old man who looked out fearfully. "Yes?" he quavered, peering past Tora at the scene outside. "Oh, dear," he muttered. "He'll be so angry! Oh, dear. I expect he'll beat me."

Tora looked at the frail figure. "Beat you? Why? What did you do?"

"It's what I didn't do. The snow." The old man gestured at the mountain that blocked the entrance.

"Nonsense. You're too old to move that snow. It'll kill you."

The old man nodded. "I know."

"Are you the pharmacist?"

"No. He's not here yet. Oh, dear. Can you stay until he comes?"

"When does he come?"

"I don't know. He doesn't like to get his shoes and clothes wet."

"You work for him?"

The old man nodded. "He bought the store from me and kept me on."

"Then you were a pharmacist yourself?"

"A long time ago. Before I lost everything."

"Can I come in?"

The old man opened the door a little wider and Tora stepped inside. With the closed shutters it was dark, but some oil lamps lit the small shop and revealed a very neat and tidy space with many shelves of labeled boxes and jars that contained medicines and ointments, and a wall of drawers that were also labeled with their contents. A spicy smell lingered. On the counter were scales and small stacks of papers to pack the purchases in. All was very clean and neat.

The old man was on his knees behind Tora, drying his wet and muddy foot prints on the wooden floor with a rag.

"Sorry. Let me do that," Tora said, taking off his sodden boots.

"No, no." The old man finished and painfully got to his feet. "I'm Mitsune," he said with a bow. "How may I serve you?"

"Do you know Sanekane by any chance?"

"Oh yes. I have had that honor. He was a good man. A kind one."

"So everybody says, but someone killed him."

"No!" The old man gaped.

"Yes. He was poisoned. I wondered if you knew the two women who kept his house for him."

The old man nodded. "The older one. He stopped by from time to time to pick up medicines and we talked sometimes. That's how I know he was a good man. He was telling me about all the people he knew and their troubles. I got the feeling he was always looking for some unfortunate person who needed his help." He turned away and wiped his eyes on his sleeve.

Tora took in the old man's threadbare clothing and wondered. "Did he help you also?" he asked gently.

"He offered help, but I couldn't take it. He was always kind and asked if I needed anything. After my wife died, I sold the shop and prepared to become a monk. But I was unworthy, and so I left the monastery. I came back here to work." He heaved a sigh. "He felt sorry for me."

"But if you sold the shop, what happened to the money?"

"When I became a monk, I gave it to the temple."

"Ah!" Tora thought Mitsune a very foolish old man, or a very unlucky one. He said, "You lost everything over grieving for your wife?"

"Yes. She was worth it." The old man said this calmly and nodded for emphasis. "She was everything to me. The shop was nothing compared to her."

Tora shook his head. He loved his Hanae, but what this man had done in his grief struck him as madness. At least Sanekane had not gone to the same extreme. "Is this why you and Sanekane became friendly?"

"Yes. He realized I was a good pharmacist and wanted to know why I worked for someone like Otomo. He said he would find a better place for me. But I like the shop. It's home to me."

Tora said helplessly, "I'm very sorry."

The old man waved that aside. "Did you wish to buy some medicine?"

"No. I need information. I wondered if those women, the ones in Sanekane's house, bought any medicines here."

"They did. At least, the mother did. Something for her aches and pains."

"Did she ever buy a powder made from apricot kernels?"

"*Xing ren?* No. But Sanekane did."

This information stunned Tora for a moment. Then he asked, "Did he say why he wanted it?"

Mitsune frowned. "I don't recall. Otomo was here that day and he was in a difficult mood. I have a notion it was to be used for cooking. I always warn customers not to use too much. *Xing ren* can make you very ill." They stared at each other. "You said he was poisoned. Do you think it was the *xing ren* that killed him?"

Tora nodded.

Mitsune chortled. "It won't kill you. It'll just make you very sick."

Before Tora could pursue this issue, they were interrupted by a pounding on the shop door. A loud voice called, "Mitsune! Open up! What is this?"

"Otomo," whispered Mitsune and hurried to the door, muttering, "Oh, dear!"

Tora watched curiously as the new owner entered the shop. He was in his thirties, short and stocky, and well-dressed. He was also furiously angry.

"You lazy dog! You didn't sweep the snow away. Look at my shoes and trousers! Do you think customers will bother to come in when they have to wade through all that wet snow?" He suddenly became aware of Tora and stopped. "Oh."

Tora eyed him angrily. "Your shop?" he barked.

Otomo bowed. "Yes, indeed, it is. How may I serve your honor?"

"You're late."

"I apologize. This weather. And I apologize for my lazy servant. I see you also got wet getting in." He glowered at Mitsune. "Quick! Get behind the counter and serve the customer. And then get outside and clear away the snow."

"Stay, Mitsune. I came to see you, Otomo."

This surprised both men. Otomo bowed again. "At your service."

"When I tried to talk to you at your house, you were out. That servant of yours, who is young, strong, and truly lazy, said you were here during the day. It seems to me, you should have brought that chatty young loafer to shovel your snow here. Mitsune is too old."

Otomo gaped at this. "You went to my house? Why?"

"Information about Sanekane. I'm from the capital, looking into Sanekane's death for Lord Fujiwara."

Otomo bowed again, more deeply this time. "I regret I know nothing about Sanekane's death."

"He died from apricot kernel poison. Mitsune says he bought the stuff here."

Otomo glowered at Mitsune. "Did you make some horrible mistake?" Mitsune shrank into a corner and shook his head. Otomo said to Tora, "He's senile. I live in fear that something terrible happens."

"Then why do you employ him?"

"Out of pity. He has nothing and no place to stay."

"Are you a trained pharmacist?"

"I have some training, yes."

"I doubt it very much. You bought this place from Mitsune and later got him to work for you. This situation should be investigated."

Otomo knelt. "Please do not make trouble for me. I have never made a mistake. And Mitsune is very careful. Always!" He cast a glance at Mitsune, who looked confused but nodded.

"Hmm. How much does he pay you, Mitsune?"

Mitsune whispered, "Twenty coppers a month."

Otomo cried, "He gets room and board too."

Mitsune said, "I live here, not having a home any longer. I watch the shop."

Tora shook his head. "Twenty coppers to work all day and watch the place all night. I think you'd be a great deal better off at one of the temples, Mitsune. They always need pharmacists. And you can work there as a lay person."

Mitsune nodded. "I know it, but I love my shop."

"It's not your shop. It belongs to me." Otomo was outraged.

Mitsune said nothing and hung his head.

Tora changed the subject and asked Otomo, "Did you have any dealings with Sanekane or the two women he shared his house with?"

Otomo shook his head. "I knew Sanekane to nod to on the street. He was a crazy man, always giving away his money. And those two women are what he squandered it on. They've told the neighbors he left them his house. It's outrageous, if he did."

"According to his son, he did leave them the house."

"I bet the son will put a stop to it."

"No, he's willing to acknowledge his father's wishes."

Otomo threw up his hands. "Another fool."

"Did the women ever come into your shop to buy anything?"

"Not while I was here. I don't encourage loose females in my business."

"It appears your servant knows them quite well."

"What do you mean?"

"That young man enjoys seducing attractive females. I was surprised you left him at your house with your wife."

Otomo turned pale. "He told you this?"

Tora grinned. "If I were you, I'd keep him here at the shop during the day. He can keep the snow from your doorway. And clean the shop."

Otomo frowned. "You have a point," he said. "I'll run home and get the lazy lout."

"Go on! I'm done here."

Otomo turned to Mitsune. "You stay here and look after the customers, Mitsune. We'll talk later." Then he put his shoes back on and braved the snow mountain again.

Mitsune looked after him. "I wonder what he'll do later. He was very angry with me about the snow."

Tora patted his back. "I think he'll get the young fellow to do the heavy work in the future. And he may pay a bit more to keep you from running off to one of the temples. It might be a good idea to mention the matter now and then."

Mitsune smiled a little. "I doubt it would work. Otomo isn't a nice man. I miss Sanekane. I've been saving to buy my shop back and Sanekane promised to help."

Tora said, "Well, maybe you'll find another way." He took most of his money and put it on the counter. "That's for you, for the information. I hope you get your shop back."

Walking home, he thought about the strange business of Sanekane buying the poison that killed him and decided to keep the matter to himself until he had done some more checking.

35

Family Honor

When Tora had left, Sadako said, "What are your plans now?"

"Someone must know something. I believe Kanren has told everything she knows. As for the others, they may know a bit more, but they are clearly not talking. The abbess almost certainly knows more, but she is afraid we'll find out something that will bring discredit to Hokkeji."

Sadako looked shocked. "But, Akitada, given the fact that two of her charges have been murdered, she's already dealing with potential scandal. Surely it reflects poorly on Hokkeji when its nuns get killed and nobody does anything."

"True, but the abbess trusts Captain Katsuura. She doesn't trust me at all. Besides, the Hachijo affair involves the court."

"But what can we do?"

Akitada gave her a fond smile. He liked the way she said "we." "As I said, someone must know something. She walked out of the convent repeatedly. What was she doing? Where did she go? Who saw her?"

"She visited the temples and worshipped."

"So they say, but they don't really know, do they?"

"Oh. It's what you expect a devout person to do in her circumstances."

"Yes. And that makes it a very good excuse."

"I see. You think she had a secret."

"At this point I have no option but that she has been killed or that she fled and is hiding somewhere."

"Yes. Or both."

"You mean she fled and then was murdered? Yes, that's also possible." Akitada sighed. "I think we must talk to the Yoshido family again. Kanren said she visited them at least once, and the brother came to speak to her."

As soon as the rain stopped, Akitada and Sadako put on their boots and went into the city. The weather was still dreary and the snow continued to melt. They passed the provincial headquarters and saw that there it was business as usual.

Akitada frowned. "I really should pay a courtesy visit to the governor."

"Yes, perhaps. He might have some information. "

"Possibly. Come to think of it, Akiko mentioned him as an admirer of the elusive Hachijo."

Sadako was instantly intrigued. "But, Akitada, that is perfect. You must speak to him as soon as possible. How could you have overlooked him?"

"Perhaps because Akiko was relating court gossip by Hachijo's enemies. There were also some other men mentioned."

"Oh." Sadako was disappointed. "It's very bad gossip to say such things about an imperial concubine."

"Exactly."

They reached the Yoshido mansion soon after and found that changes had been made. The flag still drooped wetly, but paths had been cleared in the courtyard, one leading to the next gate and one to the stables. Of course, the rain had cleared nearly all the snow anyway, but the piles of cleared snow still marked the effort. Somewhere someone was hammering.

They passed on into the inner courtyard. The hammering came from a servant who was working on the broken steps of the stairs. When he saw them, he jumped up and ran into the house.

Akitada smiled. "We are being announced this time."

They started up the stairs when the young Yoshido heir came to meet them. He was not happy to see them, but he bowed and said stiffly, "Lord and Lady Sugawara. What a surprise!"

Akitada returned the bow. "Forgive this unannounced visit. We are concerned about your sister. I know you're angry with her, but her grandparents still seem to love her."

Yoshido Masatada grimaced. "My grandparents are not well and must not be disturbed.. You'll have to deal with me."

It was still a miserable day, even though the rain was mostly over. Akitada glanced down at his wife and said, "May we come in?"

The young man stepped back ungraciously and gestured at the door. Then he turned his back and walked inside. Akitada and Sadako followed him into the same reception room they had visited last time. It was unlit and cold, but the shutters had been opened, bringing in fresh but chilly air.

There were clean cushions on the floor and Masatada pointed to them. "Please be seated. I'm afraid we're not ready for company. My apologies." He did not sound sorry at all.

Akitada decided to keep the visit short. "What have you done about finding your sister?"

Masatada said coldly. "Nothing."

"I'm told you did make a visit to court. Did you speak to His Majesty?"

The young face hardened. "He spoke to me. I'm not sufficiently important to carry on a conversation with the emperor."

"So your resentment also extends to His Majesty?"

Anger flared in the other man's eyes. "I'm a loyal subject. How dare you suggest otherwise?"

Akitada laughed. "The Yoshido are a haughty clan. Perhaps it's time to rejoin the emperor's more humble subjects."

Masatada flushed. "We're an old family. That means more than wealth."

"Not in this world. Who arranged your sister's service at court?"

The young man bit his lip. "That was a mistake."

"Why not answer my question?"

"My mother did."

"She had a claim on preferential consideration?"

He nodded reluctantly. "She should have known better. There's no honor among the Fujiwara."

"I have reason to know that there is both honor and dishonor among them. I sympathize. From what I've heard, your sister was treated badly."

"My sister forgot her family and played their dirty games."

"I think you need to explain that."

He raised his chin. "I don't have to explain anything to you. You're one of them. You live on their handouts. Even now you and your wife live in Fujiwara Kosehira's house. And you married one of them. You married a Fujiwara daughter."

A furious anger seized Akitada. He snarled, "How dare you? What have you ever done to save your family? You left for better things while your sister was sold off to save the family name."

Sadako cried out, "Please, Akitada. Surely . . ."

She was interrupted by one of the doors opening. A cracked female voice asked, "Masatada? Is that you?" Lady Yoshido appeared. "Ah, there you are. I need your help. I'm too old to dress myself." And in wandered Masatada's grandmother, trailing a silk sash in one hand, her gowns hanging open in the front, revealing grimy underclothes.

Masatada jumped to his feet. "Grandmother! Not now. We have company."

She hesitated, then came a little closer. "Oh. Is it you again?" Her free hand attempted to gather her robes together. "It's awkward, but my maid has run away and my husband went into the city."

Sadako rose and went to her. "Come, Lady Yoshido. I'll lend you a hand. We'll leave the men to their business." She took the old lady's arm and walked her out before Masatada could stop them.

Silence fell as the two men looked at each other. Masatada had flushed deep red with shame. Akitada said softly, "There is no dishonor in poverty."

Masatada turned white. He clenched his fists. "Get out! Get your wife and leave my house and don't ever come back."

Akitada sighed. "Please sit down. I'll try to help you if you'll give me a chance. If you had taken the time to ask more questions about me in the capital, you'd know that I don't engage in Fujiwara politics and that I divorced my Fujiwara wife. Kosehira is an old friend from my university days. I have no other friends among the Fujiwara and quite a few enemies."

Masatada stared at him, then looked toward the door Sadako and Lady Yoshido had left through. "Then who was that?"

"My present wife."

Masatada sat down reluctantly. "Even so," he said and fell silent.

"Even so?"

"You work for them."

"I work for my government, for the people of this country, for my emperor. If I'm not mistaken, you yourself served in the army, an army ordered into battle by Fujiwara officials."

Masatada did not acknowledge the truth of this. Instead, he said, "Why do you meddle in my affairs?"

"A young woman is missing and may be dead. If she was murdered, it becomes my business. For the time being I serve the emperor. He has, quite rightly, expressed concern that Lady Hachijo should be found safe and sound. Why are you so angry at your sister that you don't care about her at all?"

The young man flung out a hand at his surroundings. "Don't you have eyes in your head? My family is ruined. My grandparents were left destitute, and it's all her fault."

"That cannot be true. Your family fortunes were ruined long before this. Your sister was sacrificed to save all of you. She failed, but hardly for want of trying."

"'Sacrificed'? What do you mean? My mother called in a favor in order to elevate the stupid girl. She would have been an empress, but she dishonored us and herself and threw it all away. She's better off dead."

Akitada raised his brows. "She bore His Majesty a son. It isn't her fault the child died."

"If it was the emperor's."

Stunned, Akitada asked, "Do you have any proof it wasn't?"

Masatada looked away. "No. But there is plenty of proof she had lovers. I think everyone knew the child wasn't the emperor's and it wasn't allowed to live."

For a moment, Akitada was speechless as he considered the situation Masatada described. He had no love for the court, yet his mind balked at such a thing. Lady Hachijo had had no friends at court. It seemed unlikely that a flagrant affair could have taken place without some action being taken quickly. The gossip, of course, was another thing. He said, "I think you've been listening to her enemies and believing them."

Masatada hesitated for a moment. Then he said, "It explains her disappearance. She's gone to her lover."

"Do you have a name?"

"I have names. Fujiwara Noritoki, the famed poet. Fujiwara Korechika, our esteemed governor, and Minamoto Yoshitomo, the handsome captain of the guard. Take your pick. My slut of a sister slept with all of them."

Akitada was disgusted. He got to his feet. "I find it hard to believe that you are her brother, but I shall look into your allegations. Please tell my wife that we are leaving."

36

Suspects

They left the Yoshido compound without speaking. Akitada felt grim and angry, and Sadako looked thoughtful. Eventually though, she spoke up first.

"Did you come to blows, my husband?"

He looked down at her and felt his lip twitch. "No, my wife, but he made me very angry. How there can be such hate between a brother and his sister is beyond me."

"Yes, it is shocking what pride in one's heritage can do. The grandmother grieves for the young woman, but she is not allowed to interfere. It is the men who decide what is best."

"That's natural enough. They are the ones who have the knowledge of the world and are responsible for the welfare of the family, women included."

"You assume that their decisions are always wise?"

Akitada frowned. "No. Of course not. But the natural order requires it."

"So you would agree that in this case the Yoshido males made mistakes?"

"No. Not at all. The plan was a good one. It failed when a woman set her will against theirs. I simply commented on the total lack of feeling expressed by Masatada, his stated wish that his sister be dead."

Sadako bit her lip. "I imagine from his point of view that would be easier for the family to bear."

"Than what?"

"Her having run off with a lover."

Akitada stopped and stared at her. "Is that what the grandmother thinks happened?"

"She didn't say so, but I guessed that is what she fears."

"Well, the brother thinks so anyway. If this is the case, then she is beneath contempt and I can understand their feelings."

"Akitada, I ran off to be with you."

"That is altogether different. You were not the emperor's property. And you came to me to be my wife."

"I came to you to be with you. I did not expect you to marry me. And my brother objected. My becoming your lover or at best your concubine would have offended his family honor."

Akitada was speechless. "But . . ." he said, feeling foolish and resenting the fact that she had made her point at his expense.

He saw her eyes fill with tears. "I'm sorry," she whispered. "You see, I loved you. And duty to my family became so painful I could not bear it any longer."

They were still standing on the muddy street, cold wetness seeping through their boots and clothes. Akitada did not know what to say. Sadako whispered, "I'm cold."

That broke his paralysis. He took her into his arms and held her. "Oh," he murmured into her hair, "I didn't know. I have been such a fool. Come, let's go home. What do I care about the emperor's problem? Or the Yoshido family's honor?"

Back at the Fujiwara mansion, he fussed over her, helping her off with her wet boots, making her sit next to the brazier, holding her cold hands in his and rubbing them. She protested, smiled, and wept a little.

At this point, the new majordomo came to give Akitada a letter from the capital. It was from Kosehira who confirmed that Lady Hachijo had not visited Mount Koya or any of the temples in that pilgrimage route.

"I suppose that means she never left Nara," Akitada said, after sharing the news with his wife.

Sadako nodded. She still looked unhappy.

Akitada asked a little nervously, "What do you want me to do? Shall we go home? Perhaps it's best that we go home. This is an unhappy city."

She said, "You must do what seems right to you. I know too little about the world you live in."

He blinked but let it go. "Did the grandmother say anything that might help us find Hachijo?"

"Not really. She did say her granddaughter had not wanted to go to court and had frequently written, begging to be allowed to come home. But by that time, they had lived on her income from her position at court and her brother was a soldier, hoping for preferment, and so they insisted she stay and make an effort to interest His Majesty." She paused. "I felt very sorry for that young woman."

Akitada shook his head impatiently. "The brother said she had affairs. Akiko said there was a lot of ugly gossip. I don't know if it's true, but if so, it would be highly reprehensible under the circumstances."

"Then perhaps you should find out the truth?"

"Yes, but that won't be easy. Three men are said to have been involved with Hachijo if the gossip is true. They won't want to speak about it. Think of what is involved for their careers."

"Who are they?

Akitada thought back. "One is the local governor, Fujiwara Korechika. He's a cousin of the prime minister."

"Doesn't that mean he's related to the emperor also?"

Akitada blinked. "Yes. Yes, you're right. Dear heaven, they are all related."

"I don't suppose that will save him if he is indeed guilty."

"No. Perhaps not. Oh, I dislike court politics as much as I dislike their immoral behavior."

"Well, who else?"

"Minamoto Yoshitomo. He has a reputation with women, I think. They say he was involved in a contest with another silly young noble about who can seduce most of the known beauties."

Sadako said dryly, "Yes, that makes him a likely candidate, but gossip would fix on him in any case."

Akitada nodded. "The third is our renowned poet, Fujiwara Noritoki."

"Well," she said, "The governor is here, isn't he?"

"I would assume so. And she could have gone to him very easily. I think I shall pay his Excellency a courtesy visit tomorrow."

She said wistfully, "I wish I could come, but it would look peculiar."

He smiled. "I shall hurry back and report."

They were joined by Tora for their evening rice. Tora waited to have his cup filled, then asked, "Any progress, sir?"

Akitada ignored this. He put some rice into a bowl of clear broth and started eating.

Tora said complacently, "I guess not," and drank.

Sadako chuckled. "You'll have to wait, Tora. He's very hungry. It's been that kind of day. The Yoshido family did not serve refreshments."

Tora made a face. "I thought I was the only one facing uncooperative people."

Akitada set down his empty bowl. "I know you're anxious to make your report, but go ahead and eat first. We'll wait to hear about your thrilling discoveries."

"Afraid it'll upset your stomach, sir?"

"Your reports have had that effect."

Tora reached for the bowl Sadako extended. "Thanks, Lady Sadako. At least you're always kind to me."

Akitada raised his brows but said nothing. The meal continued, interrupted only by appreciative comments about the food.

Finally Akitada dabbed his lips and said, "Go ahead, Tora!"

Tora was tempted to startle Akitada with his news, but he resisted. He began his report rather woodenly, placing emphasis on the poverty of Mitsune, who had lost everything, and on the unpleasantness of his successor. Akitada listened for a while, then interrupted, "What has all of this to do with Sanekane?"

Hurt, Tora said, "Nothing. I'm reporting. You told me to visit the pharmacist. I thought you might find some clue in the strange arrangement between Otomo and Mitsune."

Sadako said brightly, "It's a very sad story. It strikes me, Akitada, that people have probably been tempted to commit murder with less provocation than this poor Mitsune. And Otomo seems a very unlikable fellow. Well done, Tora."

Mollified, Tora nodded. "Exactly. The answer may be in the detail. That's what you've always said, sir."

"Well, did anyone buy the poison from the pharmacist?" Akitada asked.

Tora shifted uncomfortably. "I couldn't get a satisfactory answer about that, sir. I think I need to ask more questions."

"No. You've done all you could."

"I don't mind."

Akitada shook his head. "I think we've gone as far as we can with Sanekane. I have another job for you."

Tora sat up eagerly. "Yes?"

"The two murdered nuns. There must be a connection. And there may be a connection to the missing imperial lady. The police think the older nun was murdered by a thief because she was found in the treasure house of the temple. It may be so. I'd like you to ask some questions in likely places about local thugs involved in theft from temples."

"You do realize that I don't know anyone here. In the capital I had my sources."

"Yes. I know. Be careful."

Tora nodded. "What about you? Did you learn anything new?"

Akitada bit his lip. "Nothing really new. We have decided I must look into some ugly gossip that was being spread about Lady Hachijo having lovers. It's all very distasteful, but it must be evaluated."

Tora, quite happy again, chuckled. "Sounds like fun to me. More than one lover?"

"Three."

Tora laughed out loud. "Good for her!" Then his face fell. "But that means she may have run away to be with one of them. That'll solve the case and we can all go home."

"Perhaps. But it will be very unpleasant news to take to the emperor."

"Ah. Yes. Sorry, sir. But it does make sense. She's been gone too long. If she'd been murdered, surely we'd have found her by now. The snow has melted."

They all looked at each other, nodded, and sighed.

37
The Governor

The weather continued dry and warmer than usual the next day. Most of the snow had melted. The streets were still muddy but there was hope they would dry out soon.

His Excellency, Governor Fujiwara Korechika, received Akitada courteously. It was one of those awkward meetings that happened frequently in the current government: Akitada had served twice as governor, but Korechika outranked him by three degrees. He was, after all, a Fujiwara, and one of the many cousins of the emperor.

Yamato Province was also a plum assignment. The closer to the capital, the more desirable governorships were. The provinces in the heart of the nation were peaceful and rich in rice land. Their incumbent governors were close to the seat of power and enjoyed a far more splendid lifestyle than their colleagues in faraway places.

Akitada was curious about Korechika. They had never met in person, and he saw now that Korechika was in his late twenties, a handsome man who dressed well and had the manners of a courtier. He looked the part of someone who might seduce an imperial concubine.

Bringing up the subject was also awkward. They exchanged courtesies, engaged in small talk about the weather, and Korechika inquired about Akitada's service in Mikawa Province. This led naturally into discussions of provincial administration. It seemed harder and harder to get to the point. Eventually the conversation flagged.

A little desperately, Akitada said, "I wonder if you have been informed that Lady Hachijo has taken refuge in Hokkeji?"

Korechika nodded. "I've heard something about it. A very sad story, though we should not think in this way about serving Buddha."

"Were you at all acquainted with her in the capital?"

Korechika smiled a little. "I knew her as someone in attendance on the emperor, but I was about to be posted here and left the court more than a year ago. I was not in attendance on His Majesty when I was in the capital."

That was surprising. Permission to attend the emperor was given only to a select few. Akitada would have expected Korechika to be among them. He expressed his surprise.

Korechika bit his lip and looked away. "I did once attend, but I was sent here and I thought it better to concentrate on my new duties." He smiled suddenly, his eyes twinkling. "One must grow up at some point."

Ah, so he had offended–his comment suggested some riotous partying–but because he was closely related to His Majesty and the prime minister, he had been given a fine governorship instead of severe punishment. In any case, it made it unlikely that he would have continued to pursue a love interest in the imperial women's quarters. It would have been much too difficult and dangerous.

Akitada decided to take him into his confidence. He had not been warned against this and consulting with the governor of the province where Lady Hachijo had disappeared was the natural thing to do.

He said, "I should have come to see you earlier, but there was some trouble at the house where we stay. The majordomo died under suspicious circumstances."

"Oh, dear. I take it the incident appealed to your special curiosity?"

"Ah. You know about me then?"

Korechika smiled again. "I have followed several of your cases with great pleasure." His smile was almost as attractive as Tora's. He really was a charming young man.

Akitada bowed. "You're too kind, sir."

"Well, please tell me all about it. It's my good fortune that you've come here."

"I'm afraid there's not much to tell. Initially, my wife and I faced the discomfort of staying in an empty house without servants. A search revealed that the man had been absent for a while. It seems he liked the wine too much. Eventually he was found, having died in the snow."

Korechika had listened eagerly. When Akitada paused, he said, "Ah, but you were suspicious?"

"My retainer was. He didn't like the women who had locked an elderly man out of his house."

Korechika clapped his hands. "Do go on. It's a fine tale."

"As I said, there's not much to tell. That's as far as he got."

"But what about you? Won't you solve the crime?"

"There may not be a crime. Besides I've been busy with another matter."

"Oh, another case?"

Well, thought Akitada, he either is a very good actor or he knows nothing about Lady Hachijo's disappearance. Since it was not likely that a man so closely related to the powers at court could be so ignorant, he said bluntly, "But surely you've been informed about the search for Lady Hachijo?"

Korechika gulped. "You're here about that?"

"Yes."

"Oh." Korechika looked uncomfortable. Guilty? Nervous? Perhaps the search for the lady was over. But what would be the fall-out if she and Korechika were found to be lovers? Certainly, nobody would thank Akitada for the news.

It struck Akitada for the first time that this assignment was always going to end badly. Either the lady was dead, possibly murdered, or she was alive and a shocking embarrassment to the emperor and the prime minister.

This realization made his voice harsh when he asked, "Why do you pretend to be unaware that the woman, whose name has been linked to yours while she still served His Majesty, has disappeared?"

Korechika flushed painfully. "I was told she has gone on a pilgrimage. And the rest is nothing but vile gossip. We met once or twice, as one does, for music and poetry, but always in company. And I have only just found out that she has left Nara. I've been on a tour of the province for the past month."

Akitada raised his brows. "Surely that was uncomfortable. The roads are barely passable in town."

Korechika snapped, "It may have escaped you, but the snow was sudden and unexpected. Besides people go hunting in winter. I finished my tour with some hunting at a friend's estate. The Nara area has many deer. Then I could not return until the snow melted."

Akitada said nothing. It was possible, even likely.

"Well," the governor snapped, "do you want me to produce witnesses?"

"No, of course not. Please understand. I have a difficult assignment, and my duty caused me to question you."

A brief silence fell. Korechika still looked deeply offended.

Stubbornness made Akitada persist. "Perhaps you may still be able to help me. You knew Lady Hachijo and her friends in the capital. Is there anyone she might have found refuge with?"

"Refuge from what? Are you insinuating that she was being threatened by someone? Driven to flee even from the peaceful convent she chose to mourn the loss of her child? Would you seriously accuse someone close to His Majesty, or even His Majesty himself, of such behavior?"

Korechika was working himself up into a passion, and Akitada was shaken by this outburst, by those accusations. Far less than this had sent men into exile.

"Of course not," he said, searching for words to defuse that anger. "But you have been hunting in the mountains and cannot be aware of recent events in Nara."

Korechika narrowed his eyes. "What events?"

"Two Hokkeji nuns have been found murdered."

The governor's eyes widened. "Murdered? How extraordinary! What happened?"

Akitada told him about Chozen, dragged from the river with a broken neck and Enchi, bludgeoned in the Hokkeji treasure house. Korechika listened attentively, frowned, then said, "Shocking. What are the police doing about it?"

"Nothing so far. They maintain that Chozen fell into the hands of some thug while running an errand and that Enchi surprised a thief."

Korechika nodded. "That sounds likely. It's shocking how unsafe our city has become. I shall immediately institute patrols of the streets. The temples will have to be informed to post guards." He pondered and added, "More police, I think."

Korechika had become the dutiful governor again and lost interest in Akitada's visit. With a sigh of relief, Akitada took his leave.

Lady Sadako received him with warm wine and the eager question, "Well?"

Akitada, looking glum, draped his outer robe over the clothing rack and sat down. "Nothing," he said. "He says he wasn't here when she left. He'd gone on a tour of the province and then for some hunting in the mountains. He was outraged by the implication that he was Hachijo's lover."

"Oh, dear."

"I didn't handle that very well. It's a touchy situation, talking to a man about seducing one of the emperor's concubines."

"Not easy. No." Sadako looked thoughtful. "The reaction was somewhat predictable, I think. What will you do?"

"I suppose I'll have to go back to the capital to talk to the other two."

She nodded. "Shall I pack?"

"No. The roads will be terrible, and I'll have to come back. I'll only be gone two days. Tora will stay with you."

She nodded. "It might be well to ask their help in finding the lady. But you must take Tora. Traveling alone isn't safe. I shall do very well here with the servants."

Akitada shook his head stubbornly. "Absolutely not. What would people think of me? I shall have my sword."

She bit her lip. "Yes, Akitada," she said obediently. "Be careful!"

38

Secret Business

Tora decided to begin his investigation in the market with the shop that sold religious objects. There he was greeted eagerly by a bald man who could have passed for a monk if he had not been wearing ordinary clothes.

"Ah!" he said in a soft, high voice when Tora entered, "the gentleman is thinking of making a special donation to one of our temples? Great merit is gained by spreading the faith to others, and what better way than to add to the splendor of our great temples."

Tora hesitated as if awed by the sheer number of small and large items resting on shelves, hanging on walls, and residing in decorated boxes. "Well," he said, "I don't really know. You see, this is rather special."

The shopkeeper rubbed his hands eagerly. "I see. It is something really important you are praying for?"

Tora strolled along the shelves, muttering, "Yes. Yes. Umm, you see my mother . . . " He let his voice trail off.

"Oh, I'm so sorry. You've lost her and are concerned about releasing her from suffering? A dutiful son, indeed."

Tora's parents had both died decades ago, and he hoped that their own merits had long since caused them to be reborn. But he sighed deeply. "So many things. It's hard to know."

"Allow me to advise you. How much were you thinking of spending?"

Tora looked at him blankly. "Does it matter?"

"Oh, yes. You see, a donation signifies a sacrifice. The bigger the sacrifice, the better."

"Oh." Tora touched his sash where he kept his funds. "I didn't bring much money on this trip. Worried about robbers and thieves, you know."

The shopkeeper's smile faltered.

Tora picked up one of the boxes. It was lacquered and beautifully decorated with flying geese and grasses. The artist had used gold and silver on the grasses, and the geese were picked out in mother of pearl.

"Careful," cried the shopkeeper. "That's priceless."

Tora grinned. "It costs nothing? Just what I had in mind. What's in it?" He shook the box.

The shopkeeper practically leaped to his side to take the box from his hands. "It's a sutra box. It contains a copy of one of the sutras, handwritten by a great and famous court lady."

"Oh," said Tora, sounding disappointed. "A book, you mean?" He gestured at all the other boxes. "There must be a lot of ladies writing sutras for you."

"No, no. Not for me. They write them to gain merit. Sometimes they donate them to temples."

"So how did *you* get them?"

The shopkeeper put the box on a higher shelf and gave Tora a sharp glance. "It's impossible now. I buy from other dealers in the capital and elsewhere. I also buy from merchants returning from sea voyages."

The shop door opened, and two nuns entered. The shopkeeper became flustered. "Is there anything specific you'd like to see?" he asked Tora. "There are some small implements used during services. A brass bell perhaps. I have some small ones."

Tora shook his head. "No, thanks. I'll have to think about it. I'll come back tomorrow."

The shopkeeper bowed him out and turned to the nuns.

It was by now midmorning. Women were doing their shopping at the market stalls. Tora looked about for more shops that sold religious items but saw only the usual vendors of cheap amulets. He decided the time was good for another visit to the noodle shop.

This time he did not visit for food. It was between meals, and he hoped to find the shop empty of customers. He was right.

Only Ushimatsu and the crippled boy were there. Sachiko, he was told, had gone to the market for vegetables and fish. The boy was sweeping, but Ushimatsu rested. Tora did not blame him. A man as fat as he did well to carry bowls of soup to Sachiko's guests and collect their money. He waved to Kosuke and then sat down beside Ushimatsu.

The fat man was tearful. "I miss Midori," he said as a greeting.

Tora felt a little guilty. He had not precisely forgotten her, but his mind was at the moment on other things. "Yes. How is her little boy?"

"Fine. He's gone with Sachiko. Sachiko is a saint."

Tora nodded. "And a brilliant cook."

Ushimatsu cheered up a little. He patted his belly. "Don't I know it. Have you come back to stay?"

The question sounded a little anxious. Tora said, "No. I'm on a new assignment. Sorry. I wish I could help, but I work for my master."

"Oh, that's all right." The fat man seemed relieved. "We manage and there will soon be another helper. There's a young woman who's pregnant. She needs a place."

"Good. Better than a man."

Ushimatsu grinned. "You said it. You know, Sanekane was all right. Generous with his money and his time. And not at all conceited, but just between us, Sachiko was growing much too fond of him." He chuckled. "Much safer to have another woman. Or two."

It suddenly struck Tora that Ushimatsu had been jealous of Sanekane as a rival for Sachiko's attentions. In fact, Sachiko had also been rather too friendly to himself. He suppressed a shudder. Then another as he pictured the two fat people making love in the loft above the shop.

Ushimatsu asked, "So what's this assignment you're on?"

Tora told him about the murdered nun in the Hokkeji treasure house. Ushimatsu had heard about it and expressed his opinion that the thieves were getting brazen in the city.

"Can you tell me who would know something about this?"

Ushimatsu raised his brows. "Is it your opinion that I belong to the thieves' guild?"

"No. Of course not. But you're a gambler. Gamblers are in touch with all sorts of people."

Ushimatsu put on a look of innocence and laid a hand on his heart. "I'm a reformed man. Thanks to my Sachiko, who has a generous heart and showed me a better way."

Tora noted that his benefactor had become "my Sachiko." He slapped Ushimatsu on the shoulder. "You two are married? Man and wife? My congratulations. She's a great woman."

Ushimatsu looked embarrassed. "Well, it's not official. But yes. As good as. Thanks, Tora."

"So how about helping me out, eh?"

Ushimatsu hesitated. "That's all in the past," he said.

Tora shook his head. "Oh, well. I'll stay till Sachiko returns and I can give her my good wishes on your marriage."

A look of panic crossed Ushimatsu's face. "You might go talk to Tabito," he said.

"About the robbery?"

"Yes. He probably doesn't know who did it, but he's close to the boss of thieves. He could ask for you."

Tora got up eagerly. "Where do I find him?"

"Outside Todaiji. He's a beggar."

Tora paused. "A beggar? There are lots of beggars around a temple."

"He has a dragon tattoo."

"Where?"

"On his right arm."

"Ushimatsu, it's winter. He's not going to sit around without clothes on."

Ushimatsu spread his hands. "Sorry. I've only seen him when it was warm. Best I can do. You'll find him if you ask."

It was better than nothing, and Tora hurried away to Todaiji. There he saw already a trickle of pilgrims gathering as well as a number of beggars. He ignored the women and looked over the men. His choice fell on a scrawny figure crouching next to a crutch. He wore rags, but they covered his arms. Tora approached.

The man's eyes lit up. "A few coppers, noble sir! Just a few coppers for a cripple."

The man seemed to be missing part of his leg. The stump looked bloody. Tora leaned closer. The beggar quickly covered the stump with a corner of his ragged robe.

"Just a copper or two, sir. I haven't eaten since yesterday. To please the Buddha, sir, and to earn you merit."

Tora straightened. "You're faking it, but never mind. I'm looking for Tabito."

A sly look came into the man's eyes. "Why?"

Instead of answering, Tora detached a few coppers from a string he carried in his sash. The beggar watched but shook his head. "Don't know him."

Holding up the coins in front of the man's face, Tora reached down and pushed up the beggar's right sleeve. There was the dragon. The beggar scrambled away, revealing a perfectly good but painted leg.

Tora said, "Wait. For a piece of silver, will you talk to me. Someplace else?"

Tabito looked around, then nodded. He seized his crutch and limped away. Tora followed.

They ended up in a wine shop around the corner. Tabito seemed to be well known here. Tora scanned the guests and their host and decided it looked promising. He ordered warm wine for both of them.

After the beggar had drunk, warming his hands on the cup and then emptying it in one long gulp, he said, "Another?"

Tora sipped. The stuff was horrible. He said, "First we talk."

"What about?"

"I want a word with the boss of the thieves."

Tabito laughed. It sounded like an angry chicken cackling. He was missing most of his front teeth. "Who's that then?" he asked.

"Ushimatsu said you'd know."

Becoming serious, the beggar asked, "Ushimatsu's a friend of yours? How is that fat bastard? He hasn't been around."

"He's trying to clean up his act."

That set off the cackle again. "Fat chance. Hah! Fat chance, very funny. Get it?" He cackled happily at his accidental quip.

"Yeah, I get it. Stop laughing. I need information."

Tabito sobered. "And I need more wine."

Muttering a curse, Tora ordered a refill for the beggar. The man drank deeply again, then asked, "Why'd you ask about the boss of the thieves?"

"It's about a murder. Now I want an answer, or I'll beat my expenses out of your lying hide behind this fine establishment."

"A murder?" Tabito hesitated just a moment. "The silver you promised?"

"Yes. But if you lie to me, I'll find you."

Tabito nodded. "I don't hold with murder. Especially of nuns. There's a man lives in the back of the shrine. He'll know if there's anything to know."

"What shrine?"

"There's only the one," snapped Tabito.

The Kasuga shrine was one of the most famous shrines in the country. Tora had visited it and knew that it consisted of many shrines. He frowned and asked, "Where in the back? You mean on the mountain?"

"There's a shed up there. You can't miss it. Ask for Takamune."

Tora nodded, passed a silver coin across, and left.

39

Kasuga Shrine

It had been a long day, and Tora had missed his midday meal. The weather was turning gray and cold. It looked like more snow. He trudged tiredly across town to the entrance of the Kasuga shrine. Here the first of many sacred gateways greeted him, *torii* painted vermilion and flanked by large stone lanterns.

Tora loved Kasuga Grand Shrine. It was large and beautiful. Behind it rose Kasugayama, the hill sacred to the god of the shrine. It was steep and densely covered with forest. He eyed it nervously. It was getting late, and he had no idea where on that hill and in that forest the thieves' den might be found.

Along with other visitors Tora passed through the familiar shrine buildings, barely conscious of more vermilion gates, pillars, and eaves, of an abundance of all sorts of lanterns, and of strips of paper with prayers left by visitors. He made his ablutions and obeisance at the main shrine, then hurried toward the woods behind.

But here were more shrines, smaller ones to the twelve lucky gods, and one of them could not be passed without a prayer of gratitude. This was *meoto daihokusha,* the marriage shrine. Not only was Tora a married man and fervently grateful for his Hanae, but now there was also his master's marriage, and after all the years of misery, he deserved all the happiness in the world.

His spiritual duties done, Tora set off along a steep path that led up the mountain. The trees were mostly cedars, and in their shade, the snow had persisted. The path grew treacherous and slippery. More troubling was the fact that few visitors had left their tracks. Tora was beginning to think that slimy Tabito had lied to him and that he would now have to go and kill the runt. Then suddenly a secondary path branched off. And all the foot traffic, thin though it was, seemed to have taken it. Tora followed.

The new path very quickly led him to a small clearing where a number of wooden buildings huddled together. Smoke curled up from one of them. It became clear that they served those who maintained the shrine. He made his way to the one with the smoke and knocked at the door.

This opened quickly and a huge bearded man looked out at him. "What do you want?"

"Is Takamune around?"

The big man's eyes narrowed. He looked Tora over carefully. "What do you want with him?"

"That's my business."

The big man slammed the door in Tora's face.

Tora instantly delivered a hard kick at it so that it flew open again and forced the big man to jump back. Tora pushed inside, used both arms to force the man away from the door, then slammed it behind him.

"Not very hospitable, are you?" he asked, looking around. The man was alone.

He was also very angry. He clenched his fists and came for Tora. "Out!" he growled.

Tora folded his arms across his chest and grinned. "Tabito sent me."

The big man paused. "What do you want?" he asked again, but this time he looked puzzled.

"Information. About a robbery and a murder."

The big man cursed. Tora heard a sound and swung around, barely missing a cloth a thin young man was trying to throw over his head. Tora ripped it from his hands with his left and hit him hard on the side of his neck with the edge of his right hand. The young man collapsed without a sound.

Swinging back, Tora faced the big man again. "Are you Takamune?"

The big man looked at the unconscious youth. "Did you kill him?"

"No. But I'll kill the next guy who tries such a trick again. So are you Takamune or not?"

The big man nodded. "I'm Takamune. And you?"

"Tora."

"A tiger, eh?" The big man smiled.

"So they said. I was younger then, but I've learned a few tricks in the meantime."

Takamune nodded. "Sorry about Yuki." He nodded toward the unconscious man. "He's the nervous type. There's some wine."

The building was filled with tools, barrels, ladders, carts, and all sorts of implements. Takamune made his way through a narrow passage to the center of the building where a fire burned in a hearth under the opening in the high roof. It was pleasantly warm here, and a stone jar rested near the embers, promising hot wine.

They sat on ragged straw mats. Takamune poured, and they drank. The wine was good, strong, and heavily spiced. Tora smacked his lips.

Takamune watched him. "I ask again, 'What do you want?'"

"Three days ago a nun was killed in Hokkeji."

Takamune did not blink. "I know. Terrible!"

"The police think she surprised a thief."

"The police don't know everything."

"That's why I'm here."

Takamune raised his brows. "You think I know who killed her?"

"Maybe, maybe not. But you probably know something."

There was brief silence, then Takamune asked, "What's it to you?"

Tora decided to be frank. "I work for Lord Sugawara. He's looking for a missing nun and he wants to know who's been killing nuns."

"Ah!" Takamune pursed his lips. "Not satisfied with the police? Thinks he's better than them?"

"He is."

Takamune laughed. "Well, I can't help you. I don't know who killed the Hokkeji nun or who's gone missing. My people don't work that way and most respect the faith."

"Fair enough. That means the police are wrong and I must look elsewhere."

Takamune became quite cheerful. "Sorry, friend. Did they steal anything?"

"I don't know. They left a mess, and the nuns don't seem too sure about what was there."

Takamune cast up his eyes. "Women! Just waiting to be plucked like chickens. I'd take a professional interest in what you tell me, but as I said, we respect the Buddha." He put his hands together and bowed in the direction of a corner where Tora could just make out a small Buddha statue.

Tora said, "That's very nice. Where'd you find that?"

Takamune bridled. "Not found. Bought."

"From that shop in the market?"

"No. That man's more of a thief than any of my people."

"Ah! He overcharges?"

"He charges too much and pays too little."

"So he buys locally? Have you done much business with him?"

The other man growled, "Look, I told you, we respect our faith."

"Don't worry. I believe you. I think maybe that he doesn't. Where does he get his goods?"

"Good point." Takamune pursed his lips again. "There are all sorts of thieves in the world."

"So there are. Anyone in particular?"

Takamune said, "Kids, beggars, riffraff that'll pick up anything handy. But a lot of that merchandise comes from inside the temple. Some lady or lord donates something, costly and very pretty, but the temple needs rice, or fabric for monks' robes, or gold paint for the pagoda, and so they sell something. Mind you, they keep that sort of thing quiet."

Tora sighed. "Yes, I should have thought of that."

"Of course, the money doesn't always go back to the temple."

"Ah!"

Takamune put a finger to his nose and nodded.

Tora asked, "Anyone in particular?"

"Ask that shopkeeper at the market. He knows."

40
The Poet

Akitada left early, thankful for a clear sky and a bright moon. It was a good thing that Sadako did not know of the corpse in Doctor Hayashi's care, the one who was likely some unfortunate official who had traveled alone and fallen into the hands of highwaymen.

He stayed alert, with his right hand near the grip of his sword, but the journey was uneventful. The sun came up, the roads were bad, but the horse was used to them and sure-footed. He arrived in the capital just before sundown. He left his horse at the Sugawara residence where he exchanged a few words with Genba and then left without eating or changing his clothes.

Ignoring his gnawing hunger pains, he rode directly to the *Daidairi* and the office of his best friend Nakatoshi, who was first secretary in the Ministry of Ceremonial. His particular work made him one of the most knowledgeable men about the hundreds of senior officials and courtiers.

Nakatoshi received him with an embrace and raised eyebrows at his travel clothing. "Don't tell me you rode back from Nara today," he said.

"I did." Akitada was secretly proud of having made good time and arrived safely.

"But your wife and Tora? Did you take them home first?"

"No, I came alone. For information." Akitada shed his heavy robe and sat down.

Nakatoshi looked uncertain, then sat down himself. "Is everything all right?"

"Yes. Thank you. Only the case of the missing Lady Hachijo is becoming difficult." He filled Nakatoshi in on what he had learned in Nara.

"Dear heaven," his friend said, shaking his head, "she disappears, you arrive, and two nuns are murdered!"

"I wish you wouldn't put it that way. I had nothing to do with the murders."

"Hmm. It wouldn't be the first time you scared someone into drastic action."

Stung, Akitada said, "So it's my fault they get killed?"

"No, my friend. Fear makes vicious people react with violence. Nothing matters to them but their own safety."

The concept still rankled. "I suppose in that case it would be best to leave them alone."

Nakatoshi smiled. "But could you guarantee that they would never murder again?"

"No."

"To return to the present, are you sure Lady Sadako is safe?"

"Tora is with her."

Nakatoshi sighed. "If something has happened to Lady Hachijo, you may all be in great danger."

Akitada snapped impatiently, "The sooner I find out what is going on, the better."

Nakatoshi raised his hands. "Forgive me. I only spoke out of concern for the risks you take."

Akitada ignored this. "I need to speak to two men who have been linked with Hachijo, Fujiwara Noritoki and Minamoto Yoshitomo. What can you tell me about them?"

"Ah! You think the Lady Hachijo has been abducted by a suitor?"

"I take it you knew all about the ugly gossip?" It was not meant as an accusation, but it sounded like it.

Nakatoshi frowned. "Why are you so angry with me? I had no idea that you were looking for her. In fact, I didn't know she was missing until very recently. You didn't consult me."

Akitada threw up his hands. "Sorry, Nakatoshi. I didn't mean it that way. And yes, I should have talked to you before going to Nara, but the situation was presented as extremely sensitive and I meant to clear it up quickly. I thought it was just another silly escapade by a court lady. I took Sadako with me for sightseeing. But as it turns out, nuns are being murdered, and I don't know what is going on or where she is. I came back to eliminate suspects, that's all."

Nakatoshi smiled. "And you're upset, what with having to leave your wife among the murderous villains of Nara. Fair enough. Minamoto Yoshitomo is a captain in the palace guard. He is young, manly, and frequently at imperial entertainments. I know nothing about any affairs with Hachijo, but his name has been linked with several ladies-in-waiting. Noritoki is our most popular poet. He's recently been asked by His Majesty to produce another collection of famous poems. The ladies like him very much, even though I think he isn't much to look at. Again, I know of nothing about him and Lady Hachijo, but they would have met frequently at court, and poets have a way with words. But Akitada, there is another man, Fujiwara Korechika. He's the emperor's cousin. He seems much more likely to me than the other two."

"I've spoken to him. He's governor of Yamato Province and doesn't seem to have been involved."

Nakatoshi said, "Just as well. I hear he has a temper and bears a grudge. The trouble is, once you imagine situations that such an ugly rumor suggests, you get quite carried away with possibilities. You'll speak to the other two?"

"Yes. Where will I find them? I'd like to get this done quickly and return to Nara."

Nakatoshi nodded. "A hard journey, and it gets dark early. You'd better see Noritoki first. The palace guard practices late in the day and won't be back in their barracks until after dark. Noritoki lives on the other side of the *Daidairi* on the corner of Ogimachi and Horokawa."

Akitada thanked his friend and got up to leave. Nakatoshi said, "Be careful, Akitada. This looks very much like a hornet's nest."

Fujiwara Noritoki occupied one of the old palaces on the wrong side of the capital. The powerful had long since left the area and squatters had moved in, but many of the fine old buildings had survived. Noritoki enjoyed privacy, a famous garden, and a peaceful life far away from court. No doubt he found the place ideal for the composition of his poetry. He emerged only occasionally to socialize and allow himself to be praised and admired.

Akitada thought it was also a perfect place to hide away an illicit lover.

The poet's household was well run. Akitada was announced, and the famous man received him in a room overlooking the snow-covered garden and the distant hills rising beyond.

Noritoki was older than Akitada had expected. He wondered how a man in his fifties could become involved in a sexual scandal at court. But Noritoki, though not handsome, had large liquid eyes and a deep, caressing voice. No doubt he was greatly admired for his recitation. His manner to Akitada was warm, his smile gentle and friendly. He seemed genuinely pleased to meet him and led him to a cushion, expressing his delight at the visit.

"Forgive me," Akitada said. "I know this must be an interruption of your work. My only excuse is that I'm on His Majesty's business."

Noritoki's eyes widened in delighted surprise. "Do tell me! And don't apologize. What an honor! I hope I may be able to help with whatever it is."

Given Noritoki's presumed close acquaintance with Lady Hachijo, this was disingenuous, but such were the games one played at court. Akitada said, "You have heard that Lady Hachijo has disappeared?"

"Not disappeared, my dear Akitada. She has, alas, left our world to observe the five-hundred precepts. She has become a nun. It's been very upsetting to her friends. His Majesty is inconsolable." He sighed. "She had many, many friends, and they all grieve."

Akitada said bluntly, "She also had powerful enemies. And she's not at Hokkeji or any other temple–at least not to anyone's knowledge. She really has disappeared."

Noritoki's brows shot up. "But where is she?"

"I came to ask you that."

The other man stared at him for a moment. Then he smiled and chuckled softly. "You think she's with me?"

"Is she?"

"The answer to your question is 'no'—though you do me a great honor to assume that she might have thought me worthy."

"In that case, do you know where she might have gone?"

"As to someone else having found favor, I don't know. I do know she was very unhappy, the last few months."

"Your name has been linked with hers in court gossip. I assume that the talk was based on something. How close were you?"

Noritoki looked away. "Not that close, or in the way you suggest, I assure you. I'm old enough to be her father. I think that is what she saw in me. She had lost her own parents, you know. I grew quite fond of her. She was very shy and had no friends. We exchanged some poems. She was trying and was quite good. As I said, I became fond of her and perhaps she of me. But it was not a romantic relationship. I frequently exchange poems with people. It means nothing."

He protests too much, thought Akitada. "Did you save some of those poems?"

"I am working on a new poetry collection. I save everything." The poet got up and walked to a book stand that held sheaves of papers. He sorted through them quickly and returned with several sheets. He handed one to Akitada. "Here. This is from a poetry party last autumn. It happens to be appropriate, I think."

The first poem was in a woman's hand: "I'm like a pine on the wave-tossed beach, wailing in the wind. My name is spread like mist."

Surprised, Akitada asked, "This surely is about the ugly gossip at court. Did she write this in a public exchange of poems by a number of people at court?"

Noritoki looked uncomfortable. "Well, no. Not quite. She sent it to me afterward."

"Do I take it that the participants, or some among the participants, took the opportunity to attack Lady Hachijo with veiled accusations?"

Noritoki sighed. "Yes, it may have happened. Some of the poems seemed rather strange in retrospect. Not all of the poems made sense to me at the time."

Akitada stretched out his hand for the other poems. After a moment, Noritoki released them. The first one was in the same hand. Hachijo had written, "I must forget, even in my own mind, the dream I had of love, lest I reveal it in some casual chat." He raised his brows and held it up. "What is this about?"

"I cannot tell. As I said, she was unhappy. I assumed it was because His Majesty had lost interest."

"Hmm. It sounds like some secret affair."

"Not necessarily. You forget that visits from His Majesty must never be talked about."

"Perhaps." Akitada looked at the next paper. This one was in a man's hand, Noritoki's perhaps? The writer had dashed off the lines, "If you would only come again tomorrow that I might know true happiness."

"Now this," he said, "looks like an invitation. Yours?"

"Not for what you imagine it to be," snapped Noritoki. "She had honored me by asking for my help in the matter of composition."

Akitada said nothing. The last sheet was again in Hachijo's handwriting. "In the blackness of my numbed heart, I lost my way. Is it a dream or real? Let others decide."

Noritoki looked and said, "This was after she left the palace. She lost the child soon after that. You can see how unhappy she was."

"Yes." Akitada returned the poems. "If she confided in you, it seems possible she might have come to you in her distress."

Noritoki snapped, "She didn't, and I shall vigorously defend my reputation and hers against such allegations."

And here it was again: the threat. There was nothing further to be gained. Akitada apologized. He said, "Do you know of anyone else she might have found refuge with? I'm told that His Majesty merely wishes to be reassured of her safety."

Noritoki relaxed a little and looked grave. "Poor Hachijo! No, I was quite convinced that she was innocent of the insinuations, but she suffered. If she left Hokkeji, something may have happened to her. I pray this is not the case."

Akitada thanked him and took his leave.

41
The Soldier

It was dark by the time Akitada found Captain Yoshitomo in his room in the barracks. He was not alone: three friends, also officers by their insignia, lounged about. All four were drinking. Between them stood a large jar of wine—or at least Akitada assumed it was wine. Their faces were red, perhaps from recent practice in the chilly air, but more likely from wine. All were less than thirty years old and wore the red and gold uniform of the palace guard.

One of the young men stood. On Akitada's question, he said, "I'm Yoshitomo." He was tall and muscular and had the typical swagger of the soldier. His room was cluttered with clothing, both military and civilian, and assorted swords, bows and quivers, but it was otherwise clean. Akitada had seen three servants in light hemp clothing squatting outside the captain's door.

All four young men stared at him in surprise. Yoshitomo asked, "Who the hell are you? Who let you in?"

"Sugawara Akitada." Akitada ignored the rest of the question. The various doorkeepers were well aware of rank insignia and had not dared to stop him. "I have some questions, CaptainYoshitomo."

Yoshitomo told his friends, "A paper pusher from one of the ministries." To Akitada, he said, "What can you possibly want with me?"

"I'd like a word in private, Captain."

Yoshitomo laughed. "I can't imagine what you could have to say that my friends can't hear."

Thoroughly irritated by now, Akitada snapped, "This concerns the Lady Hachijo."

Two of the captain's friends hooted and the third cried, "Your sins have come to haunt you, Yoshi. He's come to arrest you."

Yoshitomo had become quiet and rather pale. "Why come to me?" he asked, his voice suddenly uncertain.

His friends laughed and offered an assortment of answers, all of them of a sexual nature. Yoshitomo turned on them. "Out! Now!" He pointed at the door. The faces of his companions fell. After a moment's hesitation, they got up and stalked out, slamming the door behind them.

Yoshitomo, lips compressed, sat back down. "What has happened?" he asked, waving to one of the cushions.

Akitada sat. "She has disappeared and may have been murdered."

The young man paled even more. "What? The last I heard she'd gone into a nunnery."

"She left there and hasn't been seen since. I wondered if she's been in contact with you."

"No." Yoshitomo shook his head, frowned, clenched his fists. "Murdered?" he asked. "How? Why? They hated her enough, but even they wouldn't resort to murder."

"They?"

He raised his hands helplessly. "She had enemies. They supported the prime minister's daughter. They said she'd seduced His Majesty with witchcraft. But they didn't dare oppose her because she carried the emperor's child, and that child might become emperor some day. So they said the child was mine. Or some other man's. His Majesty withdrew his favor and did not send the customary maternity sash. Any other woman would have gone back to her family, but Hachijo was afraid to go home. She stopped eating and lost the child. It was terrible. I thought she'd also die. Or kill herself. I begged her to be my wife, but she decided to become a nun instead."

A terrible and dark tale. It had been hinted at before, but Yoshitomo's words were blunt and succinct and made the young woman's tragedy real.

"Was the child yours?"

Yoshitomo flushed. "No! No, never! She would never have betrayed His Majesty. Even if she didn't love him. She certainly did not love me." He covered his face. "Her name was Masako," he said softy. "Masako was so young, so beautiful, so trusting. She knew nothing about the life she was meant to live. She was frightened."

Silence fell. Akitada reconsidered the character of this privileged young nobleman. Only rarely did you find someone so close to life at court who valued innocence. After a long time, he asked gently, "Did you try to seduce her?"

Yoshitomo lowered his hands. He nodded bleakly. "Yes. You see, I loved her. She was very beautiful and everybody talked about her when she came to court. I'm ashamed to say we all tried, those of us who had access. Even some who were old enough to be her father tried. It was a game. A contest."

Akitada snapped, "It was reprehensible!"

Yoshitomo hung his head. "Yes. But it's the custom to fall in love with pretty ladies-in-waiting. The women usually know how to play that game."

"If I accept that you failed in your efforts, who might have been more successful?"

"There was a lot of gossip. I thought for a while that Korechika was courting her more than anyone else, but he received an appointment for provincial service and left. Later she seemed to become really fond of the poet Noritoki. But I doubt there was anything in it. By then she was very unhappy. Women write poetry when they are unhappy and he's a poet. I don't have the talent, I'm afraid."

Neither did Akitada. His sympathy with this young man grew. The atmosphere at court infected all that came into contact with it. He thought of his second wife. She had merely been in attendance on the empress, but she, too, had been seduced. She too had been very young, very beautiful and naïve. But Yukiko had been a married woman by then, and he, her husband, had been far away serving as governor of Mikawa Province.

He thanked Yoshitomo and prepared to leave.

The young man touched his sleeve. "Find her! And if you find her, please tell her I love her and want her to come to me. I shall pray that you find her, alive and well." He had tears in his eyes.

42
Tora Disobeys

For two whole days, Tora was to keep watch over Lady Sadako. His master had been firm and adamant about this. Lady Sadako had objected to these stringent orders, but to no avail. Tora had watched his master leave, feeling worried, angry, helpless in the face of such commands. On the first day, he had been so frustrated that he had spent an hour pacing the veranda of the house, and then the rest of the morning inspecting all the doors and shutters to make sure no intruders could enter. He had done so bitterly, convinced that such threats were highly unlikely.

Then he had spoken to the newly hired servants and the new majordomo, instructing all of them to admit no strangers and to raise an alarm if anyone tried to enter without permission. The whole household was like an armed camp, though without any arms. In fact, he had managed to frighten them all.

He had next exercised the horses by walking them around the Fujiwara residence.

Lady Sadako decided to visit one of the temples and Kasuga shrine in the afternoon. He had walked behind her, wearing his sword and keeping an eye out for trouble. There had been none. He went to sleep that day outside Lady Sadako's room.

She eventually became aware of this state of affairs and questioned her maid. Then she sent for Tora.

He arrived, bowed, and asked for instructions.

"Tora," she said, "are you afraid of an attack?"

"No, Lady Sadako. I'm trying to make sure there isn't one."

"But that means that you are aware of some danger."

"Not me. I think your husband may be."

"I see. Did he confide in you about this?"

"No, Lady Sadako," he said with considerable and pointed bitterness.

"Ah." Sadako was silent for a moment. Then she asked, "Did you have other plans?"

Tora blushed. "Nothing is more important than keeping you safe, Lady Sadako, but I wish I knew what I was guarding you from."

"So you did have other plans. You were following up on some investigation?"

"I was going to have another look at that shop in the market, the one that sells religious objects. I was thinking about those robbers that killed the old nun."

She nodded. "Yes. I see. That sounds like a good plan. I assume my husband did not specify why he wanted you to guard this house because he didn't know of any danger. He was feeling guilty for leaving me to go to the capital. I think I'm safe enough, so if you wish to look into that business of stolen temple objects, I think you should do so. Will it take long?"

Tora, greatly relieved, grinned. "No. I'll ask a few questions, that's all. I'll be back in time for the evening rice."

"Then go, and good luck!"

He hesitated only a moment, said, "Thanks, Lady Sadako. Be careful!" and hurried out.

Guilt cramped Tora's style. He suddenly imagined all sorts of things happening back at the house, resulting in a confrontation with his master that chilled his soul. What good was a retainer who could not be trusted to keep his master's family safe?

He stood in the market, staring at the shop that sold religious objects without any idea what to do next. You could not just walk in and ask the owner if he had lately bought any stolen goods.

There were few customers. As he watched, a couple of monks went in and came back out quickly. Then another monk arrived, peered in the door and entered. He stayed longer and then reappeared, carrying an object wrapped in silk cloth. He treated it reverently.

Most likely monks were the customers of the more expensive items. They wanted them for their own temples and monasteries. Ordinary men or women on pilgrimages purchased cheaper replicas at a market stand. The shop owner must deal in pricey merchandise to make a living.

And just as he thought this, a well dressed, tall man in the black clothes of an official entered the store. Tora frowned. Well, perhaps he needed a new Buddha for his family altar and did not mind spending some money. But the man made him curious. He followed him into the shop.

To his surprise, the man had disappeared. The shopkeeper also was absent. The shop was empty. That seemed very careless. Tora was tempted to call out for service, but on second thought, he decided to leave again as quietly as possible.

From the outside, he studied the building. The shop occupied the front of a long, one-storied building. The shop owner probably lived in the back. Most likely he did his business there also, not in the front of the store where he might be interrupted by the occasional monk or nun looking for prayer beads or incense.

There was a narrow alley on one side. On the other side, the building adjoined its neighbor, sharing a wall. Tora made for the alley and passed down it to the back. The wall was blind, but behind the long building was a garden that extended to one of the small canals. A low fence surrounded the garden which still had patches of snow under some shrubs. The back of the house had large hinged shutters. These were closed against the weather.

Tora simply stepped over the low fence and crossed the garden. When he passed a dense shrubbery and reached the other back corner, he saw a recess, and here he found a high window. It also had a shutter, but this was slightly open, perhaps to allow smoke from oil lamps and braziers to escape. And from the chink between wall and shutter, came light and the sound of low voices.

It was a safe enough arrangement for secretive meetings. In this weather and in this corner of a wintry garden facing a bleak stretch of water, one doesn't expect people to be sneaking about. Tora smiled with satisfaction and moved as close as possible to a place just below the open shutter.

Two men were inside. One sounded old and had a nasal voice. The other spoke firmly, in an educated manner and with authority. So they must be the shop owner and the well-dressed man in black who had just entered the store.

The shopkeeper said, "It's nice, but there's no market for it."

The other man snorted. "Don't give me that. I know what it's worth and know well that any number of people here in Nara would pay good gold for it."

The shopkeeper whined, "But I can't sell it here."

"Not right away. But I know you do business elsewhere."

There was some low muttering as they must have moved away from the window, and Tora could not make out the words. Then suddenly there was the sound of squeaking, as if something heavy was being opened right under the window, and the shopkeeper asked, "Did you get anything else? I could use a *mandala* or two. Either the Diamond World or the Womb one? No? I also have a request for a statue of Bishamon-Ten. It needn't be large. No? Hokkeji has a very nice small Fugen riding an elephant. I could sell that. No scrolls of any kind? They're easy to carry."

The other man finally approached. "You forget that taking anything at all is far too dangerous at the moment. The police are still there."

Tora's heart started beating faster. This was it. This was someone connected with the murder.

The shopkeeper said, "Pity you didn't pick up anything but this little Kannon. It's hardly the best Hokkeji has, and Kannon statues are as common as grains of sand. I can only give you five of the gold coins, or 25 of the silver."

The other man cursed. "You're a crook, Kanehira. It's a very fine carving and painted."

"Sorry. Business is slow."

"Very well then. Hand over the gold. And keep your mouth shut or there won't be any more."

The shopkeeper said, "You know you can trust me."

"Well, make sure the business is mutually satisfactory."

The voices faded again.

Tora took this as a signal to hurry back to the front of the shop. He was eager to see the face of the man who traded in objects belonging to Hokkeji and who knew all about the murder investigation there.

The well-dressed man emerged promptly. He had a long pale face which looked irritated as he scanned the street. Tora pretended interest in the wares of a fan seller. The man was a stranger. Who was he? Clearly he dealt in ill-gotten merchandise, but this was no ordinary thief. Still, he could be someone who bought from thieves, but if he was, surely Takamune of the Kasuga shrine would have said something.

Or maybe not.

Who can trust crooks?

Still, Takamune had told the truth about the shop. Tora decided to follow the man in black.

To his surprise, he went straight to Kofukuji, where he was recognized and admitted by the gatekeeper monk. Tora was not so lucky. The gatekeeper wanted to know who he was and what he wanted, and made no move to admit him to worship until he had handed over a piece of silver. By the time Tora was in the temple grounds, the finely dressed man had disappeared.

Tora roamed about a bit, but then remembered his duty to watch over Lady Sadako and gave it up. Just as he approached the main gate again, he saw the man in black leaving and followed.

The main route took him directly into the eastern districts. And there he suddenly turned into a quarter of residential properties. Tora was not close enough. By the time he turned into the neighborhood, his quarry had disappeared.

43
Return to Nara

It was night before Akitada left the *Daidairi* again and returned to his home. There, he finally ate a meal, though he was barely aware of it, he was so tired. He fell asleep immediately and rose at dawn to make the journey back.

Genba was waiting with a fresh horse and a package of food. He looked concerned.

"You should take some armed men, sir. It's not safe. You'll be in the dark before you're back in Nara. And the weather is changing."

Akitada glanced at the sky. To the west, cloud banks were gathering, promising early gloom and coming snow. "I promised my wife," he told Genba. Genba smiled and nodded. They were all happy for him. Suddenly he felt warm and alive and eager to be on his way. "I'll be quick and careful," he said.

And so he left, riding fast. The roads near the capital had dried out somewhat, but it had been cold and there were icy patches still. He crossed the Kamo River, in full flood after the rain and thaw, and moved south quickly along the river's eastern bank and among the temples and burial grounds of the capital. He reached Kohata in good time and headed for Uji and the bridge over the Seta River.

As he passed through the familiar landscape, his mind returned again and again to the three men who had had close ties with Lady Hachijo. All three had firmly denied a sexual relationship with her. That did not mean much. If there had been an affair, they would have denied it, either to defend her character or to cover up a behavior that would surely ruin their position and might lead to permanent exile.

How tolerant was the current emperor? Akitada knew little about him. He had come to the throne as a boy. The government was in the hands of his Fujiwara grandfather and uncles. In his relationship with Hachijo, he had appeared fickle. Choosing the naïve daughter of a family that lived in poverty and disgrace and raising her to the position of an acknowledged concubine when she conceived a child had been an act certain to cause the very gossip that had eventually haunted her and caused her to flee. By that time, His Majesty was already tired of her and turned his attention to his Fujiwara empress and her younger sister.

Akitada had begun his investigation by trying to understand the character of Lady Hachijo. He had found little helpful information. He knew he felt very sorry for her even while he considered her flight into a nunnery foolish. Of greater interest perhaps were the personalities of the men who had been close to her.

Both of the men he had met the previous day had surprised him. He admitted to himself that he had preconceived notions about courtiers. He had assumed the poet Noritoki would be an effeminate dreamer and the captain the very opposite, a boisterous drunkard given to shooting dogs from horseback. To be sure Captain Yoshitomo's companions fit his idea of a member of the imperial guards rather better, and they had been drinking. But Yoshitomo had turned out to be a surprisingly sensitive young man who seemed genuinely concerned about Hachijo's fate. Similarly, Noritoki had revealed a personality that had caused the young woman to seek him out for support. Had they taken advantage of her trust? Had she sought their help when she ran away from Hokkeji?

Akitada had come to think of her departure as flight. She had gone there for refuge from the cruel tongues at court and had been unhappy with the religious life. Not only that, but her brother had returned and taken the opportunity to visit her, no doubt to lay a heavy burden of blame on her. So she had fled again.

Was she with one of the men who had been kind to her? Living somewhere in deep hiding? Or had something happened to her? And if so, the time that had passed made it almost certain that she was dead.

At the Uji crossing, he came back to the present with a start. There was still some traffic, but gradually people had turned off as they reached their homes. In the west, dark clouds had spread as an icy wind sprang up. He was only halfway.

The highway skirted Mount Kuriko and turned south again. The sun slid lower and ahead lay the mountains that he would cross to get to Nara. As the clouds spread, the sun disappeared and the world turned gray. He wanted to increase his speed but was afraid to tire out his horse before the most strenuous part of the journey. Light still persisted faintly, eerily, as the darkness rose in the east.

Akitada cursed softly. Not only was night catching up with him, but there would be next to no light to see by. Still, he made good time and all would have been well except for the change in the weather. He patted his horse's neck for keeping up its speed so well. He had not given the poor animal any rest.

They reached the last mountain range before Nara in semi-darkness. Here the road rose and trees closed in. He could not see where he was going. But the horse, though it had slowed almost to a walk, seemed to find its way. He patted its neck again and spoke to it softly.

It started to snow when he reached the summit and started on the downward slope. Once they were over the crest, the horse moved more easily. Soon he saw faint lights ahead. He hoped for a farmhouse, but the lights bobbed and he guessed they were attached to horses. But the road was good, and the snow fell only lightly. He guessed that he was catching up to other travelers. There were at least three, he thought. He was grateful for the company, because all through the darkness of the mountain crossing, he had remembered vividly the corpse of the unknown traveler in Doctor Hayashi's morgue and kept his right hand on his sword.

Those in front became aware of him and stopped. Three horsemen. Two on one side of the road, the third on the other. They were dressed heavily against the cold, their heads covered, and cloths wrapped about their necks and faces.

Akitada called out a greeting.

They did not respond, but waited silently.

"Are you on your way to Nara?" he shouted, feeling foolish, because where else would they be going?

One of them said "No!" There was a laugh at that.

When he realized that they were not ordinary travelers, it was almost too late. He reached for his sword and drew it as all three moved their horses closer, blocking his way forward.

"Don't be a fool!" one of the men growled when he saw the sword. "Put it away. We just want a chat. We're lost. Is this the road to Nara?"

Akitada halted. His horse danced nervously. "Out of my way, or I'll report you," he snapped.

They laughed. Their speaker said, "Now, sir, that's a very unfriendly way to speak to fellow travelers. And for that matter, we're three of us, and we're armed, too."

All three drew their swords and waved them so he could see them,

Their leader went on to say that no harm would come to the honorable traveler. They just needed his horse and a bit of silver. They had starving families to feed. Akitada knew there was no truth in those words, though there might well be starving families. They would not rob him and leave him alive. He would have liked to avoid a fight, but it was not to be.

The road had leveled at this point, and he thought there was an open stretch ahead. If he could do some damage, they might decide to let him go. He thought his best option was a quick attack and a dash toward safety. The trouble was, his horse was tired.

Still, given the command, it surged forward willingly and Akitada swung his sword at the leader. Always attack the strongest. With any luck, the others might be intimidated and retreat. He did catch the man unawares. Perhaps earlier, easier encounters had made him careless. Akitada's sword, an old-fashioned long blade that had belonged to his father, bit deeply into the robber's right shoulder before he could bring his own sword up to deflect the blow. His horse reared as Akitada's horse plowed into it, and Akitada swung again. Blood spurted, and the robber tumbled from his saddle.

Swinging his horse about, Akitada faced the other two. One had come close, too close, but now spurred his horse away. As predicted, both turned tail and galloped off, followed by their leader's horse. Akitada was alone with the dying man.

Shaking with tension and shock, he climbed down and led his horse over to where the man lay. He was bleeding profusely from his right arm and neck. Akitada's second cut had been deep. The man tried to sit up but his eyes were becoming glazed.

"What's your name?" Akitada asked.

"Go to hell!" the man rasped.

"You're a coward!" Akitada snapped. "A murdering coward. It's you who'll be in hell."

The man laughed harshly. "Then I'll be one of the devils. I've killed men like you. You're the robbers who steal the food out of poor peasants' mouths. I'll wait in hell for you to die. You and the other rich nobles who think they own the earth." He spat at him and fell back.

"Did you kill a man like me about two weeks ago on this road?"

But the man was past speech. He bared his teeth in a snarl that might have been a grin and died.

Akitada left him there. When he tried to mount again, he realized that he was bleeding. His thigh throbbed and his foot slipped on blood in his boot. His horse, tired, stood with hanging head. He finally got back in the saddle awkwardly. The muscles in his right arm were painful, but not from a wound. He was very badly out of shape. It was a miracle he was still alive, and he hoped he would reach Nara before he lost too much blood.

44

Taking Risks

The snow was falling in thick flakes when Akitada finally reached the city. He headed straight for the provincial headquarters. After a brief explanation to the gate guards, he was taken to the police station.

When he dismounted, he fell to his knees, but one of the guards helped him up and walked him inside.

At this late hour, only the sergeant was there. He was startled out of a doze and had no time to sneer. Akitada propped himself against the wall and told him that he had been attacked on the highway and had left a dead man beside the road. Then he demanded to see Doctor Hayashi.

The sergeant started to ask questions, but the guard told him, "Best get the doc, or you'll have another dead man on your hands."

Akitada slid down to sit on the floor, feeling very sleepy. Things happened quickly then, or so it seemed. Hayashi appeared, had a look at Akitada's thigh, and busied himself cleaning the wound and wrapping it tightly.

"That should heal quickly," Hayashi said cheerfully. "It's a clean cut and it bled freely. A good sign. Go home and rest. I'll stop by tomorrow."

Akitada, still slightly woozy, managed to stand—mostly on one leg. "Thanks, Doctor. If someone will help me on my horse, I'll take myself home." He saw the sergeant hovering, and said, "Tomorrow, Sergeant. But you might get that body tonight before his friends get him. It's in the foothills, about five miles outside Nara."

He was not entirely sure how he made it home and inside the house, but Tora was there to help, and then Sadako. They wanted to send for a doctor, but all he wanted was to sleep. And in the end, they let him.

He woke to sunlight and Sadako watching him anxiously. He smiled. "Good morning, my love! Is it very late?"

"Not so very late. Did you sleep well?"

Akitada sat up. "Too well." He yawned and started to get up. Sadako cried out in alarm and a sudden pain reminded him of his wound and the encounter in the foothills. "I think I met those highwaymen that have been plaguing the police. I hope they can now find them and stop those attacks. Help me up. I must get dressed. I expect Captain Katsuura will show up any moment."

Sadako stopped him. "You mustn't. Wait until the doctor has been to see you."

Seeing her determination, Akitada obeyed. In fact, he did feel rather weak. "Hayashi said he would look in."

"The coroner?" Sadako sounded shocked.

Akitada laughed. "He's a good doctor. And a good coroner." Akitada sobered. "I have work to do. My trip has done little to help me find Lady Hachijo."

"Tell me about it while you drink your tea."

Akitada submitted to this subterfuge and stayed where he was, allowing his wife to serve him tea, and then his morning rice gruel while he told her about his conversations with Fujiwara Noritoki and Captain Yoshitomo.

She listened, then said, "They must have spoken freely, trying to be helpful."

He nodded. "I think I believe them. Mind you, those poems between Noritoki and Hachijo were suggestive, but I think this sort of thing doesn't mean much these days. They write ardent love poems for practice."

Sadako smiled. "You think it's all part of the loose morals of the court?"

"Probably. But what convinced me about Noritoki is his age and his concern for Hachijo, whom he seems to have treated as a student or a protégée."

"And the dashing captain?"

"Somewhat naïve and also sorry for her. Neither behaved like someone who had seduced an imperial concubine and was keeping her in some secret hideaway."

"Unlike the governor?"

"Ah! Nakatoshi thought him most likely. He warned me about the man's temper. Korechika tried very hard to convince me that he could not be involved. He claims his acquaintance with Hachijo happened before her pregnancy and the loss of her child. He said he was on a tour of the province when she was last seen in Nara."

Sadako looked thoughtful. "He may protest too much. On the other hand, there could have been someone else."

"Or she is dead."

"Or both."

Akitada was startled. "You think there is another man, and he killed her?"

"If she went to him, and he was afraid they'd be found out and he'd be sent into exile, he might have taken a desperate step."

Akitada said bleakly. "Yes. In that case, he'd guard his secret carefully. I don't know where to begin, Sadako."

As they sat, thinking about the problem, they heard Tora calling softly from outside the door.

Akitada called back, "Come in, Tora."

Tora looked vaguely guilty. He asked about Akitada's leg, was reassured, and fell silent.

Sadako gave him a smile. "Akitada, I sent Tora out yesterday and he has some new information."

Tora said quickly, "I would have stayed here, but there really was no point. I had the servants keeping watch."

Akitada frowned. "Not quite the same thing. However, report!"

Slightly nervous, Tora told about the shop that sold Buddhist objects, the well-dressed man in black, and his over-heard conversation.

Akitada listened, then said, "I must say, this was extraordinarily lucky. You couldn't have known this man would visit that day, or that he was connected to the robbers of Hokkeji, or that you would find a way to overhear their plot."

"Maybe there was a little luck," Tora said, "but I'd already been to the shop, decided it was likely the place to buy anything stolen from Hokkeji, and I talked to the thieves' boss behind the Kasuga shrine. He said it wasn't done by his people. He thought it was an inside job. So I decided to watch the place. And that's when I saw this man. I followed him to Kofukuji."

"Kofukuji?"

"He didn't stay long. I tried to see where he went after that, but there were too many people about and I didn't want him to know I was watching him."

Akitada sighed. "And you lost him."

Tora said nothing.

Sadako, clearly feeling sorry for him, pointed out, "Tora will recognize the man."

Her husband was doubtful. "First we have to find him."

Tora offered, "I can go back to that neighborhood and ask questions."

Akitada nodded. "Maybe later. I have an errand this morning and want you to come along. And this afternoon you and I shall visit Hokkeji."

Sadako was horrified. "You cannot get up and run around as if nothing had happened."

Akitada said, "I feel perfectly well. My leg is a little stiff. That's all. Movement will be good for it."

"Oh, no, Akitada! Tora help me!"

Tora said, "Your lady's right. It's too soon."

It did no good. Akitada had made up his mind. Tora left, he got up and, limping a little, got dressed with his wife's help. Sadako fussed, but he was adamant.

Doctor Hayashi arrived at this point and seemed pleased to see him up. "I see you had a good night," he said, looking Akitada up and down.

"I slept like the dead."

"Any pain?"

"Just a little tightness. I think walking will help."

Sadako said, "He limps and is in pain. Please stop him, Doctor."

Hayashi smiled. "A little exercise will probably help. But I want to have another look and put on a new bandage."

Akitada glanced at his wife. "Hah! I told you."

Sadako asked the doctor, "Are you sure he won't do himself any harm? He wants to spend the day walking everywhere."

Akitada said quickly, "I can ride."

Hayashi frowned. "Better walk. Slowly, and not too far. In a few days perhaps you can do more."

Akitada said meekly, "Yes. I'll be very careful. Thank you, Doctor."

Captain Katsuura arrived next, just as Akitada was setting out. The captain was in an exceedingly good humor.

"My compliments, my Lord," he cried. "That was very well done. You killed the Black Dragon."

"Really? I take it the man was a known troublemaker."

"Troublemaker? He has killed hundreds of travelers."

Akitada smiled. "I think you exaggerate. However, he may well be responsible for that unknown corpse in Doctor Hayashi's morgue. Have you found out who the dead man was?"

"No, sir. And I think you're right about that. That man was found on the same road not far from where you were attacked. He must have been traveling between Nara and the capital."

"Yes. Probably. Did you catch the others? There were two men with this—erh—Black Dragon."

"Yes. We got them. Thanks to you."

Akitada thought a moment. "They had horses. Did you bring those back?"

"Of course. Good horses, too. One was marked as belonging to a post station in the capital."

"Excellent. Send someone there with the horse. They may know who your unknown traveler is."

"Yes. I'd planned to do that."

Katsuura had turned surprisingly friendly all of a sudden. Akitada wasn't sure he liked it. "What about the two Hokkeji nuns? Any progress?"

"Alas, nothing. But I'm working on it."

"Hmm. Well, thank you for stopping by. I'm on my way to see the governor."

Katsuura paled slightly. "I hope you have been satisfied with my work, sir."

Akitada laughed. "Let's say, I anticipate results soon."

It had stopped snowing. Akitada saw that last night's snow had done little but dust the roofs. It was too warm and wet for it to stay long on the ground. The weather was warming. The New Year was only days away. He suddenly wished himself at home again.

At the tribunal, he asked Tora to wait and went inside.

Korechika received him coldly. "Back again, Sugawara? You must have too much time on your hands. I cannot say the same. Can you be brief?"

"Certainly. I have just returned from the capital. I'm afraid that of the three men mentioned in connection with Lady Hachijo, you are the only one who remains as a suspect in her disappearance."

Korechika burst out angrily, "Nonsense! And watch what you say or I'll charge you with insulting a senior official. I can make your future very uncomfortable."

Akitada nodded. "Yes, I know. But you must see my problem. I'm charged with finding the lady and have explored all possibilities. She left Hokkeji two months ago. The nuns thought she'd gone on a pilgrimage to Mount Koya. But the emperor sent people to all the temples there and along her way. She did not visit any of them. Thus, she could only have remained in Nara or have gone back to the capital."

"Then she must have gone to the capital, for she isn't here."

Akitada asked, astonished, "How do you know? You've been gone yourself."

Korechika blustered, "I would have been told. My people here are very thorough."

Akitada shook his head. "I doubt anyone knew. As for the capital, I've been there and I talked to the two men you mentioned. I'm convinced she did not go to either. They spoke freely to me about her. Hachijo did not love either man. That only leaves you. Your explanation that you left the capital for your appointment here is unconvincing because you could easily have traveled back and forth. I also do not accept the story of the tour of the province at the time she disappeared. It is clear that by then she had left Hokkeji repeatedly. My guess is that she came to you and you found a place where she could hide. You need not have been in Nara the day she left Hokkeji for the last time."

Korechika had turned absolutely white. His fists were clenched. Through gritted teeth he said, "Get out!"

Akitada shook his head sadly. "Was the child she lost yours, Korechika?"

The governor threw a brazier filled with live coals at him. Akitada jumped out of its way and left.

45
The Treasure House

Akitada limped out of the provincial headquarters. The sudden jump to escape the brazier with its smoldering coals had opened up the wound in his thigh. Tora wanted to take him home, but Akitada insisted on going to the police station instead. There he limped to Doctor Hayashi's morgue.

The corpse of the Black Dragon had joined the remaining dead. The nuns were gone, and so was Sanekane, all now properly laid to rest. And so were Akitada's other acquaintances: the boy who had died under his father's cart after years of being beaten, the brutal husband who had abused his wife and died in a fight, the peasant woman who died in childbirth, worn out by years of work and childbearing, and the unknown traveler. The room seemed empty, though

Akitada thought their ghosts most likely still hovered here.

Hayashi saw his limp and glanced at his leg. "Something wrong?"

"I moved too quickly and the wound opened. Would you mind wrapping it up for me again. I have another errand."

Hayashi chuckled. "I can tell you haven't been home. Your lady would have kept you."

They grinned at each other. Akitada was becoming fond of the strange doctor. As Hayashi busied himself unwrapping his thigh and examining the wound, Tora waited outside the door. He had a fear of ghosts, and like his master, he thought they might inhabit the morgue and be angry about their fate.

Akitada said, "I've been wondering about Sanekane again. This medicine that caused his death doesn't seem to be very fatal. I think you said it would just make you sick. What is it used for?"

Hayashi looked up from his work of bandaging. "Dumpling makers put it in the bean paste. So do housewives. We prescribe it sometimes for breathing problems."

"Then Sanekane's death was an accident?"

Hayashi straightened. "Well, his constitution wasn't strong. He was an old man and he drank too much. Wine also can make the effect worse. So, since you are looking for a murderer, you should look for a cook who knew Sanekane well and had a grudge against him."

Akitada sighed. "I doubt that is a charge that would be taken seriously."

"No. Even then you couldn't be sure the *xing ren* would do more than make him sick."

"Yes. But locking him out on a freezing night might have done the rest."

Tora stuck his head in. "I knew it! Those bitches in his house killed him."

Akitada shook his head. "You'll never prove it, Tora. Let it go." He turned to Hayashi, "At least we may have found the killers of your unknown traveler."

The old man nodded. "I heard. I doubt it matters to him, poor man."

And that comment was typical.

From the police station, Akitada and Tora turned toward Hokkeji, Akitada favoring a sore leg and gritting his teeth, Tora walking beside him. Tora insisted on expounding on his suspicions of the two women, but Akitada refused to consider them. He said, "We're going to speak to the abbess and maybe have another look at that treasure house where the nun was murdered. I want you with me. Keep your eyes and ears open. If your information is correct, the answer will be there."

Tora glanced up at a little bit of blue sky. "It will be good to go home for the New Year. We might have dry roads."

Akitada merely grunted.

The abbess received them quickly. Akitada thought she hid her irritation quite well, but when he asked her what lay people worked at Hokkeji, she said bluntly, "You will have to speak to someone else. As you know, such matters are handled by Kofukuji. Are you suggesting that Shosho was abducted by one of them?"

"I don't know, Abbess, but I'm looking into all possibilities. The deaths of two of your nuns may well be connected to Lady Hachijo's disappearance."

"That is nonsense. The police have explained both deaths. I remind you that Shosho disappeared long before the two murders."

"I'm aware of it, but those deaths trouble me, and the murderer has not been found."

She looked at him sharply. "Surely the deaths were quite separate. Two murders by two people."

"I don't think so. The two nuns worked together. I think Enchi knew or suspected something about what happened to Chozen."

"But you have seen the storehouse. Thieves broke in and ransacked it. Poor Enchi simply surprised them."

"What was Enchi doing there that day?"

"I have no idea. Looking after it was part of her job."

"Your storehouse, as you call it, is a veritable treasure house. It seemed to contain the temple's most valuable objects."

The abbess looked away. "Among perfectly ordinary objects used in our services are a few important items."

"Are you missing anything of value?"

"It's hard to tell. There was much."

"But I'm sure all the items in storage are listed somewhere."

"Such records are kept by the *betto.* You must speak to him. Now, if you don't mind, it's time for the Lotus Confession in the lecture hall."

"May we speak to Kanren?"

"No. She cannot be excused. I understand you've spoken to her several times already."

There was no help here. Akitada, sore from his morning's excursions, was in a bad mood. He rose with Tora's help, bowed, and they left.

Outside, Tora said, "She has something to hide, I think."

"She is afraid she'll be blamed, and the Emperor will cut His support for the temple."

"I thought they were all related."

"They are. And therefore the welfare of the clan is never far from their minds. The governor is the same."

"Do you suspect him?"

"Yes."

Tora looked at Akitada with amazement and a little glee. "Of murdering nuns?"

"No, not that. The murders have nothing to do with Hachijo. They simply confused the issue."

Tora stopped. "You mean all of what's been going on is nothing but a couple of ordinary murders?"

Akitada stopped also. He was glad for the rest. "Murder is never ordinary, Tora. And these murders were not either."

"Then you know who killed the two nuns?"

"I'm afraid not. But I'm getting close, I think. There were confusing events here also. Mixed motives, mainly. The treasure house is important."

"The man I saw. Is he part of it?"

"Almost certainly, Tora. You did good work there. Now let me go home and rest and think about all of this."

46

The Confession

Tora saw his master home where his wife received him gratefully, muttering loving concerns and reproaches. Having done his duty and begged a warm meal from the cook, he had time on his hands.

The mysterious visitor to the shop in the market was on his mind. He retraced his steps of the previous day to the point where he had lost him and wandered around for a while, staring at the houses, hoping for another sighting.

No such luck.

The neighborhood was similar to the one where Sanekane had lived. The houses were solid buildings of moderate size, each with a garden and a fence. It was quiet here. No convenient maids or servants were out sweeping. The snow was mostly gone anyway. In one of the gardens a plum tree was budding. The New Year was near. At home, there would also soon be blossoms, and the days would become warm.

Tora was feeling slightly homesick for his wife Hanae and for the festive spread she would be readying for the celebrations. His son Yuki would be home from his military training. He was already a lieutenant. Tora hoped he would be accepted into the guard. Yuki, on the other hand, dreamed of battle. This frightened his mother and grieved his father because they might lose him while he was still too young to take a wife and have a family. They both hoped for many grandchildren.

In the next block, he finally found some boys chasing each other. He stopped one of them and held up a copper coin. "This is yours," he said, "if you can tell me if anyone around here works for one of the temples."

The boy grinned, nodded, and stretched out his hand. "That's easy," he said.

"Well?"

The boy shook his head. "I'll tell you after you give me the copper."

Tora frowned at him. He was perhaps eight or nine years old. They lost their innocence quickly, he thought. Chances were he'd take the copper and run. But he decided to risk it. He dropped the coin into the boy's grimy hand.

The boy studied it suspiciously, then said, "Two on this block, three on the next, and one over there." He pointed.

"So many?"

"Where else would they work? A lot of people work for the temples or the shrine."

True enough.

"Can you tell me which temples they work for?"

The boy grinned. "That'll cost."

Tora regarded the child with disfavor. "Greedy little kid, aren't you?"

The boy grinned more widely.

Tora handed over another copper.

The boy eyed it and tucked it away. "One works for the Kasuga shrine, two are at Kofukuji, and two at Todaiji, and one at Gangoji."

"Kofukuji? Tell me where those two live."

The dirty hand appeared again, and Tora parted with another copper. The boy waved over his shoulder. "Over there."

Before Tora could ask more questions and lose more coppers, the boy ran away.

He walked on and explored the streets without finding the elusive man in black. With a sigh, he decided his quarry was probably at work now anyway and turned his steps toward the noodle shop.

They were all there–all but Midori–and the shop was full as always. Ushimatsu bustled about serving. Kosuke was washing the empty bowls, and Sachiko stirred her pot. Midori's little boy clung to her skirts and watched.

Their faces lit up when they saw Tora and they greeted him happily. Kosuke came to give him a hug, and Ushimatsu stopped long enough to slap him on the back. Sachiko ladled out a special helping for him and smiled. Even the little boy took his thumb out of his mouth and gaped.

Tora sat down near Sachiko and enjoyed his noodle soup. She said, "I thought you were gone."

Tora swallowed. "Not yet, but soon. My master and I are close to solving those crimes."

Sachiko said nothing, but she gave him a startled look.

Kosuke asked, "So who killed dear Sanekane, Tora?"

"Well," said Tora, finishing his soup and handing him the bowl, "that's still a bit of a mystery. You know Midori told me that she killed him?"

Kosuke dropped the bowl which shattered on the stone floor. This brought Ushimatsu.

"Careful, Kosuke," he warned. "We don't have many left. They cost good money, you know."

Kosuke bent to gather the shards. "I know, Ushimatsu, but Tora said Midori killed Sanekane."

"What?"

Tora said, "Yes. It's true."

Ushimatsu seemed to swell with anger. "You're blaming poor Midori, who's dead and can't defend herself. What kind of scum are you? You fooled me! Get out!"

Tora raised his hands. "Not my idea. She told me when she was dying."

Ushimatsu would not have it. "Then she must've been out of her mind. Midori loved him. She'd never hurt him. Don't you dare go about telling lies like that. Midori was the sweetest, gentlest creature in the world."

Tora noted that some of the customers were beginning to take an interest. He said, "Let's talk later, Ushimatsu."

Ushimatsu growled but he returned to his duties, and so did Kosuke.

It struck Tora that Sachiko had said nothing throughout this incident. He watched her now and noticed that she looked ill and drawn. She stirred and filled bowls automatically, but her mind seemed elsewhere.

He realized, too late, how explosive the situation was and remained quiet until the last customer had eaten his fill and departed. Kosuke was still washing dishes, but Ushimatsu came back still glowering.

"Did you hear what he said?" he asked Sachiko.

She nodded.

"And you believe him?"

She nodded again. "I believe that Midori said so. She said the same to me."

Kosuke almost dropped another bowl.

Tora said, "I didn't believe it myself. And then I talked to the old pharmacist in town. He knew Sanekane well. I was trying to find out if those two greedy women in his house bought the poison. But he said Sanekane bought it himself."

Ushimatsu shook his head. "That doesn't make sense. You mean he bought it for himself? Why would he do that?"

Sachiko suddenly collapsed on one of the barrels that held rice. She covered her face and burst into tears.

"What's the matter, Sachiko?" Ushimatsu was beside her, putting his arm around her heaving shoulders. The small boy embraced her knee and started to wail.

Kosuke stopped washing bowls and looked at Tora accusingly. "You've made Sachiko cry, Tora."

Tora bit his lip. "I'm sorry, Sachiko. Let it go. He's gone, and so is she."

Sachiko sobbed harder and wailed, "It was me! It was me! I wanted her dead. Oh, the gods hate me."

They all stared at her and at each other.

Tora snapped, "Stop it, Sachiko. What are you talking about?"

With a great effort, she pulled herself together, wiping her face with her sleeves, and sniveling a little. "Sanekane bought the Chinese powder for me. It was for Midori. The monk said it would help Midori's breathing. He said not to give her too much, because it might make her deathly ill and kill her more quickly than the disease."

"But . . ." said Ushimatsu.

"Did you give her too much?" asked Kosuke, his eyes wide with shock.

Sachiko looked at him sadly. "I gave her all of it. I put it on one of my filled buns and gave that to her for her supper."

"But," said Tora, confused, "it was Sanekane who ate it."

Sachiko nodded. "Midori gave it to him because she loved him. And he took it, because he loved her." She covered her face again and rocked back and forth in her grief.

Tora said, "Nonsense. Sanekane didn't love her."

Ushimatsu nodded. "Sanekane loved you, Sachiko. We all knew."

"No," she wailed, "Midori tried to take him from me and he was going to her. That's why I did it. I went crazy when I saw how it was between them. I meant to get rid of her." She wept again, shaking her head and rocking. "I've asked her to forgive me and she did, but she blamed herself for Sanekane dying."

Tora sat frozen with shock at what Sachiko had done.

She wiped her face and said, "You go and get the constables. Tell them I did it."

The two men cried, "No!" and turned pleading faces to Tora. Even the small boy let go of Sachiko's knee and turned his tear-stained face to Tora.

Tora said heavily, "I believe you, Sachiko. And you'll have to make it up to Midori and Sanekane. But it's not something I want to take to the police. The Chinese powder just makes people very sick. It doesn't kill them. Sanekane got drunk, then he got sick, and fell asleep in the snow. Who can tell if it was the powder that killed him, or the wine, or the cold. He was an old man."

Sachiko gaped at him. Then she shook her head. "It was me. I killed him. An ugly old woman like me has no business falling in love. But he was so good to me, so kind, so loving. I couldn't bear it when he put his arm around Midori."

Tora got to his feet. He also had tears in his eyes. "Take care of her child, Sachiko," he said gruffly. "Sanekane would have wanted that."

And then he looked at them all one last time and left the noodle shop.

It was his case. It had been left to him from the start and it was solved now. But Tora would never tell what had really happened. The story of Sachiko's desperate love for Sanekane would stay locked away in his mind. He had been told to abandon the search for Sanekane's killer and now it was done. There was no triumph in it, no joy of having succeeded.

He felt sad, helpless, and old.

47
The Nuns

Akitada spent the remainder of the day resting. His thigh was painful and hot to the touch and while he was increasingly impatient to be done with his assignment and Nara, he saw the wisdom of letting himself heal. Sadako pointed out that any problems with his recovery would jeopardize a timely return to the capital for the New Year's festivities.

They spent some time talking about the problem of Lady Hachijo. Sadako said at one point, "I think we should believe that she is alive. It will be easier to find a living woman than a dead one."

Akitada nodded. "Someone is hiding her or she is hiding herself. As for someone hiding her, I'm betting on the governor. I recall he acted exactly like a man who is desperately afraid to be found out."

"Perhaps. But I think it would be dangerous to face him again and would get you nowhere."

They pondered this for a while, then Sadako asked, "Is it possible for him to keep her in his official residence?"

"I doubt it. He has his wives with him. One is a Fujiwara cousin."

"Then he must have another house. A secret place. I'm told many men keep their lovers in separate homes so nobody finds out."

Akitada raised his brows. "Where did you hear such reprehensible tales?"

She laughed. "Oh, Akitada. You didn't marry an innocent girl, you know. You married a woman of the world."

Her husband pretended to be shocked. "What? I'm surprised, Sadako. What secret affairs have you been involved in?"

Sadako giggled. "I'll never tell."

He reached for her. "I find that strangely attractive. Come, let's make love."

She disentangled herself after a rather heated cuddle, and said, "Behave yourself, husband. We have some mysteries to solve."

On the whole, Akitada thought, his recovery would make for a very pleasant time. His new wife was a constant source of new delights, and relaxing on cushions near warm braziers and a simmering tea pot was a great deal better than limping about Nara in the wet, cold weather.

"Very well, my love. I admit I need help. What is your advice?"

"We should find out if his Excellency has other houses. Let's ask Akazoma. He's from Nara. He may know." She got up and went to the door to send for the new majordomo.

When Akazoma came in, a quiet, modest man in his gray robe and trousers, he bowed and asked anxiously, "Is there some problem, my lord?"

"No, not at all. We are very pleased with you, Akazoma," said Akitada.

The majordomo bowed again. "Thank you. I trust your wounded leg is not too painful?"

"It's improving. We have a question about your governor. Not being from here, we don't know much about him. I've met him, but he was not very chatty."

Akazoma nodded. "Yes, he's rather stiff, I hear. I suspect it's his youth. This is his first assignment as a governor. And he's so close to the capital that he must worry all the time that people will report any mistakes he makes."

Sadako said, "That's it precisely, Akitada. He's uneasy about meeting anyone from the capital, and so he seemed unfriendly."

The majordomo looked interested. "Has he been unpleasant to you, sir?"

Akitada laughed and made a face. "Let's just say I don't want to ask him any more questions."

"What is it that you want to know, sir? If I cannot answer, I have friends who may know more."

"Ah, I wondered about his personal life. Does he have his family here?"

"Yes, sir. Two of his ladies reside in the Nara residence. The third has remained in the capital. She's the daughter of the retired Emperor. The governor has three children by his ladies. They remain in the capital."

"I'm impressed. An emperor's daughter?"

"Yes. I understand she is older than the governor."

"Ah. What about his other ladies?"

"Both are well-born, sir. He is a lucky man."

"He is indeed."

But this did not naturally follow. Akitada knew well enough that marriages were arranged to consolidate property and power within a clan or a family. It certainly meant that the young man was not free to please himself. If Hachijo had gone to him, she could not expect to be raised to the position of a wife, let alone to that of a senior wife. It was an unhappy, even desperate situation.

He asked, "Does he have other women outside of his marriage?"

The majordomo smiled a little. "He's a young man, sir, a good-looking one. There have been rumors."

"What does he do with such women?"

"He visits them in their own homes or wherever they may live."

"Hmm. Then he doesn't have any convenient place himself?"

"Well, the governor is a wealthy man. He owns much property, but I don't think he takes his pretty ladies there."

"I see. Could you ask your friends if he has been visiting any of those places frequently in the last month or so?"

The majordomo made a funny sound, a suppressed chortle or snort, but he kept his face expressionless. "Certainly, sir. Anything else?"

"No, Akazoma. Thank you."

"Thank *you,* sir. My Lady." Akazoma departed with a deep bow.

The next morning, Akitada felt a good deal better. He sent for Tora.

"Tora," he informed him, "I want to see if we can find that man you saw. We're going to visit Kofukuji today."

Tora nodded. "As you wish, but is it likely that he should show up while we're there?"

"Well, perhaps we can bring him to us."

This mystified Tora, but he said nothing. The walk to Kofukuji put a strain on Akitada's leg and he had to rest frequently. When they arrived, He had himself announced to the abbot and told Tora, "Listen carefully while I'm speaking to the abbot. You are to say nothing and give no sign if by chance you see the man you've been following. Can you do that?"

"You mean he works here?"

"Perhaps. We shall soon find out. But Tora, if you give any sign it will warn him, and then we may have a hard time catching him and proving that he's guilty."

Tora grinned. "I'll be as silent as the great Buddha!"

Abbot Saison received them quickly. Akitada introduced Tora as his assistant.

"And do you bring me good news," the abbot asked with a smile. "Is our young nun found?"

"Not yet, Reverence, but I think we're quite close. This concerns the murder of the two nuns from Hokkeji."

The abbot's face fell. "Oh, dear! I hope there is no connection."

"None, I think. Lady Hachijo, or Shosho as she's known now, left Hokkeji long before the murders."

"Well, that's a relief. Though we are all upset over what happened. I thought the police had the investigation at Hokkeji in hand?"

Akitada sighed. "Maybe so, but they've made no progress. I have had an idea and for this I'd like to consult your *betto*. Is he available?"

"Yes. At least I think so. He's very busy as he goes about from temple to temple. I've meant to talk to him about that. It's all very well to lend a helping hand, but his duty is to Kofukuji. And to a lesser degree to Hokkeji."

"So he visits other temples regularly also? I suppose he advises on their record keeping?"

"Yes. He's incredibly clever with figures. We're lucky to have him. I must be careful not to offend him." The abbot chuckled.

Akitada nodded and murmured, "Ah!" This casually delivered information was very interesting. He thought it might be a good idea to look into the *betto's* work elsewhere. But the abbot had already called a young monk and sent him on a search for *betto* Wakita.

They were lucky. The *betto* was found and arrived after only a little while, during which Akitada asked questions about the other institutions that enjoyed Wakita's help.

When the young monk opened the door to let the *betto* enter, they turned to look. Akitada watched Tora's face. He saw his eyes widen and his mouth open and held his breath. But Tora caught himself and turned back toward the abbot.

Akitada saw the man with new eyes. He was middle-aged, tall, dressed in black silk, and wore his hair in a topknot. He was not handsome; his face was rather pasty in color, his lips, by contrast, were too full and red. Yes, thought Akitada, he is a womanizer for all his dry and businesslike demeanor.

Wakita glanced at them, recognized Akitada and nodded to him, then asked the abbot, "How may I serve your Reverence?"

The abbot smiled. "Very sorry to interrupt your labors, my dear Wakita. You recall Lord Sugawara, I think?"

Wakita bowed to Akitada. He ignored Tora, who stared at him fixedly.

Akitada inclined his head. "Yes, we met."

"Well, Wakita, sit down. His lordship has a few questions about your work. It has something to do with the murders."

This somewhat oddly phrased statement made Wakita tense and look sharply at Akitada. He had peculiar eyes that seemed both fixed and cold in spite of the fact that he was clearly startled.

The abbot asked, "Well, would you like me to leave you to it, Sugawara?"

"No, your Reverence. That won't be necessary. We'll be quick."

The *betto* relaxed a little. "I'll be glad to tell his lordship whatever I can. I am, of course, only involved in Hokkeji's accounts, and that really extends only to checking them and giving advice. Most of my work is here."

"So I understand. You are evidently very good at what you do. His Reverence mentioned that you also visit other temples."

Wakita hesitated and glanced at the abbot. "I do sometimes answer a question or two. It is all done to serve a greater purpose, our faith."

The abbot nodded eagerly. "Indeed, Wakita, you are very diligent and faithful. I look forward to the day when you will become one of us in every way."

"I also think about it often and pray to be found worthy," said Wakita piously.

Akitada asked, "You worked with the two nuns who died, didn't you?'

The *betto* blinked. "My work for Hokkeji consisted of checking accounts to see if they were done correctly."

"But you knew Enchi and Chozen?"

"It was mostly Enchi who handled the accounts. I believe the other nun helped sometimes."

"And the matter of the storehouse which is, as I saw, a veritable treasure house containing many beautiful things donated to Hokkeji, you also inspected it regularly?"

"Rarely. I only passed their lists of what had been given to his Reverence here."

The abbot nodded. "Our dear Wakita is the most diligent man."

Akitada nodded. "I assume that this means you know what items belong to Hokkeji and can identify what it is the robbers took?"

The *betto* had regained his confidence. He smiled a little and said, "As to that, I cannot be much help. I see so many wonderful things in my work there, here, and at other temples that they become all the same to me. I'm afraid my memory isn't what it used to be. I'm getting old."

That was a clever answer. It not only discouraged Akitada from pursuing this line of questioning, but it also made Wakita an unlikely suspect for any sexual or violent crimes.

Akitada decided to shock him out of self-satisfaction. "You're not married, I take it?"

Wakita looked at the abbot. "I used to be, but my wife died and I now follow the Buddha's teachings."

The abbot smiled benevolently. "My poor Wakita. We all grieved with you when you lost your wife. But the Buddha heals all pains and you are now on a better path."

Time for more shock techniques?

Akitada said, "I saw the body of Chozen after she was pulled from the icy waters of the canal. She was a beautiful woman, still young enough to tempt a man. Were you tempted, *Betto*?"

The abbot gasped.

Wakita turned white and then deep red. "What?" he croaked.

"It strikes me that you're the only man known to have worked closely with both nuns. So I repeat my question: were you tempted?"

"No!" Wakita almost screamed this. "I barely saw her. It was Enchi I usually worked with. And I would hardly desire her. You are insulting, sir."

"Yes," said the abbot. "That was a cruel and offensive remark."

Akitada smiled with satisfaction. "I brought my assistant for a purpose, your Reverence. You see, he witnessed a transaction in a shop in the market." He paused and saw the sudden fear in Wakita's face. But the man controlled himself quickly. Akitada went on. "This shop deals in religious objects. Many of them are very valuable." He saw that the abbot was sitting up a little. "Yes," he said, "I see you know of it. It struck us that the robbers who killed Enchi would have tried to sell what they stole as quickly and as profitably as possible. But it wasn't a thief that Tora saw. It was Wakita here."

Wakita said quickly, "So what? I go there frequently on legitimate business. I look for objects that might be of interest to the temples I serve."

The abbot nodded. "Really, Sugawara," he said coldly, "you go too far. I think this conversation is over."

"Not quite," said Akitada. "You see, Wakita, it isn't just that he saw you going in and coming out. He overheard an interesting conversation you had with the shop's owner. Please tell us what you heard, Tora."

Tora cleared his throat. "I was checking the back of the shop to see if there was another entrance or exit. That's where I found an open shutter and heard voices. I stopped a moment, and heard the shopkeeper talking to this man there. This man offered an object for sale and argued over the price. The shopkeeper asked him for other objects that were the property of Hokkeji, and this man said 'maybe later'. He said it was too dangerous right now. When he left the shop I saw his face clearly. I followed him, and he led me to a neighborhood, where they knew him to work for Kofukuji."

There was a moment's silence. Then the abbot looked at Wakita.

Wakita cried, "He lies. It's all a pack of lies. Your Reverence, please help me. I have served this temple for many years."

The abbot sighed. "It is very hard to know a man's soul."

Wakita, his face pale as snow, staggered to his feet and made for the door. Tora tripped him, and when he tried to get up, he twisted his arm behind his back until he cried out. Taking off Wakita's belt, he tied his feet together.

The abbot grimaced. "Please! No violence! Take him to the police. They'll sort out all those allegations."

Wakita wailed, "She was a devil, Reverence. Women are evil. She tempted me with her smiles and with her soft words. She came close to me so I could smell her woman's smell. I fled but she followed me to my house." Wakita sobbed. "In the end, I couldn't help myself. I'd lost my wife. It's terrible to be so alone. I touched her, begged her to comfort me. I asked for such a little thing. Just some comfort. But she started screaming, so I locked her up. When she climbed out through a window, I had to chase her. I only wanted to stop her screaming, but she suddenly went limp and when I saw she was dead, I put her in the river." He gulped and added, "I'm sorry."

The old abbot had struggled to his feet, his face a mask of horror and disgust. "Take him away!"

Akitada asked Wakita, "What about Enchi?"

Wakita had given up hope. "She knew Chozen had come to my house. I told her I wanted to inspect the storehouse. While we were there, she accused me again. I said Chozen left on her own and must have met some man in the street, but I could see she didn't believe me and would talk to the abbess. I had no choice."

The abbot covered his face.

"So you killed her and then you arranged things to look like a burglary?"

Tora butted in, "And took a couple of things with you to sell in the market!"

The *betto* whimpered, "What will they do to me?"

"A double murder," said Akitada bluntly, "means exile to hard labor in some unpleasant place like a mine. For the thefts, they'll probably just beat you."

Wakita rolled on the floor moaning.

The abbot called for help, and some young, strong monks secured Wakita with ropes, and then ran for the police. Wakita alternated between wailing in self-pity and making accusations against the two nuns.

The abbot covered his ears.

Akitada felt an intense revulsion for the man as he thought of the body of Chozen lying naked and helpless in Doctor Hayashi's morgue, the evidence of her desperate attempt to escape this man bearing witness to the torment he had put her to. It was this crime that touched him more severely. But poor old Enchi also troubled him. Had she just been foolish to confront a man she suspected of being a killer, or had she seen no other way of bringing him to justice?

Fortunately, Captain Katsuura and his constables came quickly. They listened to Akitada's account of Wakita's confession, which was supported by the abbot, and then carried the weeping *betto* away.

48

The Hidden House

After leaving Kofukuji, Akitada and Tora spent some time at the police station, informing Captain Katsuura and his sergeant more fully about Wakita's activities and his confession. The two policemen took notes, looking very pleased, and then sent for the prisoner.

The interrogation that followed was unpleasant. Wakita's guards were less than gentle with the *betto*. Perhaps they had already mistreated him earlier. He had a black eye and looked utterly spent. He wept as he answered the questions, making no more attempts to justify himself. When he was taken away, Captain Katsuura sent his sergeant and some constables to arrest the owner of the shop who had dealt so profitably with Wakita.

Akitada and Tora left at this point.

Back at the house, Akitada found a formal order from the prime minister's office. He was being told to return immediately and report. He sat for a while thinking. He could not refuse an order like this. He suspected that Korechika had complained about him, and that his uncle had decided to protect him at all cost. This suggested that Korechika was indeed behind the disappearance of Lady Hachijo, and that the prime minister must know it. Akitada's situation had just become a great deal more dangerous.

And yet, could he abandon his assignment when he was so close? If Hachijo was alive, the emperor must be told. If she was dead, then her killer must be brought to justice.

He went to find his wife. Sadako was packing. Astonished, he asked, "Are we leaving?"

She said calmly, "I think you have been told to go back."

He sighed. "Yes. Just when we are so close."

She stopped folding clothes and gave him a searching look. "You want to go on?"

He nodded. "I need just another day."

"Then you must do what your conscience tells you."

"At least until Akazoma reports."

"Tora says you found the man who killed the nuns."

"Yes."

He told her how they arrested the *betto* but spared her the uglier details. It was at this point that the majordomo arrived.

Akitada asked eagerly, 'Do you have news?"

Akazoma smiled and bowed. "My lord, my lady. I have indeed."

"Good man!. Out with it!"

"I mentioned my friend, sir?"

"Yes, yes. Did he know of a place?"

But Akazoma was not to be hurried. He said, "My friend's son happens to work in the city administration. He is a clever boy who studied hard and worked hard. That means he moved up rapidly and is now trusted with the documents referring to the city's most important citizens." He paused for effect.

Akitada bit his lip. "An admirable young man in every respect."

"He is indeed. I hold him up as an example to my grandchildren."

Akitada felt a little ashamed that he had not even been aware of Akazoma's grandchildren. He had taken the man for granted as not being his responsibility and had not inquired into anything but the bare minimum of his qualifications.

He now said, "I am sure your grandchildren are lucky to have a caring grandfather. They must give you much pleasure."

A smile lit Akazoma's face. "They do indeed. But to get back to my friend's son. Luckily he found the information you wished. The governor does have a small house on the outskirts of Nara. It isn't his own, but he pays a man for its use."

Akitada pictured a derelict hut in an overgrown garden where Korechika took his casual flings. He clearly had not wasted much money on his amorous adventures. Thinking of Hachijo in such a place, he hardened his heart against the young nobleman.

He said, "Thank you Akazoma. I will need directions."

Akazoma nodded. "I shall take you myself. It's not easy to find, but I have some more to tell you. Another friend has a cook who lives close to this place. And she says that someone is living there. Two women. And sometimes at night she hears a horse."

"Yes. That's very interesting. Thank you. Shall we go just after sunset?"

Akazoma bowed. "As you wish, sir."

When the majordomo had left, Sadako said, "It sounds a long way from here. Will you be able to walk so far?"

"I could ride, but I doubt Akazoma rides."

"A sedan chair then?"

"I would be embarrassed to use one while the old man walks. No, I feel much better."

"At least take Tora."

"Very well. I suppose he would be hurt if I left him behind."

They crossed the city, which was bustling at this hour when the light faded and colorful lanterns bloomed outside wine shops and eating places, and headed to the western outskirts where there were small farms and isolated villas. Akazoma took them to one of the latter. It lay silent and dark behind a screen of bamboo that rustled dryly in the breeze. There was no fence or gate. The property looked uninhabited. They skirted the dense bamboo and came to a place where the ground bore hoof marks near a tree. An angry crow squawked at them and flew away with a clatter of wings. Akitada jumped and Tora cursed under his breath.

Not far from the tree, they found a narrow path through the bamboo.

Akitada turned to the majordomo. "This is as far as you need to come. Thank you. I'm very grateful for your help."

Akazoma looked disappointed and peered down the path. Akitada smiled, gave him some silver and said, "You missed your evening rice. Please go and have a fine meal on your way home."

The majordomo brightened, bowed, and left at a trot. Akitada and Tora took the path. Tora kept close behind him, his hand on his sword, but no one barred their way. They reached a clearing, overgrown with weeds, and saw a small, abandoned-looking villa. The red lacquer paint peeled from the railings and eaves and the shutters had missing slats. It was deathly silent. Only the bamboo rustled drily now and then.

"Let me take a look around," Tora whispered.

Akitada nodded.

Tora walked softly around the next corner and disappeared while Akitada climbed the stairs to the veranda and tried the door. It was barred from inside. He waited.

After a few moments, Tora reappeared. "All the shutters are closed," he said, "but there's a light inside. Someone's home."

"The door is barred. Let's knock and see what happens." Akitada pounded on the wood hard enough to rattle the bar inside.

Silence.

"Let me," Tora offered. He pounded with even greater force and shouted, "Open up! It's the landlord."

Akitada raised his brows. "Must you lie?"

Tora grinned. And the bar inside was withdraw. The door opened a crack. A young girl holding a small oil lamp peered out. "What do you want?" she asked in a frightened voice, seeing two tall men outside.

Akitada said, "I'm Lord Sugawara. Announce me to your mistress."

The maid started to close the door, but Tora reached past Akitada and gave it a firm push. "No, sweetheart," he said. "You cannot leave his Excellency standing out here in the dark."

She backed away with a cry as they walked in.

Akitada closed and barred the door and looked at the maid. She had a slender figure to go with the pretty face. Her gown was plain cotton and her hair was braided as he had seen peasant women wear it in the far north. She was terrified. The lamp trembled in her hand.

"Please," she begged, "Don't hurt us."

"Calm down. Nobody's getting hurt," Tora assured her, flashing her one of his brilliant smiles. "My master would like a word with your mistress, that's all."

They were in the small front room of the house. It was completely empty. A doorway led to the back where they could see more light.

Akitada said, "Wait here, Tora," and walked toward it. The maid dashed past him and tried to bar his way but he had already reached the open doorway and seen the woman, standing there, looking at them with wide, fearful eyes.

She was extraordinarily beautiful, even to his jaded eyes. Small and delicate, with a pale oval face and huge eyes, long glossy hair falling over a silk gown in a pale rose color and spilling over the bare wood floor. Hair of such richness and length was prized above all else by the women at court, but this creature was also exquisite in all other respects.

The hair gave him pause. He had expected that it had been cut in preparation for her ordination. But surely this was Hachijo herself.

He bowed deeply in admiration and respect. "Forgive this intrusion, Lady Hachijo," he said. "I'm Sugawara Akitada. His Majesty sent me to make sure you are alive and well."

She said nothing. He saw her struggle with the best response. Would she deny her identity? No. She nodded and waited.

Akitada looked around at the plainness of her quarters. "Are you comfortable here?"

She finally spoke. "I am here through the kindness of a friend. It suits my current position."

Her voice was soft and melodious. Akitada wondered how even an emperor could turn away from such a creature.

He glanced at the maid. "May we speak privately?"

"No. Yasuro stays."

The maid scurried to her side.

Akitada closed the door behind him. "May we sit down at least?"

He saw that she did not want him to stay, but she finally nodded and sat down in a rustle of silk. The maid knelt behind her.

He sat down across from them. "I believe this friend is Fujiwara Korechika?"

She flushed a rosy red. "If you know so much, why ask?"

"Are you lovers?"

The red deepened and her eyes flashed. "No!"

"I beg your pardon. I was told he brings his women here."

Her hands began to shake. She looked down at them and tucked them into her sleeves. Then she lifted her chin. "Korechika is a friend. I had no others. I know nothing of his habits. You are insulting."

Akitada felt ashamed and nodded. "Forgive me, Lady Hachijo. I regret my plain words. I have been charged with finding you and making certain that all is well. It pains me that I have to ask such questions, but your future and that of Korechika depends on my account of the truth." He saw her anger falter and continued, "My finding you here has put all of us in a difficult position."

She said, "It would have been much better had you not found me. I only wish to be forgotten."

"But you left Hokkeji. It was as good a place to be forgotten as any."

She lowered her head. "I could not bear lying to the nuns."

"What do you mean?"

"As soon as I arrived, I knew I was not worthy. I tried to become worthy but failed. So I left."

He had suspected as much and knew now he had wished for it. The nunnery was no place for such a woman. But to flee into the arms of that proud and self-centered Korechika was quite another thing. At least he had not killed her.

Akitada said quietly, "If it becomes known that you live here under Korechika's protection, you are both lost."

She pleaded, "I live here quietly. I hurt no one. Can you not go away and forget you found me?"

He sighed. "Lady Hachijo, you must know that isn't possible. You will be found sooner or later. You must leave this place. Korechika can do nothing for you. He has a family and a position. His life is very public."

He saw she understood by the fear and despair in her face. "Then I must go," she whispered, twisting her hands in her lap.

"Can you go to your family?"

"No!" It was a pitiful wail.

"I have been to see them. Your grandmother loves you."

There were tears in her eyes. "*Obaasan*." she said softly. "Yes, but I cannot go back. I have spoken with my grandfather and with my brother. They have forbidden me to return to them. My brother is very angry."

Akitada nodded. "I have also spoken with them. I deplore their behavior, but there is nothing we can do about it. You must return to Hokkeji for a while."

She shuddered, then nodded.

"Do you still have your nun's clothes?"

"Yes."

"You must put them on and go back alone. You must tell them that you have been in retreat. Say as little as possible, but tell the abbess that you have learned through prayer that you cannot be a nun."

She watched him anxiously now. "But where will I go then?"

"The allowance made you by His Majesty will be returned to you when you leave Hokkeji. With it, you can live where you please, quietly and in comfort."

Her eyes widened. "It sounds too easy. Nothing was ever easy for me. I don't believe you."

"It won't be easy. Much depends on how well you tell the lie about where you have been. Everything depends on that. His Majesty will not abandon you.

And I shall do my best to make my report to the prime minister who will ease your way."

She looked stricken. "The prime minister will destroy me rather than help. The empress is his daughter."

"I know, but I think you do him an injustice. He serves the emperor and for His sake he will do the right thing. In any case, I see no other option."

She said softly, "Thank you for trying to help me."

He wanted to smile at her, to reassure her, but everything was still too uncertain. "Your maid works for the governor?" She nodded. "I'd like you to write to him now, to explain your decision to return to Hokkeji, and to ask him for his silence."

She asked the maid to run for her writing box and took up the brush to write a short letter. When she was done, Akitada read it and nodded. "It will do. And now you must get ready."

She looked at him. "I have never betrayed His Majesty."

And Akitada, who knew nothing of the sort, said, "I believe you."

49

A New Year

They finally returned to the capital. By then not only Tora but also Sadako had seen enough of Nara and yearned for their home. It would be a new year in another two days. There would be celebrations and a joyous anticipation of spring. Delicious foods would be prepared and friends would gather at parties. The celebrations were due not only to the New Year, but they also involved the customary promotions and new honors that the court bestowed on officials.

Akitada left Nara sunk in gloom. Ahead, he saw uncertainties, dangers, and disappointments. He found it difficult to hide this from his companions, but their relief was so palpable that it kindled a small amount of hope in him also.

They had at least two achievements to look back on. The murders of the two nuns had been solved and the abominable *betto* Wakita would pay for his crimes. And Lady Hachijo resided again in Hokkeji and awaited the emperor's decision about her future.

Akitada's plan had worked well. She had changed into her nun's garb and then she had bravely walked out of Korechika's house and along the dark Nara streets to Hokkeji, where she had been received gladly. Akitada and Tora had followed at a distance to make sure she made the journey safely.

The next morning he had received a message from Hokkeji of the return of their most celebrated guest. He had gone to meet with the abbess and Lady Hachijo. Lady Hachijo had taken the opportunity to inform him that she had decided not to go through with her ordination. The abbess had made no comment, but her compressed lips made it clear that she was bitterly disappointed. It was probably mostly the loss of the generous stipend that had come to Hokkeji with Lady Hachijo that upset her Reverence.

What remained was his report to the prime minister and this worried him. His promises to Lady Hachijo had been based mostly on what he had wished for her. Reactions from his Excellency and His Majesty were quite another matter.

There was no time to lose after he was back. Early the next morning, Akitada dressed carefully in his court robes, complete with rank ribbons on his small hat. He had finally achieved the lowest level of the fifth rank after his marriage to Kosehira's daughter. It had been a remarkable reversal of his previous years of misfortune and ignominy among officials and was entirely due to his connection by marriage to the Fujiwara clan and to Lady Yukiko's service to the reigning empress. He had taken no pleasure in it whatsoever. Now he faced a situation when he might well be stripped of his rank and worse. No doubt his divorce from Yukiko had sat badly with the Fujiwara clan and they had been hoping to demote him as soon as possible.

Sadako helped him with the tiresome process of getting ready. She had perfumed his shirt, trousers and coat for hours, it seemed, and now she stood back to admire him with shining eyes.

"Oh, you're a great man, Akitada," she breathed. "A very great man. I'd forgotten how important you are." And she bowed to him.

He snapped, "Stop that! It's nonsense. I wish to heaven I had never reached this height."

She stared at that. "But why? It means power and wealth and great happiness. And now the New Year will surely bring you more."

"No. It will not. I don't desire it. I wish I could return to the time when the *kugyo* didn't know me. Believe me, Sadako, this will bring nothing but trouble. And my report this morning may well send all of us to the outer reaches of the nation to become rice farmers."

She turned quite pale. "Oh, no," she whispered, and he immediately regretted he had spoken so vehemently and exaggerated the danger.

"Well," he said grudgingly, "it may not be quite so bad, but my dear, do not attach any value to my rank. It is the most uncertain and troublesome thing in my life."

She nodded. "Not for myself," she said. "I care nothing for it. But I love you and it gives me pleasure to see you so admired. You have frightened me now. I pray all will be well."

Ashamed, he took her in his arms, held her, and whispered in her ear, "I shall count the moments till I'm back with you. You and I need nothing but ourselves."

And then he set off to face the prime minister.

When he gave his name to His Excellency's assistant, he found himself admitted immediately. The prime minister glared at him and snapped, "About time, Sugawara. You have been gone for weeks without so much as a report. I consider your behavior extremely offensive. His Majesty is also angry."

Akitada blinked at this. "I'm sorry, your Excellency. I did not know I was supposed to report."

"Don't lie. What did you do with Lady Hachijo? You might as well both have disappeared off the face of the earth. I call it outrageous behavior."

A dreadful suspicion began to form in Akitada's mind. "Nobody told me and no messages came while I was in Nara. But there was some trouble with bandits on the highway. I encountered them myself on my way back from the capital."

The prime minister's eyes narrowed. "And that is another matter. It was reported to me that you did return to the capital at one point. Apparently you did not find it necessary to come here."

"I'm sorry, Excellency. I had not found Lady Hachijo then and had nothing to report."

The prime minister's voice was as cold as his eyes. "Are you telling me that you have finally—after taking a vacation of two weeks with your new wife—something to report?"

Put this way, it was hard to respond with a triumphant 'yes', and Akitada no longer felt triumphant—if he ever did. But he had promised Lady Hachijo that he would help her even though the prime minister was the father of the empress, an empress who had been at the center of Lady Hachijo's persecution at court. The remark about Akitada's "new" wife suggested that the Fujiwara faction also still bore him ill will over his divorce from Yukiko. So he said nothing and waited for the sword to fall.

The silence became unbearable. Finally Akitada raised his head. "I have only just found Lady Hachijo. She is alive and well. I understand that His Majesty has been anxious about her."

"Where is she?"

"In Hokkeji. But she wishes to leave."

The prime minister grunted. "Where was she all this time?"

"She was in a religious retreat at a small temple under an assumed name. She went to this place because she had doubts about being worthy of becoming a nun. In the end, she decided to return to her former life."

"She cannot possibly expect to be welcome at court!" his Excellency snapped. He bit his lip immediately.

Akitada said quickly, "No, your Excellency. She merely wishes to live quietly somewhere. Unfortunately, her family blames her for leaving His Majesty's protection . . ."

His Excellency interrupted, "Not at all surprising. A dreadful family! I've had to deal with her brother."

"Yes. So have I."

The prime minister pursed his lips and pondered. Akitada concentrated on breathing more calmly. Perhaps, just perhaps, something might yet be saved.

Finally the great man nodded. "The arrangements can be made, but they will be in His Majesty's hands. Now to get back to you."

Akitada bowed his head again and waited.

"What kept you so long?"

"Several murders, your Excellency. Two of the dead turned out to be nuns belonging to Hokkeji. When no trace of Lady Hachijo could be found, I checked with the police. In the morgue was a young woman who had been taken from the river a few days earlier. She was naked, but her hair was cut like that of a novice. I decided to find out if she might be Lady Hachijo." Akitada paused.

The prime minister looked shocked. "You went to look at naked women. In a police morgue? And you thought one of them might be Lady Hachijo? You manage to do some very strange things, Sugawara."

Akitada said calmly, "I have seen death before and I'm a married man. However, at the time there was also an unidentified male body there. A victim of the bandits who was found on the road between the capital and Nara. He might have been a messenger."

The great man nodded. "We'll look into it. Go on. What about the nuns. I think you spoke of several."

"Two. The murderer was apprehended. He turned out to be the *betto* of Kofukuji."

"Ah! I heard that he had been arrested. Shocking." The prime minister shook his head and sat lost in thought. Then, recalling Akitada, he said, "Very well. That is all. You may go."

The abrupt dismissal caused Akitada to stumble to his feet. He bowed deeply and left in a hurry–in a most inappropriate hurry, as he realized as soon as the doors closed behind him. He stood for a moment, catching his breath, blinking sightlessly at the formally gowned officials and the servants in the anteroom. They stared back, no doubt wondering what dismal future awaited him and hoping they would fare better.

He caught himself, straightened his back, and walked out as calmly as he could manage.

Outside, in the chill spring air, his head cleared. All was not lost, though an axe might yet fall. He had expected the worst and had escaped with . . . what? . . . a reprimand and a grudging acceptance of his proposition for Lady Hachijo's future. The thought cheered him and he managed to arrive at his house with a smile on his face.

The smile was wasted. Nobody was looking anxiously for his return. Smoke billowed over the cook house. The stable boy was on a ladder fixing pine branches to the gate. Tora was nowhere to be found, and his study was empty. There was neither a brazier nor a pot of water simmering for a cup of tea. Muttering under his breath, he walked to the pavilion he shared with Sadako and found it also empty. He had to struggle with his court robes by himself. Having tossed the heavy silk clothes over the clothes' rack, he dug his old, comfortable house robe from a trunk and put it on. Then he went in search of his family.

He found them in the kitchen. The cook and Sadako, liberally dusted with rice flour, were making New Year's dumplings. His daughter Yasuko was stuffing them with sweet bean paste. Yuki, newly home from the university, was dipping a finger into the bean paste and being scolded by his sister. Also present, though somewhat lost in clouds of steam among simmering pots were the wives of Tora, Genba, and Saburo, along with assorted maids and Mrs. Kurada, their housekeeper. The kitchen was full of people, and nobody paid the least attention to him. The preparations for the New Year's celebration were in full swing.

A wave of sheer happiness washed over Akitada. He went to join his son and put his finger in the sweet bean paste.

Historical Note

It is the end of the year 1034. The capital of Japan is Heian-kyo (Kyoto), and the government is firmly in the hands of the senior Fujiwara nobles. The emperor, though descended from the legendary sun goddess, is also the son, grandson, and nephew of a Fujiwara and Fujiwara women are the empresses and concubines.. His duties are largely ceremonial. He represents the native Shinto faith and those religious observances keep him busy. The administration of the country is carried out by his Fujiwara relatives and a few other noble families. Once he has heirs, he will be urged to retire so that a younger, more malleable, successor can be put in his place.

A few times in Japan's history, emperors have tried to assert themselves against outside forces. In 707, the capital was the city of Nara. In its early form, the government patterned itself after the T'ang administrative system. But instead of the Chinese meritocracy that rewarded talented officials by promoting them to the most important positions, it involved a nobility that was based on heredity and membership in the ancient Japanese family clans.

In Nara, the Buddhist faith gained power and influence over the emperors until, in 781, a new emperor, Kammu, faced with dangerous interference from the Buddhist clergy, moved his government away, first to Nagaoka, and then to Heian-kyo. In the new capital, only two temples were permitted. All others were banished to the surrounding mountains and across the river.

Nara became almost overnight a city of temples. The imperial palace was converted into provincial headquarters for the surrounding Yamato Province and occupied by an imperially appointed governor. The Fujiwara family supported one of its largest temples, Kofukuji. Other temples continued to thrive, among them the great Todaiji, where the huge statue of Daibutsu, the great Buddha, resided. Hokkeji, a smaller temple, also dates to this period. A few centuries later, the Buddhist priests and monks would again make their power felt, but for most of the Heian period relations were cordial.

In the same manner in which Chinese forms of government were combined with Japanese ancestral customs, the new religion, Buddhism, adapted itself to the native Shinto, the worship of the Japanese gods. Nara was not only the center of the Buddhist faith, but also the site of the ancient Kasuga shrine whose immanent god protected the city. While the move away of the central government should have spelled the end for the city, it became instead a center of the country's religious and spiritual life. Both the imperial family and the Fujiwara clan protected it and supplied funds that made the temples and shrines thrive. In addition, the Japanese people made it one of the important places they visited on pilgrimages. Its closeness to Heian-kyo also helped.

By far most of the temples were supported by monasteries, but a few of the smaller ones were served by nuns. In Buddhist doctrine women cannot attain the five ranks of the Buddhist cosmos. Like Confucian precepts, Buddhism teaches that women must be subservient to men (fathers, husbands, and sons). Shinto was similarly anti-feminist and considered women unclean for biological reasons. But women are strongly spiritual beings and they found some consolation and reassurance in the Lotus sutra which stipulates that a woman may find enlightenment if she assumes a male body. In any case, women frequently sought to flee the "world" by withdrawing into a religious life, either by joining a convent, or by living a celibate life in order to study Buddhist scriptures. Many of these women belonged to the upper classes and renounced the world because a husband died or because a disappointment made them seek refuge in a religious life.

Hokkeji, being a convent, did not fare well during the Heian Era. By then the religious focus was on esoteric Buddhism, and the great teachers like Saicho and Kukai imported ascetic practices from China and considered women as ritually defiling. It was not until the twelfth century that convents began to prosper again. A good scholarly text on the role of nuns in Japan is Lori Meeks' *Hokkeji and the Reemergence of Female Monastic Orders in Premodern Japan.*

Finally, the story of Lady Hachijo was suggested by *The Confessions of Lady Nijo,* a diary written by a Japanese noblewoman in 1308. It covers thirty-six years of her life and chronicles her experiences as an imperial consort who eventually withdrew from court and became a nun. Lady Nijo's banishment was well deserved, since she engaged in love affairs while serving the Emperor Go-Fukakusa. One of these affairs was with a high-ranking monk who was the emperor's half brother. Once disgraced, Lady Nijo spent the rest of her life in traveling as a nun-pilgrim. Lady Hachijo in this novel did not betray the emperor, but she was disgraced by palace gossip. In any case, we know that the life of court ladies frequently included torrid love affairs.

About the Author

I. J. Parker was born and educated in Europe and turned to mystery writing after an academic career in the U.S. She has published her Akitada stories in *Alfred Hitchcock's Mystery Magazine,* winning the Shamus award in 2000. Several stories have also appeared in collections, such as *Fifty Years of Crime and Suspense* and *Shaken.* The award-winning "Akitada's First Case" is available as a podcast.

Many of the stories have been collected in *Akitada and the Way of Justice.*

The Akitada series of crime novels features the same protagonist, an eleventh century Japanese nobleman/detective. *The Nuns of Nara* is number nineteen. The books are available as e-books, in print, and in audio format, and have been translated into twelve languages. The early novels are published by Penguin.

Books by I. J. Parker

The Akitada series in chronological order

The Dragon Scroll
Rashomon Gate
Black Arrow
Island of Exiles
The Hell Screen
The Convict's Sword
The Masuda Affair
The Fires of the Gods
Death on an Autumn River
The Emperor's Woman
Death of a Doll Maker
The Crane Pavilion
The Old Men of Omi
The Shrine Virgin
The Assassin's Daughter
The Island of the Gods
Ikiryo: Revenge and Justice
The Kindness of Dragons
The Nuns of Nara

The collection of stories

Akitada and the Way of Justice

Other Historical Novels

The HOLLOW REED saga:

Dream of a Spring Night

Dust before the Wind

The Sword Master

The Left-Handed God

Contact Information

Please visit I.J.Parker's web site at www.ijparker.com. You may contact her via e-mail from there. (This way you will be informed when new books come out.)

The novels may be ordered from Amazon or Barnes&Noble as trade paperbacks. There are electronic versions of all the works. Please do post reviews. They help sell books and keep Akitada novels coming.

Thank you for your support.

62596919R00246

Made in the USA
Middletown, DE
24 August 2019